ONE NIGHT

By Ramona Gray

Chapter 1

"Oh darling," he murmured tenderly into her ear, "Until this very moment with you in my arms, I didn't realize just how empty my life was."

"Show me just how much you love me," Kate whispered.

His mouth was warm on hers and as he rained soft kisses on her full lips, Kate pressed her body against his. He kissed her passionately and Kate tried to lose herself in the moment but was increasingly distracted by his facial hair. Did he have a beard before? She couldn't remember. She shook off the nagging feeling that something wasn't right and parted her lips further, eager to deepen the kisses. She tried to slowly slide her tongue into his mouth but was thwarted by a thick layer of his facial hair.

What the hell?

She tried to pull back but his facial hair was everywhere, in her mouth, up her nose - she couldn't breathe. She was about to be the first woman in history to die of asphyxiation from facial hair. Before she could succumb to death by beard, the loud beeping of her alarm clock jarred her awake.

"Chicken, get off me!" She grumbled, her voice muffled by the fourteen pounds of cat currently lying across her head.

When Chicken refused to budge, Kate made the error of touching her. She had adopted Chicken from the local animal shelter three years ago. She had gone in with the expectation of adopting a cute, fluffy kitten with big eyes and long hair and who would charm everyone with her sweet personality and beautiful looks. An hour later she left with an old, fat grey tabby named Chicken whose personality was described by one volunteer as "unexpectedly angry".

But, as she explained to her best friend Olivia over coffee the next day, "She was scheduled to be put down that day. How was I supposed to just walk away from her?"

"Why is your hand all bandaged like that?" Olivia asked.

"Chicken's not so, how do you say it...friendly with people? She likes her space," Kate replied.

"And those big scratches down your leg?" Olivia pointed to the painful looking scratches that started at Kate's knee and ended just above her ankle.

"Oh that? Well, you know my chair by the window in the sun room?

"Yes," Olivia replied.

"Chicken's decided that's her chair now and when I tried to move her over so I could sit down and share it with her she got a little, eh, territorial. But I'm sure she'll be fine in the next few days. She's still traumatized from being on death row," Kate said cheerfully.

In the three years since then Kate and Chicken had arrived at an unspoken agreement. Chicken wouldn't use her as a shredding post if Kate didn't try to touch her unless specifically invited to.

Kate also learned fairly quickly to warn her guests to avoid touching Chicken, resist from looking her in the eye and that it was, in fact, probably best to just refrain from looking in the general direction of the angry tabby.

This morning, however, her body's will to survive overrode her common sense and as she reached up and gave the cat a shove on the butt to get her moving, Chicken growled and flung herself off Kate's head with an irritated hiss.

"Ouch! Dammit, Chicken!" Kate cried.

She slammed her hand down on the alarm clock, silencing it's frantic beeping, and crawled out of bed to inspect the damage to her face.

"Nice," she muttered as she peered into the bathroom mirror.

Thanks to Chicken's quick exit and razor sharp nails she now had a bright red scratch down the middle of her forehead. She had been shamelessly flirting with Josh, the super cute guy from the train, for the past two weeks and she could only imagine how well the flirting would go with a giant scratch on her forehead.

Nearly an hour later Kate carefully weaved her way through the usual crowd of people on the train. Why she was even moving to the back of the train where her potential boyfriend usually sat, she wasn't sure. Her morning hadn't gotten any better with the realization that she really should have done some laundry yesterday instead of re-watching the first two seasons of 'The Walking Dead'.

Her lack of clean clothes had left her no choice but to wear one of her least flattering pairs of pants with a white shirt that had seen a few too many accidental spins in the dryer and was now a bit too snug for work. The shirt cupped her full breasts and hugged her lean stomach and as she pushed past people she could feel the unwelcoming glances of a couple of the more lecherous type fellows who rode the train.

"Excuse me, please," she murmured as she squeezed past a lady in her fifties.

"Sorry," she muttered to the young guy whose foot she had just stepped on.

She was almost at the end of the train - she could see the back of Josh's head. Just a few more steps and she'd be there, prepared to flirt her way into a dinner and movie date. With a sudden jolt the train started to move and Kate was flung sideways. Her feet tangled together and she fell with a graceless heap into the lap of a well-dressed businessman sitting on one of the side seats, her head slamming against the back of the seat with a loud bang.

With an unladylike grunt, she sat up straight and tried to scramble from the man's lap but his hands were on her waist and he was holding her firmly against him.

"Are you okay?" His deep voice washed over her.

"I'm fine, I'm so sorry..."

She trailed to a stop as her breath caught in her throat.

She was very close to the man's face, kissing distance as her mom liked to say, and she had never seen eyes that blue before. Her eyes traveled over his face before she could stop herself. He had dark hair with a hint of gray at the temples, a proud aristocratic nose and a hard angular jaw. She was mesmerized by the fullness of his bottom lip and stared in fascination when he smiled briefly and she got a glimpse of straight white teeth.

She realized abruptly that she was still sitting on his lap and tried again to struggle her way free but he refused to let her go. He was saying something to her but her newly acquired head injury and the closeness of his warm, solid body seemed to have temporarily short-circuited her brain.

"I didn't hear - what?" She stammered, still staring at his mouth.

"You've scratched your forehead on the seat," he said.

"What? Oh no, that's from Chicken in bed this morning," Kate mumbled.

"Chicken in bed?" The man arched one eyebrow and stared at her. "Do you mean you were eating chicken in bed or you share your bed with a chicken?"

"No! Chicken's my cat." Kate took a deep breath, her head had stopped ringing and she was aware of the bemused look on the faces of the other passengers around them. She was still sitting on the man's lap, his hands now placed firmly on her hips and their faces only inches apart.

"Really, I'm okay," Kate said, "I just need to stand up."

"Hold on," he said, "let me look at your head first."

Before Kate could protest he was holding her jaw with his lean fingers and turning her head to one side and then the other. He tugged gently on her chin, forcing her head down slightly. His other hand left her hip and as he slowly threaded his fingers through her thick red hair she wondered why it suddenly seemed so difficult to breathe. She winced when his fingers rubbed against the large scrape on her scalp.

"Sorry," he murmured into her ear, his warm breath sending shivers down her spine and a rush of heat to her lower body. "Looks like just a scrape, it's not bleeding."

He returned his hands to her hips. She ignored the butterflies in her stomach from the weight of his hands and cleared her throat.

"Please, let me up. I'm perfectly fine - just really embarrassed."

For the first time since she fell into his lap, the man seemed to really look at her. She could feel her face growing red as he stared at the scratch on her forehead. His astonishingly blue eyes looked briefly and intently into her light green ones and then moved lower to her mouth. Her mouth suddenly dry, she darted her tongue out to wet her lower lip. He made a low noise in his throat at the sight of her tongue. With dawning horror, Kate felt her nipples harden when his gaze fell to her breasts. The snug white shirt left no doubt to the effect his bold look was having on her and when he glanced back up at her, his large hands tightening a little on her hips, she watched a slight grin cross his face for just a moment.

Angry at herself and her reaction to him, Kate placed her hands against his hard chest and shoved herself up and out of his arms as the train came to a bumpy stop.

"Thank you for your help," she said in a loud clear voice "but this is my stop".

She wobbled her way off the train, not caring that this was actually two stops early. She needed to get away from the intensity of his gaze and her body's shameful reaction to it. In the cool morning air, Kate held her aching head and took a few deep breaths as the train pulled away.

Everything is fine. Sure, you just fell into the lap of an incredibly handsome man and then humiliated yourself further by acting like some sex-starved maniac but you'll never see him again. Everything is cool.

* * *

The law office of Harper and Thompson was a well-known law firm in the city. In 1988 Arthur Harper and Gerald Thompson had formed a partnership that had lasted almost thirty years. Over that thirty-year span the company had grown from two lawyers and an admin assistant working out of a small unassuming office, into a large, bustling company that employed over a dozen lawyers, eight legal assistants and six administrative staff. Five years ago Kate had interviewed for and was offered a job as Gerald Thompson's personal assistant. The first year had been a difficult one. Gerald Thompson was well known for his fiery temper and loud outbursts and unless she was well rested and fueled by caffeine, Kate's patience easily wore thin. Eventually they grew to an understanding. Gerald kept his temper mostly in check and stopped referring to Kate as "that girl who brings me coffee and types my letters", and Kate ignored his occasional childish tantrum and went against her nature by bringing him a coffee every morning.

Three weeks ago tragedy struck their office when Gerald Thompson suffered a fatal heart attack while playing the fifteenth hole at Westwood Golf Club. When Arthur Harper, who was as kind as Gerald had been callous, called Kate into his office the day after the funeral, she had steeled herself for the inevitable. Arthur already had a personal assistant, Olivia, and only the partners were given personal assistants. The other lawyers in the firm shared the services of three other admin assistants and there was no need for help from Kate in the admin pool. She had been shocked when instead of being handed a notice of termination, Arthur had gently patted her hand with his gnarled fingers and told her not to worry, that plans had already been put into motion and a new partner was going to be starting in a couple of weeks.

"So you see, Kate," Arthur had smiled at her "you're still very much a part of the Harper, Thompson team."

Kate had thanked him and left his office, giving a quick smile and nod of relief to Olivia on the way past her desk. She had spent the last two weeks clearing out Gerald's office in preparation for the arrival of the new partner, Edward Turner, this morning.

Kate hurried into the reception area, smiling warmly at the receptionist, Rose, who gave a brief wave and grin before answering another call on the switchboard. She walked the short distance to her desk and quickly turned on her computer, aware that her unplanned walk from the train station had made her ten minutes late.

"You're late, Katie pie." Olivia was standing by her desk, tapping one perfectly-manicured finger on the dark wood. "Wow – that's some screaming bright scratch you've got on your forehead. What happened?"

Kate grinned ruefully at her best friend, "I tried to french kiss Chicken this morning."

Olivia sighed and rolled her eyes "You really need to get laid, girl."

Kate laughed as she tucked her purse under desk. She had met Olivia four years ago when she was hired as Arthur's personal assistant and over the last four years they had grown very close. Kate had spent many evenings and weekends hanging out with Olivia and her husband Jon, an engineer for a local mining company.

Kate loved Olivia and her weird sense of humour although she always felt slightly less feminine around her. At 5'5, with her blonde hair cut in a stylish bob and her light green eyes and slender frame, Olivia was a very striking woman. She oozed sensuality and femininity. At 5'11, Kate towered over her and her womanly curves looked almost chubby compared to Olivia's sleek and slender body. But Olivia was also extremely intelligent and kind, a good listener and made a delicious and dangerous strawberry margarita.

"So you're late because you tried to french kiss Chicken this morning?" Olivia asked.

"Nope," Kate said. "I'm late because I fell into some guy's lap on the train this morning and was so embarrassed I got off two stops early and walked the rest of the way to work."

"Really?" Olivia wiggled her eyebrows at Kate. "Was this guy good looking?"

"I didn't really notice," Kate said innocently.

"Liar!" Olivia laughed. "I can tell by the look on your face that he was."

"He was somewhat attractive. Listen, I need to get ready for Mr. Turner's arrival so take your cute butt back to your desk," Kate said.

"Mr. Turner's already here," Olivia replied. "He's in Arthur's office right now. In fact, when I arrived this morning Rose told me that Arthur and Mr. Turner had just gone into his office and he had asked to not be disturbed. And apparently, Mr. Turner is, as Rose puts it 'a real dish'."

"Shit!" Kate muttered. "He wasn't supposed to be in until ten and I still haven't finished completely clearing out the desk."

"Move your ass, girl," Olivia said as she walked down the hallway.

Kate ran into Gerald's former office and began to hurriedly empty the desk drawers. A half hour later she had successfully cleaned out the desk of miscellaneous papers and office supplies. The recycling box was full and she heaved it off the floor. The top stack of papers fell out of the box and slid under the desk. Cursing to herself, Kate crawled under the desk and hurriedly scooped up the papers and tossed them back in the box. She straightened and promptly whacked her head on the desk in the same spot she had hit it on the train this morning.

"Fuck!" She cried, holding her head as she staggered to her feet. Someone cleared their throat behind her and she whirled around, her hair hanging in her face and the front of her white shirt covered in dust. There in front of her stood Arthur Harper and the stranger from the train.

"You," Kate breathed in disbelief.

"Kate, this is Edward Turner. Edward, this is Kate Jones, your personal assistant."

"We've met, but not formally," Edward replied curtly, holding out his hand. Kate shook the hair out of her face and gave his outstretched hand a quick shake.

At the touch of his hand, her face went warm and her traitorous nipples hardened again. Quickly she bent and picked up the heavy box of recycling from the floor, holding it in front of her like a shield.

"Kate, are you okay?" Arthur asked. "You're looking a little flushed, and you have a huge scratch on your forehead."

"It's from a chicken," Edward offered.

"What?" Arthur asked.

"Her scratch - it's from a chicken."

"It is not from a chicken," Kate retorted, "it's from my cat named Chicken". She frowned at her new boss who stared back at her with an inscrutable look on his face.

"I see," Arthur said slowly. "Well, this is your office, Edward. You've met Kate and she can help you with any questions. Welcome to the firm, I'm looking forward to working with you."

The two men shook hands and, as Arthur left the office, Kate shifted the box of recycling into a more comfortable position and faced Edward. As he studied his new office she took the opportunity to take a closer look at him. He was tall, she guessed about 6'4", and lean with broad shoulders and narrow hips. His height and piercing blue eyes struck an imposing figure and she felt a little shiver run through her when he turned and looked at her.

"As you can see," she said awkwardly, "I've cleaned out your desk so you can put your - "

"That won't be necessary," Edward interrupted. "I've got some new furniture coming in tomorrow afternoon. Once it arrives, I'll need your help with arranging it and organizing my files and paperwork which should be arriving this afternoon from my firm in New York."

He looked her up and down, but unlike the slow deliberate glance from the train this morning that had filled Kate with warmth, this one left her feeling like she was lacking something.

"So you used to live in New York?" She asked casually, hoping to glean a bit more information about her new boss.

"Yes," he replied. When he said nothing else, only stared at her with those disconcerting blue eyes, Kate shifted the recycling box again. Her arms were beginning to shake from the exertion of holding it.

"Okay, well, uh, I'm going to take this to the filing room, my desk is right outside your office so if you need anything you can just holler or my extension is 819."

She walked awkwardly toward the door, hugging the heavy box to her chest. As she stepped around Edward, he surprised her by reaching out and taking the box from her. As he slid his hands around the cardboard box, the back of his hand brushed up against the soft swell of her breast and she gasped and stepped back quickly. Without a word he turned and carried the box out of the room.

Kate stared dumbly at the floor. She could still feel the soft brush of his hand against her breast and her breath quickened in her throat. What was wrong with her? An accidental brushing of his hand on her body and she was acting like some horny teenager. With one last deep breath, she walked out of the office to her desk. It was going to be a long morning.

* * *

"What are the odds that the handsome devil from the train would be your new boss?" Olivia said.

After eating their lunch in the staff lunch room, they had decided to take a walk in the park adjacent to their building so Kate could fill Olivia in on the details of the morning in private.

"It would be just my luck," Kate said glumly. "This guy is worse than Gerald."

"No one was worse than Gerald," Olivia said. "Besides, he's been your boss for less than four hours. You can't tell anything about him yet, and it sounds like you had a connection on the train."

"We didn't," Kate said. "And he is worse than Gerald. I can feel it in my bones, Olivia. Half an hour after I met him, he insisted that I rearrange my entire desk so that I'm facing his door when I'm working. Is he expecting me to just sit and watch his door all day in case he needs something? Plus, I heard him on the phone talking to his previous company and he came across as an arrogant dick. I thought Gerald was bad with his 'bring me my coffee' and 'change my voicemail' but I can guarantee you Mr. Turner will be even more high maintenance."

"One," Olivia replied "you shouldn't speak ill of the dead and two – this arrogant man also caught you on the train, examined you for injuries and," she grinned impishly, "apparently makes your underwear wet just by looking at you."

Kate gave her a sour look. "You keep that to yourself or I'll super glue your stapler to your desk – I swear it. Besides, he was completely different on the train. He was warm and friendly, maybe a little too familiar, but not arrogant. I can't believe I'm saying this but I actually miss Gerald's crusty old man attitude."

"Don't worry, Katie-pie," Olivia said. "You're just having a bad day. I'm sure Mr. Turner will be just fine and if he isn't, remember how rough the first year was with Gerald. You can handle whatever Mr. Turner throws at you. Now, let's stop at the Starbucks on the way back. I need a hit of caffeine."

* * *

Olivia is right, Kate thought to herself as she sat down at her newly-arranged desk. She was just having a bad day and acting like her new boss was an asshole without any real reason wasn't like her. There was just something about Edward Turner that set her nerves on edge and she was already hating that she was attracted to him. The law firm had a strict no-dating policy between employees and besides, the secretary dating the boss was a horrible cliché and it always ended badly.

It seemed to work out for Lina.

Yeah, her baby sister was happier then Kate had ever seen her but she had literally just started dating her boss. Kate was happy for her but she was also worried that this Aiden guy would break Lina's heart.

She sighed and took a sip of her coffee as her phone rang.

"Hey, Rose. What's up?"

"Mr. Turner's things are here, should I send the couriers back with the boxes?" Rose asked.

"Yes, please." Kate hung up the phone and walked to the door of Edward's office. Knocking lightly, she said, "Mr. Turner, the couriers are here with your things. Should I have them put the boxes in here?"

"Yes," he replied without bothering to look up from the computer screen he was staring intently at. Under Kate's direction, the couriers placed the boxes in the far corner and left. Kate hovered for a moment at the office door, waiting to see if Edward had further instructions for her but when he continued to stare at his computer screen she returned to her desk.

The afternoon passed slowly. Edward remained at his desk in front of his computer and with little else to do, Kate kept reliving the incident on the train this morning. While not a classic beauty, her thick red hair, full breasts and generous smile could and did attract attention from the opposite sex but before this morning she'd never been so affected by a man simply looking at her. The way Edward had stared at her mouth and breasts and that brief tightening of his hands on her hips had left her wondering what it would be like to have him in her bed. Would he be gentle or rough? Would he be slow and tender or –

Enough, Kate!

She placed a shaky hand to her warm and flushed cheek. This type of thinking was madness. Lusting after her boss was a sure way to be fired.

At five, Kate peeked into Edward's office. "I'm leaving for the day, Mr. Turner. Have a good evening."

Still absorbed in his work, he nodded distractedly. "See you tomorrow, Ms. Jones."

Chapter 2

By the next morning Kate's mood had not improved. After eating a light supper and doing laundry, she had gone to bed early with a book but couldn't lose herself in the story. She had clicked off the light and stared at the ceiling as Chicken curled up comfortably beside her. Hours later she had fallen into a restless sleep that never quite deepened.

Now, freshly showered and dressing in her bedroom, she chatted grumpily at Chicken, who was stretched out on the bed and lazily grooming her face.

"The thing is, Chicken, why was he even on the train in the first place? He's a partner in a law firm, he should be driving a fancy car to work. And another thing - I've thought a lot about my reaction to him on the train and it's obvious to me now that it has nothing to do with Edward despite what you might think. It's exactly like Olivia said – I just need to get laid. Any woman who hadn't had sex in over a year would have reacted the same way. Right, Chicken?"

She glanced over at Chicken who lifted her leg over her head and licked her own ass.

"Nice," Kate said. "Stay classy, Chicken."

* * *

"Good morning, Kate."

Kate shifted over on the bench seat as Josh squeezed in beside her.

"Josh! How are you?"

"I'm good. I missed you yesterday."

"Sorry, I was stuck in the middle of the train."

"No problem." Josh gave her a smile that yesterday would have brought a flush of warmth to her cheeks. "Listen, I was wondering if you'd like to go to dinner this Friday?"

Kate cleared her throat nervously. Josh was handsome with his dark hair and hazel eyes and seemed like a great guy. They had been chatting on the train for a while now and he was finally asking her out. She had been waiting for this moment so why was she suddenly so disinterested? Josh was waiting patiently for her answer and she cleared her throat again.

"I, uh - yes, of course I do," she stuttered.

"Great!" Josh grinned enthusiastically, the dimples in his cheeks deepening. Kate smiled at him as they exchanged cell numbers. Josh was a very nice guy and she wasn't about to turn down the chance to get to know him better just because she had a sudden case of the 'wet panties' for her boss.

* * *

When she arrived at work, Edward's office door was closed and she dropped her stuff at her desk, turned on her computer and wandered to the kitchen. She poured herself a cup, adding a generous dollop of cream, as she grinned to herself. Olivia would freak out when she told her about her date with Josh on Friday.

Coffee in hand, she turned and bumped into Edward who was standing directly behind her. She stumbled backward and gasped in pain as the hot coffee sloshed over the top of the mug and splashed onto her hand. Edward immediately seized the mug and, setting it on the counter, put one hand on the small of her back and propelled her toward the sink. He turned on the tap and guided her hand under the cool water.

"Ouch," Kate muttered.

"Are you always this accident prone, Ms. Jones?" Edward asked with a hint of impatience in his voice.

"No," Kate replied, "You surprised me. I wasn't expecting you to be standing so close. Have you heard of respecting someone's personal space?"

"Like you respected my personal space yesterday on the train?" Edward asked.

"That was an accident. And you were the one who wouldn't let me off your lap," Kate said hotly.

"Indeed. I suppose I wanted to make sure you weren't going to pass out on me. Speaking of which, how's your head today?"

She didn't reply, suddenly distracted by how close Edward was to her. He was standing directly behind her, one hand resting on the counter beside her and his other hand wrapped lightly around her wrist, forcing her to keep her hand under the cool water. She was trapped between his body and the counter and she could feel the light pressure of his chest against her back.

Despite her own height, Edward still towered above her and she glanced up at his face. She could smell the clean scent of his skin and see the small nick on his jaw where he had cut himself shaving. His closeness was heating her skin, bringing a flush to her cheeks, and staring at her pale hand being held firmly by his large one was giving her a fluttering sensation in her stomach.

"Ms. Jones? How's your head this morning?" He repeated.

"It's better, thank you."

"Good. And I see the chicken scratch is healing nicely as well."

Kate blushed as he let go of her wrist and turned off the tap before stepping back.

"Let me see your hand," he said.

She turned to face him, holding out her hand obediently. Plucking the dish towel off the counter, he dried her hand gently and examined it closely.

"Looks like you'll be fine."

"Thanks." Her voice was husky and low and she could almost hear the lust in it.

Get it together, Kate!

He was standing close to her, too damn close, and she struggled to clear her thoughts and control her breathing. Determined to act casual, she forced her gaze to his. He was staring at her mouth and, as though they had a mind of their own, Kate's lips parted. She watched in fascination as his nostrils flared and his hand tightened around hers. She couldn't breathe as his head dipped down.

Do not kiss your boss in the office. I repeat – do not kiss your boss in the office!

Ignoring her inner voice, Kate tilted her head and leaned forward, her heart beating wildly in her chest.

"Am I interrupting something?"

Edward immediately released her wrist and turned toward the doorway of the kitchen. She peeked over Edward's shoulder and groaned silently. Melissa Saunders, one of the lawyers in the firm, was standing in the doorway. She and Melissa had been at odds since Melissa had been hired last year. The combination of Kate's quick temper and Melissa's obvious disdain for and poor treatment of the admin staff had led to more than one argument between the two of them.

"You must be Edward Turner."

Edward strode towards Melissa, extending his hand. "I am, and you are?"

"I'm Melissa Saunders. We'll be working on the Johnson case together."

"Nice to meet you, Melissa," Edward said.

"Likewise," Melissa answered. Her gaze drifted down Edward's body. "I'm looking forward to working with you."

Hidden behind Edward's back, Kate rolled her eyes and picked up her coffee. Melissa was tall and slender and had a cold type of beauty. Her porcelain skin was flawless and her light blue eyes were framed by long lashes. She radiated confidence and her ruthlessness in a court room was well known.

As Kate slipped by them Melissa said coolly, "Good morning, Kate."

"Melissa," Kate replied and left the kitchen. She dropped off her coffee at her desk and headed to reception to check her mail slot and pick up any messages for Edward.

What just about happened, did not just about happen. You absolutely, positively were not about to kiss your new boss in the kitchen.

Pushing the image of Edward's mouth out of her mind she turned the corner into reception and came face to face with a large man in a uniform with "Hank's Moving" on a small patch on his breast pocket.

"Mr. Turner's furniture has arrived, Kate," Rose said.

Kate smiled at the mover. "Let me show you where the furniture goes."

An hour later Gerald Thompson's old furniture had been removed and the new furniture was in its place. Kate trailed her fingers along the rich mahogany wood of the new desk. The room was now dominated by the large desk. A black leather couch was on the far side of the room with two black matching leather chairs placed in front of Edward's desk for clients. A matching mahogany filing cabinet was pushed up against the wall behind the desk allowing him to easily turn and access any files he might need. Two large mahogany bookshelves were placed against the wall opposite the window and four large framed photos leaned against the same wall as the couch, waiting to be hung.

As Edward set up his computer on the new desk, Kate cleared her throat. "What should I start doing first, Mr. Turner?"

"You could start by filling up the two bookshelves with the books from those four boxes there," he replied tersely.

Edward discreetly stared at Kate as she moved his books to the bookshelf. Anticipating that she would be helping him unpack she had dressed more casually today in a light pink shirt that, while not as tight as yesterday's shirt, still clung to her breasts in a very appealing way. His groin twitched when she stretched to her tip toes to place some books on the top shelf and her shirt rode up slightly, giving him a glimpse of her pale skin above the waist band of her pants. He forced his gaze to his computer screen before he had a full-blown erection and really embarrassed himself.

From the moment Kate Jones had fallen into his lap on the train, he hadn't been able to get her out of his mind. The memory of her green eyes staring into his and the image of her nipples straining at her shirt had even invaded his dreams last night. And then this morning when she had burned her hand he had jumped at the chance to touch her again, to stand close to her and breathe in the scent of her hair. Standing next to her in the kitchen, seeing the obvious desire in her eyes had been more than he could handle. All rational thought was driven from his mind, he could think only of claiming that full mouth with his own, of cupping her breast in his hand and running his thumb over her nipple until she moaned.

Edward cursed silently to himself, shifting uncomfortably in his new office chair as his attempt at preventing an erection failed miserably. He was attracted to Kate - he could admit that to himself. Her hair and eyes, the curve of her hip, the way she flushed when she was nervous, made him ache to touch her. He sighed harshly. Kate was the first woman since Tabitha to even catch his eye. Guilt immediately flooded through him at the thought of Tabitha.

It's been two years. She wouldn't expect you to remain celibate for the rest of your life.

No, she wouldn't but it didn't stop the guilt. Until Kate had literally fallen into his lap, he had honestly thought he would never be interested in being in a relationship again.

Relationship? Do you think you're ready for that? Just because you want to fuck your PA doesn't mean you want a damn relationship. You haven't even slept with another woman since Tabitha. Remember?

Yeah, he remembered. And that was probably one of the reasons he was finding it so difficult to keep his hands to himself when it came to Kate. He'd always had a healthy appetite for sex and two years was a long fucking time to go without it.

He stared idly at Kate's long hair as she pushed it away from her face and reached for another book. He wasn't ready for a relationship, that was clear, but it didn't mean he couldn't consider the possibility of having a no-strings-attached night of sex with Kate.

Nice. Could you be more of an asshole?

Maybe she'd be happy with a night of meaningless sex. Ask her. No one in the office needs to know.

He shut his inner voice down with a snap. He could only imagine the look on Kate's face when he casually asked if she wanted to risk her job by fucking him. She'd either punch him or have him fired for sexual harassment. Hell, she'd probably do both. Just because he thought they had a moment on the train didn't mean that she did.

He resolved to keep his distance from her, to keep things strictly professional between them and to ignore his growing attraction to her. In front of him Kate bent over to pick up a stack of books from the box on the floor and at the sight of her ass, he groaned softly to himself. Maintaining professionalism was going to be more difficult than he thought.

* * *

Olivia poked her head into Edward's office. "Hey, girlie, ready for lunch?"

Kate blew a few stray pieces of hair from her face. She was hot and sweaty and in the last couple of hours had succeeded in filling only one bookshelf. She still had two boxes and a bookshelf to go. It was slow work, the books were heavy, her lower back was throbbing and Edward had asked for the books to be placed on the bookshelf in alphabetical order. Consequently, she had spent most of the time arranging and rearranging the books on the shelf.

"More than ready," she sighed and returned the book she was holding into the cardboard box. Edward had left an hour ago, gruffly informing her that he and Melissa were going for an early lunch to go over the details of the Johnson case. She followed Olivia out of Edward's office and grabbed her purse.

"I was thinking sushi for lunch," Olivia said. "Yay or nay?"

"Definite yay," Kate replied. "And it's my turn to buy."

* * *

"So tell me why, after pining for cute Josh from the bus for weeks, you're not looking so thrilled at going out with him?" Olivia asked before popping the avocado roll into her mouth.

"What are you talking about?" Kate asked. "I'm happy about it."

"Sure you are," Olivia said. "What are you planning on wearing?"

"Well, depending on what restaurant he suggests, I was thinking of that cute blue dress I wore to Arwin's wedding last year."

"Eh," Olivia said.

"What?" Kate asked indignantly. "You told me I looked cute in that dress."

"Yeah, I lied. I mean, you looked cute, but too cute. Like little girl cute. I think you want to go for a more grown-up look with Josh," Olivia said.

"What do you suggest then, oh wise one?" Kate asked.

"What about that sexy green dress you wore last year to Julian and Liz's party?"

"I wore that dress to their Halloween party. It was my 'vampire hooker' dress, remember?"

Olivia laughed. "Of course I remember. And as long as you don't pair the dress with the fishnet stockings, stiletto heels and fake fangs, no one will know it was your vampire hooker dress."

"I don't know," Kate replied doubtfully. "It's shorter then what I would normally wear plus it's pretty low cut."

"I remember," Olivia said. "Make sure you wear the push up bra with it. The spectacular view of the girls will leave Josh drooling."

"I'll think about it," Kate laughed.

* * *

Kate stood and placed her hands on the small of her back, grimacing slightly she stretched. It had taken another hour and a half but she was finally finished filling the bookshelf with the various law books in Edward's collection. She stretched again, arching her back, and relished the feel of her spine stretching.

From his position at the doorway Edward watched as Kate stretched, his eyes drawn to the prominent curve of her breasts as she placed her hands in the small of her back and rubbed gently. She had put her long hair up, twisting it at the back and somehow managing to keep the mass of hair up with nothing more than one of his pencils from his desk.

How did she do that, he wondered to himself. A few stray tendrils of hair had fallen from the twist and curled against her cheeks. She looked warm and flushed and he was struck with the sudden urge to cross the room and place a path of soft kisses across the nape of her neck. Instead he cleared his throat and walked towards his desk. Kate jumped before turning and smiling politely at him.

"How was your lunch meeting, Mr. Turner?"

"Fine thank you, Ms. Jones," he replied. "I need you to type up the notes from my meeting with Melissa, photocopy the sections I've marked in these two files and arrange a meeting with Mr. Johnson for Friday afternoon. We'll probably need about two hours of time so if you can book off the time in my calendar, I'd appreciate it."

"Of course," Kate replied. She took the notes and the file folders from him and headed toward the door.

Edward stared at her retreating ass before dropping into his chair and staring moodily out the window.

* * *

"So, you guys hear the latest office rumour?" Rose asked.

It was Friday afternoon and Kate and Olivia had joined Rose for her daily lunch walk.

"No, what is it?" Olivia asked.

"Melissa and Mr. Turner are having sex," Rose said gleefully.

Kate stumbled and nearly fell. Olivia grabbed her arm and kept her upright as Kate stared blankly at Rose. "You're kidding me."

"Nope," Rose replied. "You've both seen how much time they've been spending together, and Sheila says she saw Melissa practically sitting in Mr. Turner's lap in his office when she came back from the court run yesterday afternoon."

Olivia rolled her eyes. "That doesn't mean they're sleeping together. Melissa is a flirt."

"Yeah, but Sheila said that Mr. Turner wasn't exactly pushing her away."

Kate's stomach twisted weirdly. Over the last two days, Edward and Melissa had been spending plenty of time in his office with Melissa divulging the details of the Johnson case to Edward.

"They're working on the Johnson case together," Kate said. "I highly doubt that Mr. Turner would be stupid enough to jeopardize his partnership with the firm by sleeping with Melissa. He's been here less than a week for God's sake."

Rose shrugged. "I'm just telling you what the latest rumour is."

"Ridiculous," Olivia snorted. "Seriously, the employees in our damn office are so desperate for scandal that they make up shit all the time."

She glanced at Kate as they turned the corner and started toward the office. "Are you excited about your date tonight?"

"Ooh, you have a date? Who with?" Rose asked.

"His name is Josh and I met him on the train," Kate said.

"I want all the date details first thing Monday, especially the dirty ones," Rose demanded as she opened the door to the building and Kate and Olivia followed her into the lobby.

Kate grinned at her. "A lady never kisses and tells, Rose."

"Tease," Rose said before stepping into the elevator. "You know I live vicariously through you single girls. The last time my Bob and I did anything dirty was when we participated in the 'Mud, Sweat and Tears' competition last year."

* * *

Kate picked up her phone, "Hey, Rose, what's up?"

"Mr. Johnson is here for his meeting with Mr. Turner," Rose replied.

"Thank you, I'll be right out." She stopped briefly at the door to Edward's office where he and Melissa were reviewing a file on his desk. "Mr. Johnson is here. Should I show him to your office?"

Edward looked up briefly. "Yes, please."

Kate headed towards reception. She smiled at the short, balding man who was standing next to the reception desk chatting with Rose. "Hello, Mr. Johnson."

"Katie!" He exclaimed delightedly. "It's fantastic to see you again, my dear."

He clasped her hand warmly and stood on his tip-toes to kiss her lightly on the cheek. "You're looking as lovely as ever."

"Thank you, Mr. Johnson," Kate said.

"Now, Katie, how many times do I have to tell you to call me Alfred?"

She took his offered arm and they walked toward Edward's office. "Can I get you a coffee, Alfred?"

"No thanks, my dear. I'm afraid at my age, coffee this late in the afternoon will keep me awake most of the night," he replied.

They had reached Edward's office and Kate knocked lightly and led Alfred into the room.

"Edward Turner, this is Alfred Johnson, one of our favourite clients. Alfred, this is Edward, our new partner, and of course you know Melissa Saunders."

"Nice to meet you, Turner," Alfred said in a booming voice as he shook Edward's hand. "I've heard good things about you. Melissa, it's good to see you again."

"Alfred," Melissa nodded to him, "please have a seat".

Kate squeezed Alfred's arm before walking towards the door.

"A pleasure as always, Katie," Alfred called after her. Edward's stomach twisted when Kate turned and favoured him with a heart-stopping smile.

It was ridiculous to be jealous of the old man, he thought but it didn't stop the jealousy twisting through his stomach. Pushing the image of Kate's smile out of his head he sat down and focused on the task at hand.

* * *

"Okay, Chicken, be honest with me. Do I look like a hooker?"

Kate turned from the full-length mirror and faced Chicken who was currently trying to shred the window blinds. When Chicken declined to answer, she turned and faced herself in the mirror once again. She thought she looked okay, she had chosen to wear her hair up in a French twist with a few tendrils framing her face. She had applied a little more make-up then she normally wore and she thought the combination of smoky grey eye shadow and the lip gloss with just a hint of red in it was a nice look for her. She had followed Olivia's advice and worn her black push-up bra under the infamous green dress. She'd gone one step further and paired the bra with a black thong and a matching garter belt and stockings. Black modest heels had completed the outfit.

"Not that I'm planning on doing anything," she assured Chicken. "But a girl likes to look her best under her clothes too."

She felt very feminine and more than a little daring as she did a small turn in front of the mirror. The green dress had a tight plunging neckline that combined with the push-up bra showed off a generous amount of cleavage. She worried that it was both too tight and short but after trying a few test sittings, decided that she could live with the length the dress rode up when she sat down.

"I'm not showing off my hooch so I think we're good, Chicken."

Having given up on her burning quest to destroy the blinds, Chicken yawned in her general direction before jumping off the bed and leaving the room.

Kate checked her cell phone. She still had nearly two hours until her date and she thought briefly about driving over to Olivia's house and seeing what she thought of her outfit. If she stuck around at home, she'd just end up covered in Chicken's fur. The phone beside her bed rang and Kate rolled her eyes. The only person who ever called her on her landline was Olivia and she picked it up with a small grin.

"Yes, Olivia, I'm wearing the push-up bra and yes, the girls look fantastic in it."

There was a moment of stunned silence and then a thoroughly masculine voice said, "Ms. Jones?"

Her mouth dropped open in dismay and she cursed inwardly before saying, "Yes?"

"This is Edward Turner. Have I caught you at a bad time?"

"Um, no. Of course not. What can I do for you, Mr. Turner?" Kate said as she closed her eyes and prayed for the floor to swallow her whole.

After another brief moment of silence, Edward said, "I'm sorry to call you at home, but I have a bit of an emergency situation. Alfred just left my office and we have some urgent papers that need to be filed tomorrow morning. I could really use some help with making the corrections to them."

"You're filing on Saturday?" Kate asked.

"Yes, I realize it's unusual but the whole situation is a bit unusual. Could I ask you to come in this evening or do you have other plans?"

Kate thought fast. It was six thirty, and if she left for the office now she could probably have the typing done by seven thirty and still catch the train to the restaurant for eight. "I have plans for eight but I could stop by the office right now. Do you think I'd be finished by seven-thirty?"

"Absolutely," Edward replied.

"I'll see you in about half an hour then," Kate said and hung up the phone. She took a moment to take one last look in the mirror, smoothing the dress down over her hips, and then left the bedroom.

* * *

Kate let herself into the office but didn't bother to turn on the lights in reception. She hurried to her desk, switched on the small lamp on her desk, dropped her purse and her jacket on her chair and headed into Edward's office.

"Hi," she said as she walked into the room. He had the overhead lights off, the room was lit only by the lamp on his desk, and his tie and suit jacket were lying across the couch. His sleeves were rolled up on his forearms and he had unbuttoned the top two buttons of his shirt. She stared at the hint of dark hair visible on his chest. He looked up at her, his expression hidden in shadows. He didn't say anything and after a moment of silence, Kate cleared her throat nervously and looked around the room

"Where's Melissa?"

"She took Alfred out for dinner," Edward replied in a low and weirdly strangled voice.

"Are you okay, Mr. Turner?" Kate asked.

"Fine," he replied abruptly. "The typing is on your desk."

He looked down at his computer, clearly dismissing her. Kate's temper flared but she bit her tongue and left the room. She waited impatiently for her laptop to turn on, steaming inwardly at Edward's rude behaviour.

Edward took a deep steadying breath as he looked at the darkening sky outside the large window in his office. He felt like he'd been punched in the stomach when he'd looked up and seen Kate standing in his office, a goddess in green. The dress she was wearing hugged every curve, the low neckline showed off the creamy swells of her breasts and the short hemline revealed a heart-stopping amount of thigh clad in black nylon. His body had reacted with an immediate erection and it had taken everything he had not to walk across the office and pull Kate against him, to force her to feel how much he wanted her. Obviously her plans for tonight were a date and, as another twinge of jealousy ripped through him, he cursed under his breath and pounded angrily at his keyboard.

When Kate returned half an hour later and dropped the papers on the desk in front of him, he stared grimly at his screen. If he looked at her again, he'd try and fuck her senseless.

"If you take a look at this, I'll stick around for a few minutes longer and make any changes needed," she said.

"Thank you, Ms. Jones," he replied tersely.

Kate stared silently at Edward. His eyes were glued to his computer screen and his hands were clenched together in a tight fist.

She turned and wasn't able to stop from muttering an extremely childish but oddly satisfying, "asshole" under her breath before starting toward the door.

She had barely taken a few steps when her arm was seized and she was turned around so roughly that she stumbled in her high heels. She would have fallen if Edward hadn't caught her around the waist.

"What - " she breathed before Edward lowered his head to hers and captured her mouth in a hard punishing kiss. She gasped and he thrust his tongue deep into her mouth, stroking her tongue with rough urgency. She put her hands up against his chest, meaning to push him away but he wrapped his arms around her waist and pulled her against his firm body. She could feel his erection pushing against her hip and she moaned into his mouth when he slid one hand down to her ass and squeezed gently, forcing her tighter against his body.

She clung to his neck and returned his kiss, sucking his lower lip into her mouth and forcing a low groan from his throat. Edward cupped the back of her neck and tugged her head back. He pressed feather-soft kisses down her neck and she moaned lightly when he traced her collarbone with his tongue. She was light-headed and she clung desperately to Edward's broad shoulders as he kissed his way back up her neck, stopping to nuzzle lightly at her earlobe.

He ran his hand up her ribs and cupped her left breast. She cried out and arched her back, moaning when he ran his thumb over her nipple. It hardened immediately under his touch and with a small groan he lifted her and sat her on his desk. He pushed her legs apart impatiently and, grasping a nylon-clad thigh in each hand, pulled her up against his erection.

She could feel his hard cock directly against her pussy, separated only by his clothing and the thin material of her panties, and she moaned loudly when he slid his hands under her dress and traced the lace top of her stockings with the tips of his fingers. Before she could stop him, his hands had moved to her hair and he deftly plucked out the hair pins.

"Wait," she murmured as her carefully constructed French twist fell apart. He ignored her and continued to remove the hair pins.

"I want your hair down," he whispered. He finished removing the pins and ran his fingers through her hair. Pulling gently on it, he forced her face upward so he could capture her mouth again but she turned her head so that his mouth grazed across her cheek.

Trying hard to hang onto the last remnants of her sanity she gasped, "Mr. Turner, please. I – we need to stop."

"Edward," he growled.

"What?"

"Say my name." He nipped lightly at her lower lip. "Say Edward."

"Edward," she whispered obediently.

His hand tightened on her thigh as he muttered, "Kate."

The sound of her name coming from his lips sent a shiver down her spine, thoughts of stopping fled her mind and she pulled his head towards her so she could place soft kisses along the line of his jaw. He groaned into her ear and reached around to the back of her dress. Quickly he unzipped it and yanked it down her body, pulling her arms free of the sleeves and letting it pool around her waist. She reached up and undid the buttons on his shirt, anxious to feel his skin against hers.

She pushed his shirt off his shoulders and he shrugged out of it, letting it fall to the floor. She leaned back and admired his broad chest. His biceps rippled when she traced her fingers over his upper arms and she studied the dark hair on his chest before lowering her gaze. She could see the outline of his erection against his pants but when she slowly reached out to grasp him, he took her hand in his and placed a gentle kiss on the palm. He pulled her against him, wrapping her thighs around his waist, and kissed her repeatedly. She shivered when he lowered his mouth and kissed the top of her breast and then cried out when he traced the hard outline of her nipple through the lacy material of her bra with his tongue. He teased her nipple through the material, nipping at it lightly with his teeth and then sucking long and hard on the lace-covered tip.

"Edward!" She moaned. She wanted desperately to feel his warm mouth directly on her sensitive nipples and she pressed eagerly against him as he kissed her again. He trailed his fingers along her spine, making her squirm, and then reached for the clasps of her bra.

"Yes," she moaned again when he grasped the flimsy material in his fingers. Before he could undo the clasps, his cell phone rang and they both jumped.

"Fuck!" Edward muttered before leaning away from her and looking down at his phone.

"It's Melissa," he muttered and stepped away from her, answering the phone with a low growl.

"Edward speaking. Yes, Kate finished the typing for us. No, I'll have to pass on meeting you for drinks. I still need to finish a few other things if we're going to make the filing deadline by tomorrow morning."

Kate slipped off the desk and shrugged her way back into her dress, struggling to zip it up. She collected the hair pins he had dropped on the desk and as he finished up his conversation with Melissa, he slipped into his shirt but didn't bother with the buttons.

"Yes, I'll meet you here at the office tomorrow at eight. See you then."

He set his cell phone on the desk and stared at Kate. She had backed away from him, putting the desk between them, and was staring at him with large shocked eyes. He stared at her for a moment. Her pale skin was flushed, her nipples still hard and aroused against the outline of her dress and her generous mouth was red and swollen from his kisses. Her red hair fell in waves to her shoulders and he stared at the flame-coloured locks before taking a deep steadying breath.

"Kate, I…"

"Nope." She shook her head. "This never happened. It was a moment of insanity, that's all."

She was talking rapidly with a mild note of hysteria in her voice. "I won't say anything to anyone, you won't say anything to anyone, and it'll be like it never happened. Right?"

She stared at him, mouth trembling slightly and he nodded. "Yes. It was a mistake and I apologize."

She looked almost hurt for a moment before glancing at the clock on his wall. "I have to go. I'm supposed to be on a da – I'm supposed to be meeting someone in half an hour."

He watched as she tried to gather her hair back into the twist. Her hands were trembling too much and after a few moments she gave up.

"I have to go," she repeated herself. "I - I'll see you Monday, Mr. Turner." She turned and left his office without looking back.

Chapter 3

Kate, her heart thudding in her chest, grabbed her purse and jacket and fled the building. On the train to the restaurant she caught a glimpse of her reflection in the window. She was horrified by what she saw. Her hair surrounded her face in a red cloud. Her lips were red and swollen and the paleness of her skin only emphasized the burning patches of red on her cheeks. Edward's late evening stubble had left red marks on her exposed cleavage and her breasts felt heavy and swollen. Her lower body ached and throbbed with need and she couldn't stop thinking of what would have happened if Melissa hadn't phoned.

She knew that if they hadn't been interrupted she would still be back in his office with Edward's hardness taking care of that deep aching want. She shivered uncontrollably at the thought of the two of them connected in the most intimate of ways, Edward whispering her name as he made her his. She balled up her fist and hit her thigh in frustration. She had to stop this. She was almost at the restaurant for her date with Josh and she needed to get herself under control before then.

Hands shaking, she attempted to fix her hair, tucking it behind her ears and smoothing down the back. She pulled a small compact from her purse and quickly powdered her face and chest, trying to minimize the redness before closing her eyes and taking deep breaths, willing her racing heart to slow down. She concentrated on taking one breath after the other, pulling the good air in and pushing the bad air out.

Twenty minutes later, as she stepped off the train and started walking the few blocks to the restaurant, she felt more in control, more like herself. Josh was waiting for her outside the restaurant and he greeted her with a warm kiss on the cheek.

"You look wonderful." He smiled appreciatively at her. "That's a beautiful dress."

"Thank you," she said before taking his arm. He led her into the restaurant and she took another calming breath. She could do this.

* * *

Josh sipped at his coffee as the server cleared away their dinner plates. "So, is it just me or are you really distracted tonight?"

"I'm sorry," Kate said. "It's been a long day, I had to work late and I'm a little tired."

"Do you often work late?" Josh asked.

"No, but I have a new boss and he's a - a little demanding," Kate said. Unbidden, the memory of Edward's rough kisses popped into her mind.

Swallowing hard, Kate smiled at Josh. "I'm having a really great time though, honest."

"Maybe we could try this again next Friday," he suggested.

"I'd like that," Kate replied.

They finished their coffee and when Josh offered to see her home, she declined politely. He walked her to the train station and she didn't object when he took her hands and leaned in to place a soft kiss on her lips. She closed her eyes and tried to enjoy it. Josh's lips were warm and his kisses were sweet but she couldn't help comparing his soft, gentle touch to the rough demands of Edward.

Stop it, Kate!

She pulled away and gave Josh an apologetic smile but was saved from trying to explain by the arrival of her train.

"Next Friday?" Josh asked as the doors opened.

"Yes," Kate said. "Call me, okay?"

"I will," Josh said. He squeezed her hand and she smiled again at him before ducking into the train and finding a seat.

Well, you really fucked that up, Kate. If Josh calls you for a second date, it'll be a damn miracle.

She rubbed at her forehead before leaning it against the cool glass of the window. Within minutes she was thinking of Edward again, of the way he said her name in that low voice of his, and the feel of his mouth, and slow waves of lust were rolling through her lower body. She shifted in the seat and rubbed at her forehead again. What the hell was happening to her?

* * *

Just over three years ago Kate had purchased a modest bungalow twenty minutes outside of the city. It was small and cozy and Kate thought it was perfect for her and Chicken. On a normal Saturday she loved sleeping in and puttering around her house in her pajamas with a cup of tea in one hand and a book in the other. On this Saturday, after tossing and turning for most of the night, Kate carefully eased past Chicken who was sleeping peacefully on the bed and headed into the kitchen to make a cup of coffee. It was just after five and she sighed wearily and looked out the window over the sink into the darkness.

She thought briefly about calling her sister, Lina. Lina had just started a relationship with her boss and she thought ironically about their conversation last week when Lina was visiting her. She had teased Kate about what would happen if her new boss had been young and attractive and Kate had flatly stated she would never date her boss.

She groaned loudly and took a sip of coffee. She didn't need to talk to Lina about dating her boss. She had no intention of doing anything that wasn't work related with Edward. She'd be fired if she slept with him and she had bills and a mortgage to pay. No, it was best to just simply forget what had happened last night.

That afternoon, Kate was trying to immerse herself in a book when the doorbell rang. Olivia was standing on her doorstep, a coffee in each hand.

"Hello, Katie pie. Jon was tired of me talking about what could have happened on the date and sent me over here to get all the gory details." Olivia's smile faltered as she took a closer look at Kate's face. "Honey, what's wrong?"

"I did something incredibly stupid, Olivia," Kate said as Olivia stepped past her.

"Uh oh," Olivia said before handing her the coffee. "Tell me all about it."

An hour later, Olivia sipped thoughtfully at her lukewarm coffee. "God, Katie, you sure know how to pick the exact wrong guy for you. It's like your damn super power."

"I didn't pick Edward," Kate protested. "I just – I lost my mind for a few minutes."

"Well, I can't blame you. Edward is a handsome devil but still, you're playing a dangerous game."

"I didn't mean to do it," Kate said. "It just sort of happened. But it totally ruined my date with Josh."

"How do you feel about him?" Olivia asked.

"Josh is good looking and a nice guy. Not a lot of chemistry, I guess, but – "

"Not Josh," Olivia interrupted. "Edward."

"I don't feel anything for him. I don't even know the man. I know nothing about him and I can't believe that I…"

Kate trailed off into silence.

"Jumped your boss in his office like some love-starved sex monkey?" Olivia piped up helpfully.

"You're not helping, Olivia."

"Okay, so let's recap," Olivia said. "You had a date with the guy you've been mooning over for months, nearly had sex with your boss in his office, and you – owch! Goddammit, Chicken!"

She glared at the fat tabby who hissed at her and swatted again at her bare leg.

"Chicken, get out of here, you rotten cat!"

She flinched and tucked her legs up under her as Chicken hissed again and growled quietly.

"That cat has serious anger issues."

"Tell me about it," Kate said as Chicken glared at both of them and then sauntered out of the living room.

"Where was I?" Olivia asked. "Right – nearly sleeping with your boss. What are you going to do, Katie?"

"Do? I'm not going to do anything. I'm going to pretend it never happened and be a professional. I don't even like Edward. He's arrogant and kind of a jerk."

"Your hooch seems to like him just fine," Olivia said.

Kate threw the pillow from the couch at her. "Yeah well, my hooch makes bad decisions. We both know that."

"True," Olivia conceded. "But you really haven't known Edward for that long, so at least promise me that you'll give him more than a week before deciding he's rude and arrogant."

"Fine," Kate said. "I'll try."

"Good." Olivia stood and held out her hand. "Get your shoes on. You're coming back to our place for the afternoon. Jon's barbequing and there's more than enough for three.

* * *

Monday morning Kate squeezed her way onto the train. It was a particularly busy morning and there wasn't a seat to spare. She resigned herself to standing the entire way and, as she held on to the small strap that hung down from the metal bar running across the upper section of the train, she stared blankly out the window. A familiar smell assaulted her nose and she turned to look behind her, groaning inwardly.

Henry Dobson was slowly pushing his way through the bleary-eyed crowd in her direction. Henry was a partner for one of their biggest competitors and often took this particular morning train. He was well known for both his ability in the courtroom and his horrible taste in cologne. Today was no exception and as he drew closer Kate took shallow breaths through her mouth.

"Good morning, Kate!" He puffed enthusiastically, "How's my girl this morning?"

"Fine," Kate replied shortly. Henry had hit on her once at a lawyer/banker function and she hadn't trusted him since. His idea of hitting on her had been to corner her in the coat room and offer her a new job with more pay if she'd go home with him after the party. The man was shameless in his pursuit of women and she knew he would stand close and bump up against her on the train ride. Sure enough, he had only been standing beside her for less than a minute before he was standing uncomfortably close, the smell of his cologne making her feel a little nauseous.

At six feet Henry was only a little taller than her but he used his slight height advantage to loom over her. His face only inches from hers he said, "So listen, Kate, I think you really should consider coming to work for us. You know we have a great benefits package."

He dropped a lecherous wink at her and keeping a polite smile on her face she edged backward, trying to gain some distance. Just one more step and she might actually have a little fresh air to breathe. As she took that last step, she stepped solidly on someone's foot behind her.

"Oh, I'm so sorry." She looked over her shoulder to see Edward standing behind her.

"We meet again," he said with a large grin. "Have you noticed that every time we're on the train together, somebody gets hurt?"

Shit, he's gorgeous when he smiles, Kate thought as tingles of warmth traveled down her spine. She gripped the strap tightly as the train came to a jolting stop. The doors opened and as more people piled in behind them, Edward stepped closer until she could feel the solid warmth of his chest against her back, his body both protecting hers from the jostling of the crowd and preventing Henry from moving closer.

"Henry, this is our new partner Edward Turner. Edward, this is Henry Dobson, he's a partner over at Russell, Dobson," Kate said as Edward's crotch brushed against her ass.

Edward nodded to Henry. "It's nice to meet you."

"Same here," Henry replied. "Your reputation precedes you. I've heard you stop at nothing to get what your client wants."

"I do my best," Edward said. "We like to make our clients happy."

"Of course," Henry agreed, "and I was just telling Kate that her presence at our office would make both me and our clients happy. You'd better be careful. I'm determined to steal her away for myself. I've got the perfect position for her at Russell, Dobson."

Forcing another polite smile, Kate said, "You're very kind, Henry, but I'm quite happy in my current position."

"Of course, my dear Kate, but just remember my door is always open."

As Henry prattled on about his weekend to Kate, Edward took the opportunity to stare at her unnoticed. In stark contrast to Friday night's cleavage-bearing dress she was wearing a plain white shirt buttoned to her throat and a blue knee-length skirt. Her hair was braided neatly but a few strands had escaped the braid and were curling around her face.

If she had made the effort to cover up her curves for him, it had been a futile effort, he thought wryly. The image of her breasts in that black bra was burned into his head. He wondered idly if the nylons she was wearing under her skirt were stockings or if she saved those for special occasions only. He realized a moment too late that Kate had said something to him and both she and Henry were now staring at him.

"I'm sorry?" He asked.

"I said this is our stop," Kate replied.

"Right," he said. They said their goodbyes to Henry and pushed their way off the train.

"Kate," he said as they started the short walk to the office, "I think we got off on the wrong foot last week and I want to apologize. And Friday night - "

"Can we just forget Friday night happened?" Kate interrupted. "Because I'm not in the habit of boinking my boss, despite what Henry Dobson might think or wish, and I'm horribly mortified at what almost happened."

Edward surprised her by laughing loudly, "Boinking your boss?"

"Yes, boinking the boss," Kate replied firmly.

"I don't believe I've heard the term 'boinking' since I was in high school," Edward said thoughtfully.

Kate flushed slightly. "I'm not sure if you've read the employee handbook but relationships between coworkers isn't allowed."

"I've read it," Edward said.

"Good. Then you know what happened on Friday was a mistake. Can we start over this week? Just pretend last week never happened?"

"Yes. I think that's for the best," he replied as they crossed the street to their office building.

She sighed with relief. "Thank you."

She followed him into the elevator and stood against the far wall as Edward pushed the button.

"Did you get the documents filed?" She asked politely.

"We did. Thanks for working some overtime, it really helped," he said.

"No problem."

"How was the rest of your weekend?"

"Quiet," she said briefly. "I went to a barbeque at Olivia's on Saturday."

"You and Olivia are close?" He asked.

"We are," she replied as the elevator stopped and the doors opened.

"How was your weekend?" She asked tentatively.

"I mostly unpacked," he replied.

The elevator doors opened and they walked silently down the hall to the office.

"Kate, these arrived for you not five minutes ago," Rose gushed as Kate and Edward entered the office. She pointed delightedly to a dozen red roses in a beautiful crystal vase.

"I guess your date with Josh went well?" She teased.

Kate looked at Edward, the easy grin was gone from his face and he was staring at the flowers with a strange expression on his face.

"So?" Rose asked curiously.

Blushing a little, Kate hurried forward to take the flowers.

"Let's talk at lunch." She smiled distractedly at Rose and, carrying the roses, followed Edward toward her desk. As he went into his office, she set the flowers down and opened the card.

Thanks for a wonderful evening. Looking forward to this Friday. Josh

Olivia passed by Kate's desk, stopping to lean in and take a deep breath of the fragrant roses. "Ooh lovely! From Josh?"

"Yes," Kate said.

"Nice. Good morning, Mr. Turner." Olivia smiled at Edward as he walked towards Kate's desk.

"Good morning, Olivia. How are you?"

"Very well thanks," Olivia said cheerfully before leaving.

Kate smiled nervously at Edward. She had the feeling their truce from the train this morning had already ended and was relieved when he gave her a small smile in return.

"Nice flowers," he said nonchalantly.

"Thanks," she replied briefly. "What can I help you with?"

"Do we have a court runner in the office?"

"Sheila usually does our court run every day at two."

"Could you ask her to take these in this morning? Also, can you get started on the paperwork for the real estate transaction for the Henderson file?"

"Sure," Kate replied.

Edward hesitated before smiling at her. "I'm getting a coffee. Can I get you one?"

A grin crossed Kate's face and Edward stared at her curiously.

"It's just that, I always had to..."

She trailed off and shook her head. "Never mind, I would love a coffee please. Cream only." She smiled warmly at him as he walked away and he shrugged off the pleasure he felt at her smile.

* * *

"Okay, date details," Rose said with a grin as she poured dressing over her salad.

"He's really nice. He's a finance consultant for a small firm about five blocks from here, has one older brother, his parents live in a suburb about an hour from the city. He has dark hair and hazel eyes and he enjoys sports and going to the movies."

Rose laughed. "You sound like you're reading a personal ad. I want to know whether he's a good kisser."

Kate grinned at her. "Yup, he's a good kisser."

She wasn't lying. Josh was a good kisser. It wasn't his fault that she liked Edward's demanding and forceful kisses better. If she hadn't kissed Edward beforehand, Josh's sweet kisses would have been perfectly acceptable.

"Kate? Hello?" Rose said.

"Sorry?"

"I asked if you're going to see him again."

"Probably," Kate replied.

Rose smiled happily. "That's awesome. You're such a sweetheart, Kate. You deserve to be happy."

"Thanks, Rose," Kate said. "How was your weekend?"

Chapter 4

Kate stretched tiredly. It was Thursday afternoon and she was more than ready to go home. It had been a long week, Edward and Melissa had been out of the office for most of it, working at Alfred Johnson's office and Kate had been kept busy with emails from both Edward and Melissa. She was looking forward to a quick supper and a hot bath. Maybe she'd splurge and have a glass of wine with her bath. Her phone rang and she grimaced and answered it.

"Good afternoon, Kate speaking."

"Kate, it's Edward."

Despite herself, Kate's heart quickened at the sound of his voice in her ear and she gripped her phone tightly.

"Hi, Edward."

"Hi. Can you do me a huge favour? Melissa and I are just coming back to the office now with that document you typed yesterday and it has a lot of changes to it. Can you stay a bit late and finish it?"

"Sure," Kate replied.

"Great, we'll be there in five minutes."

An hour and a half later Kate's back and neck were aching, her eyes were blurry from staring at the computer screen and she was starving. The office had long since emptied, leaving just her, Edward and Melissa. As she hunched over her keyboard again, Edward's door opened and he and Melissa stepped into the hallway.

"Edward, I can stay. I really don't mind," Melissa pouted prettily.

"No, everything's good, you should go home and relax. We'll have another busy day tomorrow," Edward replied firmly.

"Of course, but if you need anything, you have my cell phone number – call it anytime day or night." Melissa smiled at Edward and headed for reception before stopping and looking at Edward over her shoulder.

"Anytime, Edward," she repeated.

"You bet, Melissa," Edward said before turning to Kate. "How's the document coming along?"

"Fine," she replied. "Another half hour or so and it should be done."

"Great. I'm hungry. Are you hungry?"

Surprised, Kate nodded.

"Do you like Chinese food? I was thinking maybe we should order something to eat."

"Sure," Kate said. "I know a great place."

* * *

"You're right, this is delicious." Edward helped himself to more lemon chicken as Kate took a little more of the steamed vegetables. She had ordered the food and while she was finishing typing the document, Edward had picked it up. The smell of the food was irresistible and even though she was finished her part of the document, her growling tummy convinced her to stay and eat. They were sitting comfortably on the black leather couch in the corner of the office. She had been sure to keep a safe distance between them when they sat down but if Edward noticed, he gave no indication.

"Tell me something," Kate said. "Why do you take the train to work? You strike me as the type who…"

She paused as Edward glanced at her curiously.

"Who what?"

"Drives a fancy car," she said.

"I happen to think it's crucial for people to realize the importance of using public transportation in an effort to support the local economy. Studies have proven that...."

He trailed off as Kate gave him a dry look.

"You're not falling for this are you?" He said.

She shook her head and he gave her a boyish grin. "I thought it was worth a try. My car is in the shop. It should be ready by the end of next week."

"I knew it," she teased.

"What about you? Why do you use public transportation?" He asked.

She took a sip of water. "I don't know, I guess it's just easier and sometimes you meet interesting people."

"Like Josh?" Edward asked.

"Like Josh," Kate replied.

She nervously smoothed her skirt down her legs before hurrying on. "Plus, a monthly pass for the train is less expensive then the amount it would cost in gas to drive my car from home to the office every day for a month."

Edward stood and held out his hand for her plate. She handed it to him and he carried both plates to his desk. He helped himself to the other bottle of water and returned to the couch as Kate stared at him thoughtfully. He was wearing casual pants with a dark brown sweater. She could see a bit of the white t-shirt he was wearing under the sweater and he looked more comfortable and relaxed then she'd seen before. He dropped on to the couch with a small sigh and turned to face her.

"Kate I just wanted to say thanks for –"

He was interrupted by a small laugh from Kate.

"What?"

"You have sauce on your face," she said. "Nope, the other side, a little to the left. No, your other left."

Kate dissolved into laughter as he wiped ineffectively at his face. "Here, let me."

She scooted forward until their legs were touching and wiped away the sauce with her thumb. Edward gripped her hand and stared at her. Without a word he drew her hand toward his mouth and, closing his lips over her thumb, slowly licked off the sauce. At the feel of his warm tongue gliding across her thumb, Kate moaned low in her throat. She pulled her hand away from him.

"This is a bad idea, Edward," she muttered shakily.

"Probably," he replied.

"I should probably go," Kate whispered as he leaned forward and slid one arm around her upper back and the other around her waist.

"Probably," he said again before effortlessly pulling her into his lap. She was sitting sideways on his lap while one large warm hand rubbed slow circles on her back and the other kneaded gently at one thigh. She could feel his warm breath on her face but resolutely stared at a spot on the wall. She wanted to touch him, to feel the strength in his upper arms and shoulders, but she suppressed the urge and let her hands dangle at her sides.

"Kate," he whispered and leaned forward to kiss the tender spot below her ear lobe. She shuddered as he kissed his way down her throat and nuzzled her collarbone.

With the last of her willpower she leaned back and, still refusing to look at him, said, "Edward, I really think we should stop."

"Yes, we really should," he agreed amiably. "Just give me one kiss and I'll let you go."

She looked at him, saw the hunger in his eyes and was lost. She leaned forward and kissed him. He kissed her back greedily. Feasting on her full lips like he was starving, he traced his tongue across her bottom lip before plunging it between her lips.

Kate moaned and slid her tongue into his mouth, lightly running it across his teeth as she pressed against him. She skimmed her hands along his arms, feeling the rough fabric of his sweater and the muscles tightening in response to her touch. She pulled her mouth from his and dipped her head to the side so she could trace his ear with her tongue. He groaned when she sucked gently on his earlobe before kissing her way back to his mouth. She couldn't get enough of him, the feel of his mouth on hers, his hands rubbing her back and thighs, it filled her entire body with a warm aching need and she sighed into his mouth when he cupped one breast with a warm hand.

She pressed herself against him, desperate to feel his hard body against hers and with a low groan he shifted her on his lap so that she was straddling his hips. Her breasts were directly in front of his face and she gasped with pleasure when he lightly pinched her nipple through her shirt with his fingers. She leaned down to kiss him, and he cupped her face in his hand and kissed her slowly and thoroughly while fumbling to release the clip that was holding up her hair. Her hair fell around their faces like a thick, silky curtain and he slid one hand through the soft tresses. Still kissing her, he grabbed the hem of her shirt and tugged it upwards, tearing his mouth from hers for a moment to rasp, "Raise your arms, Kate."

Without hesitation she lifted her arms so he could pull off her shirt. He groaned appreciatively at the sight of her nipples straining against her light pink bra and gently traced a path from her neck to the soft valley between her breasts.

"Edward," she moaned.

He flicked open the front clasp of her bra. As her breasts spilled from the silk fabric his breath caught in his throat and he groaned, "So beautiful."

He pulled off her bra, tossing it indifferently to the floor and leaned forward to take one rose tipped breast into his mouth. Heat flooded through her at the feel of his lips on her nipple and she moaned and arched her back, gripping his head in her hands and holding it to her breast. He licked and suckled gently at her nipple until she was gasping for air. He kissed his way to her other breast and teased her other nipple into the same aching hardness. Desire coursed through her body and Kate thrust her hips against him. She could feel his erection against her and she moaned as she rocked against him. She thrust harder as he nipped lightly at her breast, clutching his shoulders in her hands.

"Kate stop," he said with a low groan.

When she didn't, he lifted her roughly off his lap and pressed her down on the couch. He yanked off his sweater and shirt and leaned over her.

"You were about to make me come in my pants," he whispered into her ear, making her shiver. With one hand he pushed at her thighs and she parted them willingly so that he could settle his body between them. She gasped a little when he ground his erection against her. She ran a finger teasingly across his bare ribs and smiled when he squirmed.

"You're ticklish," she said and ran her fingers up and down his sides. He squirmed again and captured her hands in his. He pinned her arms above her head, admiring the way the motion lifted her breasts, her erect nipples pushing against his chest. Holding her wrists in one large hand he ran his other hand down her ribs.

She grinned at him. "I'm not ticklish."

"No? Then let's see what else I can do to torment you."

She gasped and twisted as he bent his dark head to her breasts and ran his tongue back and forth over the tip of her nipple. He released her hands and she reached down to grip his head, urging him to take her nipple into his mouth. He obliged and suckled hard at her nipple as bolts of heat ran up her legs and she shifted restlessly underneath him. He reached down and trailed one hand under her skirt up her thigh.

"So you do wear them for more than special occasions," he said into her ear.

"What?" She gasped, distracted by the feel of his fingers tugging gently on the garter that held her stockings up.

"Stockings, you wear them for more than just special occasions."

When she only looked at him blankly, he said, "I've been wondering all week if you wear stockings only on special occasions like your date, or if you wear them to work too."

Her face paled and he frowned. "Kate, what's wrong?"

"This is wrong," she said. "We said we weren't going to do this, remember? I have to go." She pushed him back and sat up before grabbing her bra and shirt from the floor. With her back to him she dressed hurriedly. When she turned to face him, he was standing behind her and she groaned softly at the very obvious sight of his erection.

She forced herself to look him in the eye. "Edward, we agreed on Monday, that – that we weren't going to do this. The secretary sleeping with the boss? It's so inappropriate. What if someone in the office found out we were doing this? I'd be fired. And there's Josh, I've sort of started seeing him and it's not fair to him."

At the mention of Josh's name Edward swore loudly and ran a hand through his hair. "You're right, it's not appropriate. I apologize."

"Don't apologize," Kate said. "It's as much my fault as it is yours, I shouldn't have touched you."

He laughed a little bitterly. "I don't normally act like this from a single touch, Kate. I just, with you - "

He gave her an almost helpless look and then snatched his shirt from the floor and pulled it over his head. "It's been a long time that's all."

Kate nodded. "Yes, me too. So, we'll just avoid touching each other and everything will be fine."

"Right," he said.

"I think I should go. The document is finished and sitting on my desk."

"Thanks. I'll see you tomorrow."

"Good night, Edward," Kate said and walked out of his office, acutely aware of his stare at her retreating back.

Edward slammed his fist down on his thigh before stalking to his desk. He collapsed in his chair and stared out the window at the darkening sky. Fuck, he had really screwed that up. What the hell was it about Kate that made him act like a horny, teenage boy? When she touched him, even innocently, it set his whole body on fire.

He closed his eyes and made himself remember Tabitha's funeral. It immediately dampened his desire and he rubbed absently at his temples. He really should call Tabitha's parents. It had been weeks since he'd spoken to them and he had promised to keep in touch when he'd moved from New York. He pictured Tabitha's sweet face, her dark curls and dark eyes and cleared his throat roughly. God, he missed her. She'd have the perfect advice for him and –

He snorted loudly. Wishing his dead wife was alive so she could give him advice about lusting after his PA was unbelievably stupid. He was losing his damn mind.

No, my love. You're just ready to move on.

No, I'm not," he argued. *It's too soon.*

His dead wife laughed in his head. *It's been two years, my love. You're more than ready. Did you think I would expect you to be alone for the rest of your life?*

I'm not ready for a relationship, he argued again.

Maybe not. But you are ready for sex.

Not with my PA.

She laughed again. *Perhaps that's not the wisest idea but you always did like to do things the hard way.*

He didn't reply and he could almost hear her sighing in his head.

Ask her for one night, my love. We both know you won't be able to get her out of your head or make your dick behave until you do. She's attracted to you, that's obvious. Maybe all you need is one night in her bed to curb the attraction. It's time to get back in the saddle.

You have such a way with words, Tabitha.

I always did, my love. Trust me – I know what's best for you.

Kate isn't going to want a night of sex with me.

You won't know until you ask. Besides, she won't be able to resist your charming ass. I couldn't.

He smiled a little. *I miss you, Tabitha.*

She remained silent on that topic and after a moment he stood and walked out of his office.

* * *

The next morning, Kate paused for a moment outside of reception to give herself a quick pep talk. She had taken an earlier train this morning to be sure to avoid running into Edward and she was determined to keep things professional.

No more getting all inwardly giggly when you hear his voice, you will not find reasons to go into his office and you will not, I repeat, you will not under any circumstance remember what it felt like to have him between your legs. Keep it together, girl!

She nodded hello to Rose before walking quickly to her desk. Olivia was sitting in her chair, writing a note on a yellow stickie.

"Hey, beautiful! How was your evening? Did you end up working super late?"

"It was just fine, thank you," Kate replied primly. "I only worked a couple extra hours and then I went straight home and had a hot bath and a glass of wine. It was a lovely and *ordinary* evening."

"All right, you weirdo, what's going on?" Olivia asked immediately.

"Nothing. Why do you ask?" Kate said innocently.

"Because you're all…"

Olivia paused as Edward turned the corner from reception and walked towards them.

"Good morning, Mr. Turner."

"Good morning, Olivia. Kate."

"Good morning, Edward," Kate said. "How are you today?"

"Very well, thank you. There are a few more changes to that document that I'll need by eight thirty," he replied.

"Of course," she said as he went into his office and shut the door.

"You two so did it," Olivia said.

"Olivia!" Kate hissed through clenched teeth "Edward and I did not do it. And keep your voice down for goodness sake."

"Well, you came awfully close then. Go ahead – deny it."

"We didn't…."

Kate trailed off as a hot blush rose in her cheeks.

"Uh-huh," Olivia said smugly. "I knew it. We're going for sushi at lunch today and you're giving me all the dirty details."

"Fine," Kate sighed. "Now shoo, I have to get those changes done."

* * *

"I think you two just need to do it," Olivia said around a mouthful of sushi.

Kate glanced around nervously. The restaurant was full and she searched for any sign of their coworkers before sighing. "Could you try and give me some helpful ideas? Honestly, be serious."

"I am being serious," Olivia said earnestly. "Obviously you're attracted to each other and if it really is because you both haven't had sex in a while, then this might be the solution to your problem. You have sex once, get it out of your system and boom you're both able to concentrate on working again instead of what colour each other's underwear is."

Kate shook her head. "If anyone found out, I'd be fired."

"So be discreet," Olivia replied.

"It's a very bad idea."

Olivia shrugged. "It might not be the best idea but the sexual tension between you two is off the charts. People at work are going to start noticing, Kate."

"No, they're not."

"Yeah, they are. I noticed it right away this morning."

"You're more perceptive than most."

Olivia rolled her eyes. "What about Josh? Are you still going out with him tonight?"

"Yes," Kate replied.

"Really?"

"Really, really Olivia," Kate insisted. "Even if I went ahead and did what you suggested with Edward, it's not a relationship. Josh is a nice guy and I have an actual chance of having a relationship with him."

"But are you sexually attracted to him?" Olivia asked with one raised eyebrow.

"I barely know him. We've been out on one date, and I don't know if I'm sexually attracted to him yet. These things take time," Kate said.

"Oh really? Because all it took was Edward looking at you with those pretty blue eyes of his and you wanted to jump his bones immediately. Don't give me that, 'get to know him crap', Katie pie. It might work with someone else, but not with me."

"Subject change!" Kate said brightly. "How is that handsome husband of yours?"

Olivia laughed, "Fine, we'll change the subject but you know I'm going to bring it up again sooner or later."

Kate sighed "I know, Olivia. I know."

* * *

At ten to five, Kate ducked into the bathroom and changed into her jeans and a dark green t-shirt. She hurried back to her desk and logged out of her computer before grabbing her purse.

"Hi, Kate."

She twitched and stared up at Josh standing next to her desk.

"Josh, uh, hi," she said.

"Hello." He smiled at her. "The receptionist sent me back. I hope that's okay."

"Of course," she said with a nervous look at Edward's door. "Just give me a minute and I'm ready to go.

"Sure," Josh replied.

She closed her laptop, her heart sinking when Edward emerged from his office.

"Kate, can you scan this document and email it to - "

He stopped, a scowl flickering across his face when he saw Josh.

"Josh, this is Edward Turner, one of our partners. Edward this is Josh Dumont." She watched a bit nervously as Edward and Josh shook hands. There was a moment of awkward silence that Kate hurried to break.

"We're um, we're just heading out for a quick dinner and a movie," she said uneasily.

"I know a place that has great Chinese food. You should take Josh there," Edward replied.

Her face red, Kate reached for the paper he held in his hand. "I'll just scan and email this before I leave."

"No," Edward said. "I can do it."

"I don't mind," Kate protested. "It'll only take a minute."

"It's fine, really. Josh, it was nice to meet you."

"Nice to meet you," Josh replied.

"Okay, well, have a nice weekend, Edward," Kate said before she and Josh walked toward reception. Edward didn't reply and she couldn't stop from glancing briefly over her shoulder. Edward was standing by her desk staring at her, his expression unreadable.

As Kate and Josh walked away, Edward felt a streak of jealousy rip through him when Josh put a possessive hand at the small of Kate's back. She looked back briefly before they turned the corner to reception and he hoped the jealousy he was feeling didn't show. His hands tightened on the paper he was holding and he forced himself to relax. The paper was crumpled and he smoothed it out on Kate's desk, sighing harshly to himself.

It is ridiculous to feel this way about a woman you hardly know and even more ridiculous to feel this way about your assistant. You will not find excuses to walk by her desk, you will not stand close enough to touch her and you will not, under any circumstances, remember what it felt like to be between her legs.

Chapter 5

Sunday afternoon, Kate took another look at her reflection in the mirror before grinning at Chicken, who was currently weaving between her feet and purring loudly.

"Damn, Chicken, I look good."

Yesterday morning when Olivia had phoned to invite her to an impromptu get together for this afternoon, she had decided to splurge and buy a new dress for the occasion. The moment she had put on the dress she knew she was going to buy it, despite its hefty price tag.

"I probably shouldn't have but I couldn't resist. I look fantastic in it." She struck a pose for Chicken, throwing her shoulders back and tossing her hair. Chicken stared at her for a moment and with a loud disgruntled meow, turned and stalked from the room.

"Everyone's a critic," Kate called after her and turned to look at herself again. She was wearing a light green, sleeveless empire waist dress. The dress fell to just below her knees and accentuated her curves and creamy white skin. The silky material felt wonderful against her skin and she twirled once, enjoying the way the material billowed softly around her bare legs.

"I'm leaving, Chicky-Chick, Chicken" she called as she headed to the front door. "I shouldn't be too late. Try and stay out of trouble while I'm gone would you?"

As she drove to Olivia and Jon's she thought about her date with Josh on Friday night. She felt like it had gone better than the first one. After dinner and the movie, they had gone for coffee. Josh was funny and sweet and, she thought wryly, perfect. Too bad she felt zero chemistry with him.

He had driven her back to the office to get her car and as she was unlocking the door, he had leaned in for a soft and thorough kiss. She had tried to concentrate on the feel of his mouth on hers and when he had lightly traced her lips with his tongue, she had opened her mouth and let him deepen the kiss. His mouth was gentle and his hands warm around her waist but as hard as she tried, she couldn't get lost in the moment. Thoughts of Edward and the way he made her insides weak kept intruding. If Josh noticed her hesitation, he made no mention of it. Instead, he had invited her to go to a local art exhibit on Wednesday night. She had accepted despite the lack of spark she felt for him.

She parked on the street, the driveway was already full of cars, and made her way to the back yard. Olivia's idea of an impromptu get-together usually consisted of about fifty of her closest friends, and this one was no different. She rounded the corner of the house and, spotting Jon at the barbeque, she weaved her way through the crowd, waving at Rose and Sheila from the office and at Leslie, one of the members of the book club she and Olivia both belonged to.

"Hello, handsome." She smiled at Jon and gave him a quick squeeze around the waist. Jon was handsome with his blond hair and brown eyes and lithe, swimmer's body. His easy going nature and good sense of humour fitted Olivia's personality perfectly and Kate was envious of the obvious love they had for each other.

"Katie-pie!" Jon exclaimed delightedly. "You look great, darling." He gave her an enthusiastic one-armed bear hug, placing an affectionate kiss on her forehead.

"You're not too shabby yourself," she said. "Where's that hot wife of yours?"

"Check the kitchen, last I heard she was on the look-out for more potato salad." Jon waved to an older gentleman who was crossing the lawn towards them. "Better go find her before Jim gets here. Nice guy, but he'll talk your ear off about golf if you let him." He winked at her as she escaped toward the house. She was a few feet from the house when Rose and Sheila caught up to her.

"So, how was the Friday night date?" Rose grinned at her.

"We want all the details," Sheila said.

Kate laughed and shook her head. "Sorry, girls, but a lady never kisses and tells." She looked over her shoulder at them, "I need to have some secrets."

Still grinning at them and not watching in front of her, she walked straight into and bounced off a familiar hard body. She gave an unladylike yelp and pin-wheeled her arms madly, trying to keep her balance as she tipped backwards. With cat-like quickness Edward reached out and wrapped an arm around her waist, pulling her forward against his hard chest.

"Hello, Kate." He steadied her against him as she looked up at him and groaned to herself.

"What are you doing here?" She asked.

He was dressed in jeans and a dark blue t-shirt that emphasized the muscles in his arms, and she could feel the ridges of his abs against her belly as he tightened his grip about her waist for a brief heart-stopping moment before letting her go.

"My goodness, Kate, it seems like every time I see you you're throwing yourself at Edward." drawled an icy cool voice just to the left of them.

Kate blinked in shock at Melissa before clearing her throat. "Sorry, Edward. I'm a little clumsy."

"It's fine," Edward replied as Melissa stepped a little closer to him.

"Please excuse me," Kate said politely before walking rapidly to the house. She found Olivia in the kitchen rummaging in the fridge and poked her lightly in the side.

"Why on earth are Edward and Melissa here?" She asked.

"Kate, it was a huge coincidence, I – "

She stopped and looked her up and down. "Katie-pie, you look fantastic. Is that a new dress?"

"It is," Kate said. "Do you really like it? I wasn't sure if it was a bit much or – "

"It's definitely not too much," Olivia said. "I love the colour!"

"Thanks, honey," Kate said happily. "It was frackin' expensive but I - wait! Stop changing the subject. Why are Melissa and Edward here?"

"Oh right. That." Olivia made a face. "You know Jim, Jon's golfing buddy from way back? And you know that Jim lived in New York for ten years right? It turns out that Edward did quite a bit of work for him when he lived there. They've kept in touch over the years and Jim actually invited Edward to go golfing with him and Jon yesterday. It was a complete coincidence and Jon didn't even know who Edward was until Jim told him. The next thing you know Jon had invited Edward to the barbeque. I should have called and warned you but it's been a bit crazy around here."

"That doesn't explain why Melissa is here," Kate said.

"You can blame Arthur for that. I was at the office for about two hours yesterday morning - you know the Wilson case is heating up and Arthur's having fits over it - and I invited him and Sylvia to the barbeque. Melissa was in the office as well and Arthur assumed I invited everyone from the office. He brought it up in front of her and I had no choice but to invite her. I never thought she'd actually show."

Olivia paused. "Between you and me – pretty sure it's because she was hoping Edward would be here too. She's been glued to his side the minute he showed up."

Kate made a face. "What do you want to bet they start sleeping together?"

A little curdle of jealousy went through her at the thought as Olivia shook her head. "Melissa has to follow the same 'no fucking the coworkers rule' as you do, Kate."

Kate shrugged. "I doubt Arthur would fire her or Edward if they were sleeping together. She's one of his best lawyers and Edward's the new partner."

"I wouldn't worry, Katie-pie. I don't think Edward's interested in her."

"Of course he isn't. She's only gorgeous and brilliant and one of the best lawyers in the city," Kate said. "Why on earth would Edward be interested in her?"

She sighed loudly. "God, my jealousy is super attractive, huh?"

Olivia laughed. "I have a feeling Edward prefers redheads. Besides, how do you think I feel about Melissa at my house? She's going to be using my bathroom and probably going through my medicine cabinet. What do you want to bet that I catch her trying to sabotage my birth control in an effort to get me out of the office?"

Kate burst out laughing as Olivia handed her the bowl of potato salad to carry. "I'd be more concerned that she finds those 'toys' you and Jon ordered off the internet."

Olivia laughed and gave Kate a playful swat on the ass. "Cork it, sister. Now carry out that potato salad while I grab more beer."

* * *

"Honestly, Kate, you must try golfing. It's the finest sport there is," Jim said earnestly. He leaned forward and tapped her on the arm. "I'd be happy to give you a few lessons."

"That's really nice of you to offer, Jim," Kate said politely, "but I'm pretty sure I'm a hopeless case when it comes to golfing."

"Nonsense!" Jim bellowed. "Everyone can be taught to golf!"

As Jim began to talk animatedly about the proper way to swing a golf club, Kate glanced unobtrusively about her, looking for someone or something to help distract Jim's attention. His wife Marlene shot her a sympathetic wink and a grin before disappearing into the crowd. Kate had just resigned herself to another half hour of golfing tips when Olivia magically appeared at her side.

"Now, Jim, you can't keep my Katie all to yourself. I need her help," she said as Kate shot her a look of gratitude. "Katie, my love, can you do me a favour and run to the fridge in the laundry room and grab another case of beer? We're getting low."

"Of course." Kate gave Jim an apologetic look and, mouthing a silent thank you to Olivia, walked rapidly toward the house.

She sighed with relief and took a moment to savour the quietness of the laundry room. She grabbed the case of beer off the bottom shelf of the fridge and, with a small grunt of effort, lifted it and turned toward the door of the laundry room. Edward stood in the doorway and she gasped and jumped, losing her grip on the case of beer. As she fumbled with the heavy case, Edward crossed the small room and took it from her. Their fingers touched and a burst of heat blossomed in her belly. Already her muscles were tightening in unconscious reaction to his closeness, to the notion that he had been watching her. Her breath quickened in her throat as he placed the case of beer on the washer and moved back to lean against the door, crossing his arms across his chest. The bulk of his body covered the door and she felt a tingle of fear and excitement when she realized she was trapped with him.

Edward stared hungrily at Kate. Just being in the same room with her affected his body and he grimaced at the uncomfortable tightness of his jeans. She was slightly flushed and taking quick rapid breaths. His eyes drifted to her breasts in that remarkable dress and his nostrils flared when her nipples visibly hardened against the thin material of her dress. She self-consciously crossed her arms across her breasts and he let his eyes drift lower. Her bare legs looked smooth and silky soft and he wanted nothing more than to run his hand up her leg to see if her skin was as soft as it looked.

Kate cleared her throat nervously. The way Edward was looking at her was making her nerve endings sing with anticipation. "Is there something you wanted, Edward?"

He gave her a smile that made her pussy throb and she forced herself to look away for a moment. When a stray piece of hair fell across her face she blew it back impatiently and met his gaze almost defiantly.

"Well?" She prompted.

"How was your date with Josh?" He asked.

"Fine."

"Good."

He took a step toward her and she automatically took a step back.

"I like your dress."

"Thank you, it's new. I bought it yesterday at this little shop on Bearn Street. I really like it." Her nervousness was making her babble and she forced herself to stop talking.

As Edward took another step towards her, she swallowed hard. "I need to take the beer to Olivia."

"Sure." He took another step and Kate backed away until her ass hit the dryer.

Trapped!

Edward gave her a decidedly predatory grin and stepped forward again. He was only inches from her now and she could feel the heat between them as he reached out and wrapped a tendril of her hair around one finger.

"Do you know how crazy you're driving me?" He muttered.

She shook her head, ignoring the urge to lean forward until their bodies were touching.

"I didn't sleep at all Friday night," he confessed. "I spent the entire night wondering if you were allowing Josh to touch you like I had touched you the night before in my office."

He took a small step forward so that the tips of her breasts brushed against his chest. She moaned at the contact.

"I kept wondering if he had tasted the sweetness of your mouth or enjoyed the warmth of your bed and the feel of those long legs wrapped around him."

He gave her a scorching look that left her breathless. "Tried my best to not think about you moaning his name instead of mine."

He leaned forward and lightly brushed his lips against hers. She opened her mouth immediately for him but he pulled his mouth from hers without deepening the kiss.

"It was driving me insane thinking that he might be doing this to you." Edward reached out and slowly circled one hardened nipple with his thumb, forcing another low moan from her throat.

"Or this." He slid his hand to her shoulder to tug gently at the thin strap of her dress before lightly running his hand down her arm.

"Did he touch you like this, Katie-did?" He whispered as he lowered his hand and traced her navel through her dress with his finger. Her legs trembled violently and she leaned back against the dryer as he studied her closely. "Did you invite him into your bed?"

"That's none of your business." She tried to speak forcefully but it came out in a breathless squeak.

"Probably not," he agreed before sliding his hand inside both her dress and her bra to caress her breast. At the feel of his warm, rough fingers trailing across her sensitive nipple, her knees buckled and she braced her hands against the dryer, trying to stand straight.

"Did he enjoy the warmth of my Katie's bed?" He asked again.

"No," she said shakily.

"Good girl," he murmured possessively.

He bent his dark head toward her and took her mouth with his. She sighed into his mouth and when he placed one hand on the nape of her neck and deepened the kiss, she surrendered willingly. Small moans and whimpers escaped her mouth as he slid his arms around her body to cup her ass. He pulled her roughly against him and tore his mouth from hers.

"Do you feel what you do to me, Katie-did?" He whispered into her ear.

She shuddered violently when he ground his hips against hers and moaned when he slid one hand under the silky material of her dress and grasped her knee in his hand. He pulled her leg up around his hip, forcing her to widen her stance so he could fit himself comfortably in the juncture of her thighs. He dipped his head and ran his tongue over the sensitive skin of her throat while his rough hand caressed the smoothness of her thigh and calf.

"Edward" she sighed as he kissed the delicate column of her throat. She groaned when he slid his hand up her leg and under the edge of her panties to squeeze her bare ass. She reached down and tugged his shirt free from his jeans. She traced across his abs, liking the way he shuddered under her touch before she ran her fingers through the dark hair on his chest. Her nails grazed one flat nipple and he groaned loudly, his body twitching against hers.

"Are you wet, Katie?" He asked quietly.

Before she could react he anchored an arm firmly around her waist and slid his hand into the front of her panties, the palm of his hand flat against her lower abdomen, his fingers gliding through the soft curls between her thighs. She twisted in surprise and clamped her thighs together but he had shoved his leg between hers and her thighs closed uselessly around his, leaving plenty of room for his hand to touch and caress.

"Edward," she gasped and tugged frantically at his arm.

He kissed her roughly, sliding his tongue into her mouth as he pushed one finger into her damp heat.

"You're so wet, Katie," he groaned against her mouth. "You have no idea how much I want to fuck you."

She trembled and clung to him as he thrust his finger back and forth before rubbing her clit with his thumb. He swallowed her loud cry of pleasure with his mouth and kissed her fiercely, their tongues tangling together as he rubbed her clit in slow, steady circles. She thrust her hips against him frantically and when her pussy clenched around his finger, he flicked her clit lightly with his thumb. She shuddered all over and shoved her face into his neck, muffling her cries of pleasure as she came against him, her body shaking madly. He slipped his finger free of her tight pussy and kneaded her ass roughly as she shuddered and trembled against him.

"Oh boy," she muttered shakily and leaned back to look at him. He smiled at her and brushed away a stray strand of hair that clung to her cheek. She stared at him for a moment, her eyes hazy and unfocused, before kissing him hungrily. She sucked on his lower lip, making him groan with pleasure and thrust his erection against her.

"Your turn," she whispered into his ear and reached for his belt buckle.

The door to the laundry room swung open and Olivia poked her head in "God, Kate, did you get lost?"

Her eyes widened as she stared at Edward and Kate locked together against the dryer.

"Sorry!" She said cheerfully and slammed the door shut.

"Shit!" Kate muttered as the sound of Olivia's footsteps faded down the hallway. "Shit, shit, shit!"

She pushed Edward away from her and frantically straightened her dress.

"It's okay, Katie, relax," Edward said. "It was only Olivia."

"Thank God!" She hissed at him. "What if it had been Rose? Or Melissa?"

She paced back and forth in the small room, her hair streaming behind her and her face flushed. "I've gone mad. Completely mad."

"Katie, it's okay. Just calm down."

She turned on him. "One - you need to stop calling me Katie. Calling me Katie suggests we are more familiar with each other than we are and two – "

"That's not fair. Olivia calls you Katie and unless she's given you an orgasm in her laundry room, then I'd say you and I are more familiar with each other than you and Olivia are," Edward protested with a hint of laughter in his voice.

She blushed furiously but ignored his comment "And two – it's your fault I've gone mad. Your fault completely." She crossed her arms over her chest and glared at him. "You and your stupid blue eyes and hard body and your 'Katie, just kiss me once'."

"Can I help it if I'm irresistible?" Edward said. "I'm naturally charming."

He ignored her sigh of exasperation. "The real question is - do you want to finish what we started now or wait until later? I'm willing to wait until later when we can enjoy the privacy of your bed, but since you find me so hard to resist...."

He trailed off, giving her a flirty little smile that sent a flash of heat through her body.

"Gah!" Kate yelled and pushed her way past him. She stopped at the door of the laundry room and turned to face him. "You're too arrogant for your own good. There is no 'we' in my bed, Edward."

"Right — your 'no boinking the boss' rule," Edward said solemnly. "Say listen, is that a rule set in stone or more of a guideline? What if we didn't actually 'boink' but just made each other come repeatedly? Is that allowable?"

Kate stared wide-eyed at him. "What is wrong with you? Are you deliberately trying to get me fired?"

"Of course not," he said quickly. "I want you, Katie and you want me too. We'll be discreet and no one at the office will find out. Give me one night - that's all I'm asking."

She hesitated, biting at her bottom lip with indecision, and a ridiculous surge of hope went through him. "No one will find out, I promise."

Kate hesitated a moment longer before shaking her head. "We were just caught by Olivia. People will find out, Edward. They always do. I'm starting to think I'm not the one who has gone mad. What we just did, what we — we almost were about to do was a mistake. You know it was."

She stalked from the room and headed for the upstairs bathroom. She stared at herself in the mirror. Her face was flushed and she was wide-eyed and a little crazed looking. She splashed cold water on her face and then sat on the edge of the tub, willing her heart to stop racing. There was a soft knock on the door and she looked up as Olivia poked her head into the room.

"You okay?" She asked.

"Oh, fan-fucking-tastic." Kate grimaced and buried her face in her hands as Olivia shut the door and perched on the tub beside her.

"So Edward just strolled into the backyard looking like the cat that swallowed the canary."

"Jerk," Kate muttered.

Olivia laughed. "Listen, not to be too personal, but should I be disinfecting the top of my dryer for Edward and Katie cooties?"

"No!" Kate lifted her head from her hands and stared at Olivia. "I've gone mad. The old sane Kate would never make out with her boss in your laundry room."

"That's true, honey, but Gerald wasn't much in the looks department."

"What am I going to do, Olivia? I can't even get near him without my insides turning to mush. All he has to do is look at me and I want to drag him to the nearest bed. It's like I completely forget that my job is on the fucking line."

Olivia sighed before draping her arm across Kate's shoulders. "I don't know what to tell you, Katie-pie."

"I just need to forget how damn hot he is and remember that I have bills to pay. I just have to get through this week and then Edward's in New York for a week," Kate said. "We'll have a break from each other and this stupid sexual tension will end. Right?"

"Sure," Olivia said doubtfully.

Kate closed her eyes for a moment. "How do I look?"

"You look fine - a little flushed, but fine," Olivia said. "Let's get back to the party before Jon comes looking for us."

Kate clutched Olivia's shoulder. "Listen, as my best friend it's your duty to make sure that I am not alone with Edward. Do you understand and accept your mission?"

Olivia gave her a thumbs up. "Absolutely - I'm here for you. Let's go have a beer. You look like you could use one."

* * *

"Kate?"

Kate glanced up from the photocopier. Edward was standing in the small room and he gave her a look that loosened her thighs and made her panties wet.

"Stop looking at me like that," she muttered before shoving more paper into the copier.

It was Wednesday and she was feeling the strain of trying to ignore her attraction to Edward and working closely with him and Melissa. The work on the Johnson case was coming to an end and it felt frantic and chaotic as she, Melissa and Edward worked long hours to ensure that Alfred's purchase of his new company went smoothly. Edward had made no mention of what had happened in the laundry room between them but that hadn't stopped her from replaying it over and over in her head.

Edward just grinned at her and she took a step back when he moved toward her. "Relax, Katie," he said in a low voice. "I'm not going to try and fuck you in the copy room. Unless," he gave her a hopeful look that almost made her grin, "you're into that type of thing?"

"I'm not into getting fired from my job."

"Discretion," he said. "I'm all about the discretion, Katie-did."

"Having sex in the copy room is about as far from discretion as you can get, Mr. Turner," she said.

He laughed quietly. "Good point. How about drinks at my place tonight?"

"I have plans," she said.

"With Josh?"

Before she could reply, Melissa had joined them in the copy room. "Edward? Alfred's on the phone and would like to speak to you."

"Thanks," Edward replied. He left the room and Melissa gave Kate an appraising look.

"I see the way you look at Edward," she said. "It's inappropriate."

Kate rolled her eyes. "Like I care what you think, Melissa."

"You'll care when I go to Arthur and get you fired for sleeping with your boss."

"You're losing it, Melissa. I barely know Edward and I'm certainly not sleeping with him," Kate snapped. "And until you have proof that I am, you can take your empty threats and get lost."

Melissa made a snort of disgust before walking away and Kate took a deep breath. She needed to be extremely careful how she behaved around Edward, Melissa hated her and would gleefully get her ass fired, so why was she still thinking about Edward's suggestion of one night only? She sighed quietly and grabbed the stack of papers before heading to her desk. She had a date with Josh tonight and that was what she needed to concentrate on – not what it would be like to sleep with her damn boss.

* * *

"I had a really good time tonight, Kate," Josh said as he walked her to her door.

"I did too, Josh. Thanks for inviting me." Kate opened her front door and there was an awkward pause as Josh smiled at her.

"Um, would you like to come in for a drink?" Kate asked.

"I'd love to."

He followed her into the house and she fumbled for the hallway light. As she flicked the switch, she stumbled over the running shoes she had left in the hallway. Josh reached out and caught her before turning her toward him. He gave her a slow and thorough kiss and she hesitated before putting her arms around his shoulders and returning his kiss.

See, this is nice. It's a perfectly nice kiss that you're enjoying and it doesn't matter if there aren't sparks flying or if doesn't make you breathless like stupid Edward's kisses do.

As Josh rubbed her back there was a low growl behind them. He broke the kiss and stared at her. "Did you hear that?"

There was another growl and Kate pulled away from Josh before turning around. He peered over her shoulder at the fat grey cat staring balefully at them.

"Chicken, go on!" She muttered, stamping her foot at the cat. Chicken refused to move. Her tail twitched menacingly and she gave Josh a murderous look before hissing loudly.

"That's some attack cat you have there," Josh said. "Should I try and make friends with it?"

"Oh God, no," Kate said. "If you want to keep all of your limbs, it's best to stay away from her. In fact, try not to look her in the eye – it makes her even angrier."

She shooed Chicken down the hallway toward the guest bedroom. With another growl, a swat at Kate's hand and a few irritated hisses, Chicken flounced into the room. Kate quickly shut the door behind her.

"The living room is to the right," she said as Josh took off his suit jacket and hung it on the hook. "Make yourself comfortable while I grab the wine and some glasses."

She disappeared into the kitchen, returning a few minutes later with a bottle of wine and two wine glasses.

"White, okay?"

"Sounds good," Josh said. "So, your cat's name is Chicken?"

Kate nodded as she opened the bottle of wine.

"And why did you name her Chicken?" Josh said with a grin.

"That's the name she came with. I adopted her from the humane society a few years ago," Kate said. She poured wine into both their glasses and handed one to Josh. "I was going to change it but then I thought – how would I like it if someone just started calling me a different name – so I kept it. Truthfully, it doesn't really suit her. She's the angriest cat I've ever met."

Josh laughed. "Did the humane society have an explanation for why she was so angry?"

"Nope. They just said she was dropped off because her family was moving. I guess her owner said she was a lovely cat and very friendly. Then she tore a big chunk out of the hand of the first volunteer who tried to touch her and that's when they realized she wasn't exactly as friendly as her previous owner said."

"So why did you adopt her?" Josh asked curiously.

"I went there to pick out a kitten and there was Chicken sitting in the back of her cage, all puffed up and angry at the world, with a bright yellow tag stuck to the front of her kennel. I asked a volunteer what the tag meant and when I found out it meant she was scheduled to be euthanized that day, I adopted her. I took her home and tried to make friends which she wasn't having any part in. She did eventually warm up to me – mostly – but she really doesn't like strangers."

"It was nice of you to adopt her," Josh said.

Kate laughed. "I'm a glutton for punishment, apparently."

Josh grinned at her before picking up a framed photo of her and her sister from the bookshelf beside him. "Who's this?"

"That's my baby sister, Lina."

"Are you close?"

"Yes. She doesn't live in California though so we don't get to spend as much time together as I'd like. She was just out for a visit not that long ago. Would you like more wine?"

Josh set the picture and his wineglass on the bookshelf. "Honestly? I'm not all that interested in wine."

He took her wineglass and set it beside his before tugging her into his arms.

"You're so gorgeous, Kate," he whispered before bending his head and kissing her full lips. When he cupped one full breast she tried to push away the immediate image of Edward and his rough fingers caressing her breast but it stubbornly remained. Frustrated and tense, she gave Josh an apologetic look when he broke the kiss. He stared down at her for a moment and then stepped back, putting some distance between them.

"I think I should go," he said softly.

"I'm sorry, Josh, I just…"

She trailed off, trying to think of a way to explain without hurting his feelings.

He smiled ruefully at her. "You don't need to explain, Kate. You're obviously not feeling for me what I am for you. No hard feelings - we tried, right?"

She followed him to the front door and at the look of misery on her face he gave her a gentle squeeze and kiss on the cheek. "It's fine, really. If there's no chemistry for you, there's no chemistry. I'll see you around, okay?"

"I really am sorry, Josh. I wish it could have been different."

"I know," he said. "Take care, Kate."

She watched him back his car out of the driveway before closing the front door. She released Chicken from her imprisonment in the spare room before pouring herself more wine and sitting at the kitchen table. She rested her head on the table, letting the wood cool her heated cheek as Chicken jumped up on the table and batted at her hair.

"Chicken, what's wrong with me?" Kate said. "Why can't I get Edward out of my head?"

She lifted her head and stared morosely at the cat. "I really have gone mad, haven't I?"

Chicken purred loudly and butted her head against Kate's chin. Kate scratched the side of Chicken's face and stared at her thoughtfully for a moment.

"You certainly put on a fine display with Josh, didn't you? Even if I do eventually find someone to have a relationship with, you'll probably scare them away."

Chicken yawned and flopped down on the table, rolling over and exposing her generous belly.

"Like I'm going to rub your belly," Kate said. She took another sip of wine before checking the time. It was late but she suddenly, desperately needed to talk to Lina.

"Please be awake, please be awake," she muttered as she held her cell phone to her ear.

She breathed a sigh of relief when she heard Lina's voice. "Hi, Kate!"

"Hi, Lina. How are you?"

"I'm fine," Lina said. "Did mom call you and get you all in a panic? I told her not to and that I'd call you on the weekend and tell you myself."

"Tell me what?" Kate said. "What's going on?"

She heard the low murmur of a deep voice and Lina said, "Give me half an hour, Aiden. Go on to bed, I'll meet you up there."

"Lina? What's going on?" Kate repeated.

"Sorry," Lina said. "I was just saying goodnight to Aiden."

"He's at your house?"

"Well, actually I'm at his place. I'm kind of – sort of – living here now."

"What?" Kate said. "You just started formally dating like a week and a half ago."

"Yeah, a lot has happened in the last few days," Lina said.

"Start talking," Kate replied.

* * *

"Oh God, Lina. You should have called me. I could have flown in and – "

"I'm fine, Katie. Honest," Lina said. "And Daisy is doing much better. She's coming home from the vet clinic tomorrow."

"So now you're selling your house and moving in with Aiden? That seems awfully fast," Kate said.

Lina laughed. "Honestly, Aiden's not giving me much choice. He's gone from – I'll never be in a relationship to you're mine and you're moving in with me - so fast it kind of makes my head spin."

"Lina," Kate said cautiously, "are you sure that this is the right thing to do? If Aiden has that many issues with relationships, what happens if it doesn't work out? You'll be homeless."

"I'm sure," Lina said. She hesitated and then lowered her voice. "I spoke with Aiden earlier tonight about talking to a therapist about his mom and dad and how he feels about relationships in general and he was surprisingly agreeable to it. He wants to make this work, Katie. He loves me and I love him."

"Well, I'm really happy for you, honey," Kate said. "And I'm so glad you're safe."

"Thanks, Kate. Now, tell me what's wrong."

"There's nothing wrong."

"Don't give me that. I can tell there's something wrong," Lina said.

Kate sighed. "How do you do that? Ever since we were kids, you could always tell."

"It's a gift," Lina said. "Now it's your turn – start talking."

* * *

"Lina? Are you still there?" Kate asked half an hour later. She had just finished telling her every gritty detail about what was happening between her and Edward and had been greeted with silence.

"I'm still here," Lina said.

"You're trying not to laugh, aren't you?" Kate said.

Lina snickered loudly. "I totally am. I'm sorry, Kate, I know this isn't funny but seriously, two weeks ago we were just talking about what would happen if you were attracted to your new boss."

"This is all your fault," Kate said. "You jinxed me."

"So, what are you going to do?"

"I have no idea. I was hoping you could give me some advice since you were basically in the exact same situation."

"Well," Lina said, "it's not exactly the same. I was in no danger of being fired from my job for sleeping with Aiden. I guess the real question is – do you want to risk your job for one night with Edward?"

"I kind of do," Kate said. "Stupid, huh?"

"No, I don't think so," Lina replied. "Even if there was the chance of being fired, I would have still slept with Aiden. You can't help being attracted to someone. Have you thought about quitting your job?"

"No," Kate said. "I'm not quitting my job on the off-chance that I might have some type of relationship with Edward."

"Probably wise. Especially if he's only asking for one night. Besides, you really don't know a lot about him. He could turn out to be a first-class asshole."

"Maybe," Kate said.

"But you don't think so."

"No, I don't. He seems like a good guy but I guess that isn't really something I can say with any confidence."

There was a moment of silence and then Kate sighed. "I should let you go. It's been way longer than half an hour."

"We can talk as long as you need to, Katie," Lina said.

"I'm good."

"Listen, honey, the only bit of advice I can actually give is that if you really are attracted to this guy and you think you can do one night with him without losing your job, then go for it. Life is short and sometimes you just need to do something wild and crazy."

Kate laughed. "Wild and crazy isn't really me, Lina."

"Maybe it should be," Lina said thoughtfully. "At least for one night."

"Maybe, but how awkward will it be at work after we sleep together?" Kate said.

"Hey, you're both adults. Lay down some ground rules, make sure that you both know exactly what it is, and you'll be fine, "Lina said. "Just one – don't get caught sleeping with your boss and two – be sure that all you want is just one night with him. If you end up wanting more, that'll be a problem."

"Yeah," Kate said moodily.

"I'm super helpful, huh?" Lina laughed. "You probably shouldn't listen to anything I say – I'm deep in the throes of new love, and that makes people say and do stupid things."

"I'm so happy for you, honey."

"Thanks, Katie. You'll have to fly out and meet Aiden soon, okay? He's got this giant penthouse right downtown and there's plenty of space for you to stay with us."

"Giant penthouse? Nice," Kate said.

"I know, right? The guy's super rich," Lina said with a small laugh. "I can still hardly believe that he's in love with my chubby, broke ass."

"I'm not," Kate said. "I'd better go. Your handsome rich-as-hell boyfriend is waiting for you."

"I love you, Katie. Call me again if you need to talk. Any time, okay?"

"Thanks, Lina. I love you too."

Chapter 6

Friday morning Kate arrived at the office an hour early. It was the closing date for Alfred Johnson's purchase and the day would be a busy one. She let herself into reception and walked quickly to her desk. Edward's door was open and she popped her head into his office as she headed towards the kitchen.

"Good morning, Edward."

He looked up from his computer and stared blankly at her for a moment. He looked tired and a little out of sorts. His normally clean-shaven jaw was covered in a shadow of stubble and he had the top buttons of his shirt undone and his tie loose around his neck.

"Have you been at the office all night?" She asked. She had left the office at nine last night and Edward and Melissa had still been in his office going over some final documentation.

"No. I got here about an hour ago. Do I look like I spent the night?"

"You just look a little tired," Kate said. "Do you want a coffee?"

"That sounds good. Thanks, Katie," he replied distractedly.

Her stomach did a lazy little flip flop when he called her Katie. Her brain was inundated with memories of last weekend's adventure in the laundry room and she shivered a little at the memory of his low voice asking her if she was wet and the way it had felt to have him touching her. She turned swiftly and walked towards the kitchen, giving herself a light smack on the forehead.

Keep it professional, she warned herself for the umpteenth time as she started brewing some coffee. *One more day and you've got a whole week to regain your self-control.*

* * *

"Kate? Melissa is looking for you." Sheila stuck her head into the copy room and gave her a sympathetic grin.

"Thanks, Sheila."

Kate grabbed the stack of papers and hurried back to her desk. It was nearly three and the day had been long and tiring. She'd skipped lunch and her stomach growled at her as she skirted past one of the lawyers in the firm, Doug, who was standing in the hallway and talking animatedly on his cell phone.

"Where were you?" Melissa snapped impatiently when she walked into Edward's office.

"Copying the papers you asked me for," Kate replied patiently. She handed the stack of papers to Melissa before turning to Edward.

"How do they look?" She asked.

"Good. Alfred will be here in fifteen minutes to leave for the shareholder meeting. Do you think you enough have time to make these last few changes and make twenty copies?"

"Yes," she replied.

He handed the document to her and gave her a distracted smile. "Thank you, Katie."

"You're welcome," Kate replied. She gave Melissa a brittle smile. The woman was staring suspiciously at her and she glanced briefly at Edward, her eyes narrowing, before returning her gaze to Kate.

Kate, willing herself not to flush, slipped around her and left Edward's office.

* * *

"Almost finished?" Edward strode into the copy room as Kate put the last batch of papers into the photocopier. "Alfred's at reception and we're leaving in five."

"Just finishing up," Kate replied. Edward stood beside her and she breathed in the good, clean scent of him and felt a little lightheaded.

Professional, Kate. Be professional.

"Are you going to tighten your tie?"

"Thanks for the reminder." He buttoned his shirt and tightened his tie. "How do I look?"

She gave his tie a quick tug to the right. "Much better," she said with a small grin. "Tie is straight, no sauce on your face, I think you're good to go. Good luck."

She handed him the stack of papers and licked her lips nervously when he wrapped his lean fingers around her wrist.

"A good luck wish is usually accompanied by a good luck kiss, Katie-did," he murmured and captured her lips with his.

Shivers coursing down her spine, berating herself internally but unable to stop herself, she returned his kiss eagerly. He coaxed his tongue between her lips and stroked hers just once before breaking the kiss.

"Better," he whispered and ran his thumb across her bottom lip before leaving.

"Nice work at being professional, Kate," she muttered to herself.

* * *

"Kate? What are you still doing here?"

She glanced up from her computer and smiled at Arthur. "Just finishing up a few things."

"You've been working late all week. It's Friday and after six – go home," Arthur said.

"Well, I should probably – "

"Nope," Arthur chided gently as he shifted his briefcase to his other hand. "It's just you and me left in the office and I'm leaving and officially telling you to go home, Kate."

"All right," she said with a small smile. "Thank you, Arthur."

"You're welcome. Have a good weekend."

"You as well."

She shut down her laptop and tidied her desk. It was close to six and she refused to admit to herself that she was waiting around for Edward to return from his meeting with Alfred. She wouldn't see him again for an entire week and the thought was making her surprisingly anxious. Not seeing him for a week was a good thing, she reminded herself. It would give her time to get her libido under control and realize that sleeping with her boss was a very bad idea.

* * *

"That went remarkably smooth," Melissa said as Edward sat down in his chair. "Don't you think?"

"Hmm," he replied absentmindedly. He had been hoping that Kate would still be in the office which was stupid considering that it was almost six-thirty. Still, there had been a part of him that had thought she might still be here and waiting for him. He was absurdly disappointed that he wouldn't see her before he left for New York.

"Edward?"

He glanced up. Melissa was perched on the edge of his desk in front of him. Her slender legs were crossed and her short skirt showed a generous amount of thigh. She leaned back, resting her hands on his desk so that her small, pert breasts pulled against her expensive silk blouse and lightly bit her lower lip.

"We make a good team," she said quietly.

"We do," he replied before discreetly pushing back his chair.

"I think we could make a good team in other areas too," she said.

"Sleeping together is against the rules," he said shortly.

"Rules are meant to be broken," she said.

"Not this one."

"Honestly, I think Arthur and Gerald made the rule more to keep the lawyers from banging their assistants," she replied. "Apparently, a lawyer was sleeping with his assistant about ten years ago and it caused a lot of issues when he finally broke it off with her. She threatened to sue him for sexual harassment and Gerald and Arthur had to fire him. They implemented the no romantic involvement between coworkers shortly after that."

He pushed his chair back a little more. "Which is exactly why this isn't happening."

"The thing is, Edward, I'm not some dumb little PA lusting after her powerful boss. I can be discreet – I don't gossip like so many women do – and I know for a fact that there's been a few," she paused and grinned at him, "hook-ups between lawyers in this office over the last decade."

"Melissa, I'm not inte – "

His protest was cut short when she pushed herself off the desk and pressed her body against his. Shocked, he stared dumbly at her as she sat on his lap and then kissed him, sliding her tongue aggressively between his lips.

* * *

Kate, still grumbling to herself about leaving her phone at the office, trudged through the dark reception. She had been at the train station for nearly ten minutes before she realized she'd forgotten her phone and she was seriously considering taking a taxi home. It would be another forty minutes before the next train arrived and she was starving and her head was starting to ache. She rounded the corner and when she saw the light on in Edward's office, she forgot her weariness. She grabbed her phone, tossing it into her purse before moving toward his office. She would just pop her head in, find out how the meeting went, and wish him a safe trip. No harm in that – it was being perfectly professional. She stopped at the doorway, Edward's name freezing on her lips as she stared at the scene in front of her.

Edward pushed hard at Melissa's waist, forcing her away from him and pulling his mouth from hers.

"Melissa, don't ever do that again. I'm not –"

There was a flicker of movement in the doorway and he swore violently when he realized Kate was standing there. Her face was pale and she bit at her bottom lip as he stood, dumping Melissa from his lap. She caught herself on his desk and straightened gracefully before giving Kate a cold smile.

"Can we help you with something, Kate?"

"My phone," Kate said. "I – I forgot my phone. I'm sorry."

She turned and fled.

"Kate, hold on!" Edward chased after her, catching up to her in reception, and grabbed her elbow. He pulled her to a stop and forced her to turn around. She wrenched her arm free and glared at him.

"Don't touch me, Edward."

He recoiled at the venom in her voice. "Katie, it wasn't what it looked like. Let me explain."

"You have nothing to explain. Have a safe trip to New York." She tried to leave and Edward cursed loudly and grabbed her again. He held her firmly by her upper arms and gave her a tiny shake.

"Kate, I swear to you, it's a misunderstanding. Just listen to me for a moment."

"You're hurting me," she said mildly. He looked down to see he was squeezing her upper arms. His thumbs had almost disappeared into her soft flesh. Appalled at himself, he let her go and made a small hurt sound in his throat when the spots where his fingers were turned a dull red.

"I'm sorry, Katie, I..."

"Don't call me Katie," she said dully. "I have to go, I'm going to miss my train and Melissa is waiting for you." She gestured with her chin to a spot behind him and he looked to see Melissa standing a few feet behind them. He turned back just as Kate slipped out the front door and slammed his fist down on the reception desk in frustration.

He strode past Melissa, she put a hand on his arm and he shrugged it off angrily and snapped, "Go home, Melissa."

He stalked back to his office, slamming the door so hard it shook in the frame.

* * *

Kate stared blindly out the train window. The tears that had been threatening to fall since she left the office spilled down her cheeks. She wiped them off angrily and swallowed hard.

Don't you dare cry, she told herself fiercely. *He's not worth crying over.*

The lump in her throat grew larger and she felt sick to her stomach at the memory of Melissa's slender body sitting on Edward's lap, of the way they were kissing. She choked back a sob and moved to the door of the train as it rolled to a stop. She would have a hot bath and a glass of wine and forget all about her stupid boss.

An hour later she was up to her chin in hot water and bubbles. Music played softly in the background, a glass of wine was in her hand and Chicken sat on the side of the tub, purring softly as Kate talked to her.

"From now on, it's just you and me, Chicken. I know you've been making google eyes through the living room window at that handsome little Siamese cross who lives next door but that? Is a very bad idea. Stay away from men, Chicken. They suck. It's just you and me, girl, against the world." She tipped her wine glass to Chicken before taking a long swallow.

"And here's another thing about men that you might not realize, they - "

She broke off as Chicken leaped from the edge of the tub, her tail straight in the air and her head tilted to one side as she stared out the open bathroom door.

"What?" Kate asked.

Seconds later the doorbell rang and with a soft hiss Chicken ran from the room. Kate sunk lower into the tub as the doorbell rang again, loud and insistent.

"Go away!" Kate yelled. "I'm not interested in converting to a new religion!"

After a few moments the doorbell rang for a third time. Grumbling, Kate clambered out of the tub and reached for her towel.

Edward stood nervously at Kate's doorstep. He was about to ring the doorbell for a fourth time when the door opened a crack and Kate glared at him through the crack.

"Go away, Edward."

"Kate, let me in, please. I want to explain."

"I told you before, there's nothing to explain." She tried to close the door but he reached out and held it open.

"Five minutes, that's all I'm asking," he pleaded.

She stared at him for a moment, biting her lower lip with indecision. Finally, with a harsh sigh, she opened the door.

"You have exactly five minutes," she warned as he stepped into the dark front hallway and shut the door behind him. He took off his shoes and followed her into the living room.

"Well?" She turned to face him, hands on her hips. "The clock is ticking."

"Kate, I..."

He stuttered to a stop as he took a good look at her for the first time. Her long red hair was piled on top of her head and her skin was flushed and damp looking. She was wearing pink cotton pajama bottoms that had little white bunnies printed on them and a thin white tank top without, he swallowed hard, a bra. She had obviously just come from the tub and the shirt clung damply to her, her nipples erect against the fabric. He dragged his eyes away from her magnificent breasts and looked her in the eye.

"I like your pajamas," he said.

She sighed impatiently. "Are you going to waste your five minutes complimenting me on my choice of sleepwear, Edward?"

Before he could answer she paced back and forth in front of the small fireplace. She slowed and then stopped completely. "How do you know where I live?"

"I phoned Olivia," he confessed.

"You called Olivia? Did you tell her why you needed my home address so urgently?"

"I told her we had a misunderstanding and that you were angry and I needed to explain," he replied.

"And she just handed over my address," Kate sighed. "She is totally banned from the Christmas card list."

"Kate, what happened at the office with Melissa and me? What you walked in on – it wasn't what it seemed," Edward said. "She kissed me and it totally took me by surprise. I was actually pushing her away when you arrived, I swear. I have no interest in Melissa." He stared at her, willing her to believe him.

She looked at him for a long moment, her green eyes staring into his blue ones and her body tense before taking a deep breath and releasing it harshly. "I believe you, Edward."

He sighed with relief and moved towards her. "Thank God."

He reached for her and she backed away from him.

"My believing you doesn't change anything between us. It would be a huge mistake for us to be involved and we both know that. I think you should go."

He shook his head and took her hand. She yanked her hand away immediately.

"Please, Edward," she pleaded, "don't touch me."

"I have to," he said quietly.

He pulled her into his embrace and buried his face in her hair, inhaling the faint flowery smell of her shampoo before he murmured into her ear, "I can't stop thinking about you, Kate. You're the last thing I think of when I go to sleep and the first thing I think of when I wake up. You invade my dreams, I smell your perfume even when you're not around, and I can't stop thinking about how you taste and the way you moan when I touch you. I'm going insane."

He gently grasped her chin in his hand and tilted her face up before placing a soft kiss on her generous mouth. "One night, Katie-did. Just give me one night."

Her cheeks flushed and she stared silently at him. He waited patiently, outwardly calm while his insides churned.

"Only one," she finally said. "And no one can ever find out. I don't want to lose my job."

"You won't," he said. "I promise you won't."

She blinked at him when he said, "What about Josh?"

"Josh and I agreed we were better off as friends," she replied. Suddenly nervous, she glanced down at the floor. "So, now what?"

He flashed her a smile that turned her insides to jelly. "Now I get to admire those cute bunny pajamas up close."

He angled his mouth across hers and as his tongue explored the depths of her warm mouth she moaned and pressed herself up against him. They kissed for long moments, clinging tightly as they tasted each other. She rubbed her flat abdomen against his erection and, without breaking the kiss, he reached down and picked her up. She wrapped her legs around his waist and clung to him as he carried her from the living room.

"Bedroom?" He groaned against her lips.

She nipped at his bottom lip before answering, "Down the hallway, last door on the right."

He moved quickly down the dark hallway and into the bedroom. He crossed the room to the bed and tossed Kate gently on to it. She giggled as she bounced a little and held her arms out to him.

He stripped off his jacket, shirt and tie, dropping them to the floor of her bedroom before lying down beside her. He propped himself up on one elbow, his head resting in his hand and placed his large, warm hand on her belly. She shivered a little at his touch as he smiled and leaned down to kiss the tip of her nose.

"Hello, Katie-did," he murmured.

"Why do you call me that, Edward?" She asked curiously.

He just shrugged before bending his head and kissing her again, softly and slowly. He was determined to make it nice for her, to keep it slow and gentle, even though his body cried out for release. He ached to be deep inside of her, feeling the warmth of her surrounding him while he took long deep strokes. As his erection pushed and throbbed against the confines of his pants, he had to stop himself from tearing off Kate's shirt. Instead, he gently circled one nipple until it beaded under his fingers. He bent his head and sucked gently on her nipple through the thin material. She moaned and grasped the back of his head, holding his mouth to her nipple. He nipped and licked at the sensitive peak until she was gasping uncontrollably. She ran her hands down his bare back as his hand slipped under her shirt and he cupped one pale velvety breast with his warm hand.

"Edward, please," she said.

"Katie," he whispered against her neck. He leaned back and grabbed the hem of her shirt. She sat up a little and he pulled off her shirt. He drank in the sight of her full breasts with their rose-tinged nipples and bent his head again. He licked her nipple and then blew gently on it, enjoying her small gasp and shiver. He switched his attention to her other nipple, licking and sucking gently until she was moving restlessly beside him.

He moved lower down her body, placing a soft kiss on her flat belly just above her navel. She moaned loudly when he slowly traced his tongue along the waistband of her pajamas. When he grabbed the waistband, she lifted her hips up off the bed so that he could slide the pajamas down her legs. She was naked beneath them and he groaned loudly as he stared at her pussy.

Kate moaned when Edward's warm hand caressed her knee. She let her thighs fall apart, anxious for his touch on her aching, throbbing pussy but he teased her by lightly stroking her inner thigh.

"Edward," she whispered pleadingly.

He pushed himself back up beside her and with one hand still making lazy circles on her thigh, kissed her lightly on the mouth. Frustrated, she reached up and grabbed the back of his head, forcing his mouth down on hers so that she could slide her tongue between his lips. She ran her hands down his back, enjoying the way his muscles clenched under her touch. She placed soft open-mouthed kisses on his throat and he groaned and, without warning, brushed his fingers through the red curls at the apex of her thighs before sliding the pads of his fingers over her swollen, wet clit. Kate cried out as warmth exploded in her belly, followed quickly by a deep, needy ache as Edward rubbed firmly. When he bent his head and took one nipple into his warm mouth, she gasped and arched her back, her hands clenching the bed sheets as he brought her closer and closer to her climax.

When he moved his hand from her clit and rested it lightly against her thigh, Kate groaned in frustration and shoved her hips towards him. He placed a light kiss on her swollen mouth.

"Open your eyes, Katie-did," he whispered.

She blinked hazily at him and gave him a look of hunger and need. With a small groan he touched her again, this time sliding one finger into her pussy while his thumb pressed firmly against her clit. She cried out and came immediately, her hips bucking against his hand and her fingers digging into the muscles of his upper arms.

Wave after wave of pleasure coursed through Kate's body. Her legs trembled weakly and she shuddered repeatedly as Edward pulled her up against him. His hard chest brushing against her sensitive nipples made her moan, and she traced one hand lightly over his chest, enjoying his sharp intake of breath when her fingernails brushed lightly against his nipples. She licked and nibbled her way down his neck, stopping to nip lightly on his shoulder as he moaned softly. She moved her hand down his body and fumbled to unbutton his pants. He helped her, panting harshly, and as he raked down the zipper, she slipped her hand into his underwear and wrapped her hand around his cock. He gasped loudly and jerked against her. She stroked him firmly, rubbing her thumb across the head as he arched against her.

"Kate stop!" He moaned.

She stroked him a little slower and grinned at him. "Are you okay, Mr. Turner?"

"Just fine, Ms. Jones," he gritted out as she tightened her grip on him. "Do you have a condom?"

"Nightstand - second drawer."

She watched as he stood and pushed his pants and briefs down his hips. His cock was hard and dripping precum, and the slow cycle of heat started up again in the pit of her stomach. He quickly rolled on the condom and she gave him a slow, lazy smile and spread her thighs.

He positioned himself over her, settling into the cradle of her hips as he reached between them and guided his cock to her wet entrance. One small push was all that was needed but he waited until Kate made a small moan of need.

"Are you ready for me, Katie?" He asked leaning down to give her a hard kiss.

"God, yes," she breathed against his mouth.

He plunged forward, sheathing himself entirely in her wetness and warmth and they made mutual gasps of pleasure.

"You feel so good, Katie," he moaned against her throat as she urged him to move with small thrusts of her hips.

He tried to move with long, slow strokes but after two years of nothing but his own hand, he was helpless to stop from thrusting wildly. Kate's hips rose up from the bed as she matched him stroke for stroke, her thighs squeezing his waist, her breath exploding from her throat in ragged gasps. He was on the edge of his climax and before he lost all control he slipped a hand between them and rubbed Kate's clit. She jerked in surprise and he cried out at the feel of her inner muscles squeezing around him.

"Fuck!" She cried.

He plunged harder and deeper, their hips slapping together in a loud rhythm as Kate tightened exquisitely around him. She cried out with pleasure as she came, her legs falling away and her body pulsating around him. He thrust into her furiously until, with a hoarse shout, he came deep inside of her. He shuddered wildly, before collapsing against Kate's soft body. She wrapped her legs around his hips and her arms around his neck, kissing him gently on the shoulder. He rolled off of her and disposed of the condom before settling on to his back in the bed. Kate pulled up the quilt before curling against his side, one pale thigh thrown carelessly over his and her arm around his waist. He stroked her back soothingly and it didn't take long before she dozed off.

He laid in the darkness, waiting for the guilt to start and when it didn't, he didn't know whether to be upset or relieved. He had expected to feel guilty - Kate was the first woman he'd slept with since Tabitha died - and when it didn't happen he closed his eyes and tried to summon Tabitha's face. Panic flooded through him when instead of seeing Tabitha, Kate's pale face, her red hair floating around her shoulders, surfaced. He stared blankly at the ceiling, listening to Kate's soft breathing as she turned away from him and curled up on her side.

Tabitha, I'm sorry.

You have nothing to be sorry about, my love. Go to sleep.

He turned and spooned his body around Kate's, resting his hand on her hip before moving her hair and burying his face in the back of her neck.

* * *

Kate pressed her ass against Edward's growing erection. They had only been sleeping for an hour or so but already she wanted him again. He made a low sigh into her ear before his hand slid from her hip to her breast. She sighed and arched her back when Edward's fingers pulled lightly at her nipple.

He kissed the back of her shoulder before nuzzling her neck and she made a soft sound of encouragement when he tugged on her nipple again. He rolled it gently between his index finger and thumb before pinching it and she gasped sharply.

"I can't get enough of you, Katie-did," he rumbled into her ear.

He slipped his hand between her thighs and she parted them immediately so he could caress her pussy. He circled her clit, rubbing and tugging on it lightly until it was hard and swollen and she was moving restlessly against him. When he slid two fingers deep inside of her, she moaned and pushed her ass against him. He rubbed her clit firmly with the ball of his thumb and when she started to shudder and toss her head back and forth, he stopped abruptly.

She moaned in frustration and he kissed her lightly on the back. "Just a minute."

He fumbled for a condom from the drawer, ripping it open and rolling it on to his dick. Kate was making low noises of impatience and when she started to turn toward him, he stopped her with one large hand on her hip.

He lifted her thigh and pulled her leg back until it was resting over his. He pushed her forward a little, tilting her hips and repositioning her until the head of his cock brushed against her wet opening. She moaned and pushed back against him, trying to take his cock into her body but he held her still with his hand on her hip.

"Edward, hurry!" She groaned.

"Patience is a virtue," he replied.

"Jackass," she muttered under her breath. He laughed and with one quick thrust, shoved his cock into her wetness and heat.

She moaned happily as he reached around her to tease one erect nipple. She pushed her ass against him urging him to move, but he pulled her firmly against him. She was unbelievably tight and when she wiggled against him, he made a low sound of disapproval.

"Be good, Katie," he admonished lightly. He cupped her pussy with one hard hand and bit gently into her shoulder, holding her against him with his mouth and hand, as he moved with slow strokes.

She moaned and gasped and made tiny pleading noises that nearly drove him crazy with desire. She placed her hand on top of his, urging him silently to move his fingers and he obliged, sliding his fingers through the soft curls to rub gently and slowly at her clit.

Kate arched her back as Edward continued to thrust slowly. The combination of his slow strokes, his warm fingers and his mouth on her shoulder were heightening her need for him to an unbearable level. She urged him to move faster with little gasps and whimpers but he ignored her and continued on with the same slow strokes.

"Edward, faster," she begged.

He didn't reply and she squeezed his wrist, digging her nails into his skin. He made a low curse before tugging on her clit. She cried out, her ass pressing against his pelvis, and he quickened both the stroke of his cock and the stroke of his fingers. He tugged again on her clit, smiling with satisfaction when she came with a loud squeal, and he thrust in and out of her as she quivered around him. He leaned away, placing one hand on her hip and the other on the back of her neck and fucked her with hard, driving strokes until, his balls tightening and the base of his spine tingling, he came inside of her with a harsh shout.

He wrapped his arm around her waist and clung tightly to her as he softened inside of her. She stroked his arm with the tips of her fingers and smiled up at him when he leaned over her and placed a soft kiss on her mouth.

"What time is it?" She asked.

Edward craned his neck to look at the alarm clock behind him. "Almost ten. Why?"

"Because I'm - "

Her stomach growled loudly and she grinned at him. "Hungry."

He slipped out of her and she sat up on the side of the bed. "Let's order pizza."

"Sure," Edward replied as Kate walked nude to what he assumed was the master bathroom. He relaxed on the bed, folding his hands under his head and staring at the ceiling. They had agreed to only one night and already he was regretting it.

When the large grey cat jumped up on the foot of the bed, its yellow-green eyes shining in the dim light, he made a small tsking sound in his throat and wiggled his fingers on the quilt. "You must be Chicken. Here kitty, kitty."

Kate stared at herself in the bathroom mirror. Her hair was hanging haphazardly from the hair pins and her full mouth was red and swollen. She smiled a little at how utterly shameless she looked and pulled the remaining pins from her hair before running her fingers through it. As she shut off the light and opened the bathroom door she heard Edward's low voice calling for the cat.

"Gah! Edward no!" Kate cried. "Don't touch the cat!"

She sprinted toward the bed, visions of Edward torn and bleeding while Chicken calmly cleaned bits of his flesh from her paws running through her head. She was shocked into silence when she turned on the bedside light and, instead of the bloody carnage she was expecting, she found Edward lying on the bed staring at her with Chicken curled up calmly beside him.

"What?" He asked as he gently stroked Chicken from her head to her tail. The old cat purred loudly at his touch, stretching out and showing him her belly. He gave it a quick rub before scratching under her chin. "What about the cat?"

"How are you doing that?" She breathed.

"Doing what?" He asked.

"Chicken doesn't like anyone. She barely likes me." Kate sat down on the bed and gave Chicken the stink eye. "I can't believe she likes you."

Edward laughed. "I told you I was irresistible."

Kate rolled her eyes and smacked him lightly on his flat stomach. "Uh-huh. I'm going to order the pizza."

She shook her head in disbelief as Chicken climbed on top of Edward and sat on his chest, purring contently.

Chapter 7

"That was so good," Kate said as she closed the pizza box and set it on the floor. "Although I suppose coming from New York, you weren't that impressed with it."

"Actually, it was pretty good," Edward said. He was leaning back against the headboard, naked except for the sheet draped across his lap, and he popped the last of his pizza into his mouth before grinning at her. "You seemed to have worked up quite an appetite."

She blushed a little before asking, "When do you leave for New York?"

"Tomorrow. Why? Are you anxious to get rid of me? You did promise me one entire night remember," he said teasingly.

"I remember," Kate replied. She picked at a string on the quilt. She didn't dare look at him for a few minutes, positive he would see just how badly she regretted their "one night" agreement. The thought of having him for this night only ripped at her insides.

You can't keep doing this, she told herself sternly, *so just enjoy tonight for what it is and stop thinking about tomorrow.*

"You okay, Katie-did?" Edward asked quietly.

She forced herself to smile at him. "Never better."

She took a deep breath and tugged her short nightgown down over her knees. He was still sitting up against the headboard, the sheet pooled around his waist. She stared at him for a few moments. His broad chest was covered in dark hair and she envied the deep natural tan that covered him. She followed the narrow path of hair below his navel to where the sheet covered him. When his reaction to her stare became obvious against the sheets, she smiled and glanced up at him.

"What are you thinking about, Kate?"

"How jealous I am of your tanned skin," she said as she crawled across the bed and climbed into his lap. She straddled him, her pale thighs on either side of his hips and leaned forward to graze her lips across his. He slid his hands under her nightgown to cup her ass and pull her against his erection. She moaned a little and place feathery-light kisses across his chest.

"I like your pale skin," he whispered. "In fact, I think it's time to see more of it."

He grabbed the hem of her nightgown and tugged it off her body. He leaned back a little, staring greedily at her before cupping both her breasts. The stark contrast between her pale skin and his tanned skin was erotic and she couldn't stop the small moan escaping from her lips when he rubbed his callused thumbs across her nipples. They hardened under his touch and she arched her back and grasped his head in her hands when he leaned forward and nibbled and laved at her nipples.

He moved his hands to her waist, holding her firmly while he kissed her breasts, the tender side swell and the soft underside and then placed light kisses on her ribs. She moaned and ran her fingers down his ribs, laughing softly when he jerked and squirmed away.

"Right, you're ticklish."

She ran her hands back over his ribs and with a low growl he grabbed her wrists and held them at her sides before leaning forward and kissing her breasts again. He licked and sucked and pulled gently on her nipples until she was breathless and rocking her hips against him. She tried to tug her hands free but he tightened his grip and continued to tease her nipples with small kisses and nips.

"Edward please!"

He released her hands and she reached under the sheet to take him into her hand. His relentless assault on her breasts had driven her crazy with need and she pulled the sheet back with her other hand, exposing his thick cock. She ran her hand lightly down the shaft, slowly stroking him before running her fingers across the smooth skin of the tip. She leaned forward and positioned herself above him and made a loud cry of frustration when he prevented her from sliding him into her warmth.

"Condom," he groaned breathlessly.

Kate grabbed the foil package from the drawer. Hands shaking, she quickly tore it open and with rough impatience placed the condom on him. She scooted forward and, holding the base of his cock, raised herself up and forced herself down on to him. They groaned in mutual pleasure as her body stretched around his hardness.

Kate's need for relief was like a white-hot fire inside of her and, bracing her hands on Edward's broad shoulders, she rode him hard. He held her around the waist as she rocked and thrust quickly against him. She leaned forward and kissed him, pushing her tongue deep into his mouth as she let her breasts rub gently across his chest. He moaned into her mouth and tightened his hands on her hips as she increased the pace. When her breath was coming in hard gasps, he reached between them and touched her clit with rough fingers. At his touch, Kate cried his name and froze in mid thrust. She shook and trembled around him as her orgasm raced through her and he held her tightly against his hard body as he thrust and withdrew rapidly until his own orgasm washed over him.

Kate collapsed against Edward, panting heavily. His heart was pounding and he was breathing raggedly and she stroked his chest with her fingers before sitting up.

"That was good," she said.

"Good?" He arched his eyebrow at her before pinching her nipple playfully. "If all I'm getting is a good, I need to try harder."

She laughed and rested her forehead against his. "It was magnificent. I've never come so hard in my life."

He laughed. "Now you're just mocking me."

She climbed off of him and curled up on her side as he disposed of the condom. He shifted down to lie beside her and pulled her against him.

"Sleepy?" He asked.

"Yes," she replied. "Are you – do you want to stay the night?"

He nodded before cupping one full breast possessively. "If you're good with that?"

"Yes," she said before yawning.

"Good night, Katie-did."

"Good night, Edward," she whispered as Chicken leaped on to the bed and draped her heavy body across their hips.

* * *

"I really have to leave, Katie," Edward muttered against her lips. "My flight leaves in three hours and I still have to go home and shower and pack."

"Right," Kate said before kissing him again. He groaned and slipped his hand under her tank top to caress her breast. They were standing in the front hallway and as Edward gave her a final squeeze and moved away to put on his shoes, Kate sighed inwardly.

Edward had woken her at eight with his warm mouth and hands and they'd had another round of sex before she had made them pancakes for breakfast. When they were done eating, she was alarmed to realize that she wanted him again – hell, she could have spent the entire day with him in her bed - but it was time to return to reality. They had said one night and that night was finished.

"I had a really great time, Katie," Edward said.

"I did too," she replied. "Um, thanks?"

He laughed. "You're welcome?"

She hesitated before forcing herself to smile cheerfully at him. "Have a safe trip."

He stopped with his hand on the doorknob before turning around and pulling her against him. He took her mouth in a hard and demanding kiss and she sucked at his tongue as she clung to him.

He pulled his mouth away from hers and rasped, "Good-bye, Kate."

She smiled shakily as he opened the front door and then leaned down and gave her one final breathtaking kiss. This time he cupped her breast, stroking her nipple with his thumb and she moaned into his mouth.

"If you don't stop that, I'm dragging you back to my bed and you'll miss your plane," she whispered.

"I'm tempted," he muttered.

She forced herself to take a step away and blushed furiously when she glanced over his shoulder. Olivia was standing in the open doorway, one hand raised to knock and her other holding a tray of two coffees.

Edward glanced at Kate. Her pale skin was a fiery red and he gave Olivia a rather smug grin. "Hello, Olivia."

"Uh - hello, Mr. Turner," Olivia said as he slipped past her and headed to his car.

Olivia stared wide-eyed at Kate as she ushered her into the hallway and shut the door behind her.

"What the fuck, Kate?"

"What?" Kate said as she took the tray of coffees from her.

"Don't you what me, Kate Jones," Olivia said. "What the hell is going on? I get this weird phone call from Edward last night saying you had a disagreement and asking for your home address and now he's standing in your damn house and you're sucking face. Get your ass into the living room and start talking."

Kate sat down on the couch and sipped her coffee as Olivia made herself comfortable in the chair across from her. "Give me all the details."

Kate laughed. "I'm not giving you all the details."

"Fine, but at least tell me how you went from a disagreement to having sex. You did have sex, right?"

"Yes."

"And? How was it? At least tell me that," Olivia said.

"It was good. Really good."

"We talking top five?"

Kate laughed again. "Yes, definitely."

"Nice," Olivia said before sipping at her coffee. "Now what?"

"We go back to the way it was before," Kate said.

"So you have a night of sex and now you're just going to act like it never happened?"

"Of course not. But we're not going to do it again. We agreed to one night to relieve the, um, tension between us."

Olivia just stared at her and Kate gave her a defensive look. "You thought it was a good idea. You told me to do it, remember?"

"Yeah, but, Katie, I didn't think you would actually do it. You're not the type of person to just sleep with someone for the hell of it. Are you telling me that you're just going to go back to working with him like you've never seen him naked?"

"Yes. That was our agreement."

"But how do you really feel about it?" Olivia asked.

"What does it matter how I feel, Olivia?" Kate snapped. "The situation is what it is. He's my boss, I'm his assistant. We can't date and we agreed to one night only and now that night is over. I don't regret it, I don't, but there's nothing more to talk about."

At the look on Olivia's face, Kate was immediately ashamed of herself. She crossed the room and sat on the floor beside her chair, laying her head on Olivia's knee. "I'm sorry, Olivia." she said "I shouldn't have snapped at you like that."

"It's fine, Katie. I'm prying too much."

"You're not. It's just – I feel so stupid. I agreed to one night thinking it would be fine and now I feel awful."

"Awful that you had sex with your boss?" Olivia asked.

"Awful that I don't get to have sex with him again," Kate sighed. She sat up and stared at Olivia. "He's really fucking good in bed."

Olivia grinned. "Well, maybe you could do more than one night. I mean, as long as you're careful, no one at the office will find out."

"I hate that idea. Sneaking around - always worried that someone from the office will find out."

"It's not ideal but if the alternative is not getting to ride Edward like a pony whenever you want, maybe it's worth a try," Olivia said.

Kate laughed. "You have such a way with words, Olivia. Even Chicken liked him."

"Chicken liked him?" Olivia blinked at her. "You are fucking kidding me."

"I'm not. She let him pet her right away and she even stretched out on him and purred," Kate said as the topic of their conversation wandered into the living room. The cat glared at Olivia before hissing lightly under her breath.

"You little tart," Olivia said to the cat. "I've known you for three years and still can't touch you and thirty seconds after you meet Edward, you're all over him like a shameless hussy."

Kate smiled and patted the old cat when she butted her head against her leg. She rested her head on Olivia's knee again and Olivia stroked her long red hair.

"You could always quit your job, Katie," she said quietly.

"I like my job."

"I know, but if you think there could be something with Edward…"

"I have no idea if there could be. I'm just feeling sad because I had really great sex last night and I won't get it again."

They sat quietly for a few moments before Olivia nudged her. "C'mon, Katie, hop in the shower and then we're going shopping. There's no point in you moping around for the day. I need a new dress for Lana and Robert's wedding and I need someone to tell me how fantastic I look in it."

* * *

Kate added a few more drops of peppermint oil to the steaming water in the tub. She had spent the day with Olivia and for the most part was able to keep thoughts of Edward out of her head but now that she was alone, she could feel the depression creeping in.

Don't think about it, Kate. God, just let it go.

She eased her body into the tub. She was tired and, she thought ruefully, sore. She had used muscles in her body last night that she hadn't used for a while and the lack of sleep was catching up to her. She made a small hiss of pain as the hot water surrounded her aching body and Chicken looked up at her from her spot on the bathroom rug.

"My girlie bits are sore, Chicken," Kate said conversationally.

The cat growled quietly before she turned her back and lazily cleaned her face with one paw.

"There's the Chicken we all know and love."

Kate sunk lower into the tub. The hot water felt good and she forced herself to empty her mind and think about nothing. Twenty minutes later she was close to dozing when her cell phone rang. She picked it up from the floor and glanced at it, her heart beginning to pound as she recognized Edward's number.

"Hi there."

"Did I wake you, Katie-did?" Edward's slow, deep voice washed over her.

Kate shifted in the tub, water spilled over the edge and landed on Chicken who made a loud yowl of indignation and fled the room.

"What was that?" Edward asked.

"Chicken. She's mad because I spilled water on her."

Edward laughed and warmth flooded through her. "Did I wake you, Katie?"

"No, I'm not sleeping. I'm in the tub."

"You're in the tub." Edward said.

"Yes."

"Let me get this straight - you're naked and wet in the tub at this very moment?"

All of the muscles in her lower abdomen clenched at the dark lust in his voice.

"I am very naked and very wet," she said.

He groaned softly into the phone. "You're killing me."

"So I shouldn't be bathing?" She teased.

"No, but you should answer the phone and tell me you're doing something like dusting even though you're actually naked and wet in the tub, or you should refrain from answering the phone when you're naked and wet in the tub."

"Fine. I'm dusting, Edward."

"Liar. You deserve a spanking for that," he replied softly.

"Yes, well it's too bad that you're all the way in New York and I'm here safe and sound in my nice warm bath water. Did I mention I'm naked and wet?"

Edward burst out laughing "You win. How was the rest of your day?"

"It was good," Kate replied as Chicken crept back into the bathroom to resume her spot on the rug. "I spent the day with Olivia. How about you? How was your flight?"

"Fine," he replied. "Have you been to New York City before?"

"No. Not yet. It's on the bucket list though. I'd like to see Central Park and Times Square and do all the other totally cliché touristy stuff."

"Nothing wrong with doing the tourist thing," he said.

"Does your family live in New York?"

"Yes, my parents are here and my younger brother. I'm having dinner with my mom and dad tomorrow night and then dinner at my brother's place on Wednesday. I'm heading out with some friends to our favourite pub in about half an hour. I'm trying to squeeze in as much visiting in between work commitments as I can."

"That sounds nice," she replied. She ignored the stab of jealousy at the thought of Edward going for drinks and perhaps meeting another woman.

"I should probably go. I need a quick nap. Someone kept me up last night with their insatiable appetite," he said.

"Me?" Kate said indignantly and Edward laughed.

"Yes." He hesitated and then said, "Is it breaking our one-night rule if I asked you to touch yourself?"

Her cheeks flushed and her nipples hardened almost immediately. She bit her bottom lip as Edward cleared his throat.

"Too far, Katie?"

"No," she said as her hand slid between her thighs. She rubbed at her clit, a little surprised to find it swollen and aching already.

"Touch yourself, Katie-did," he whispered.

"I already am," she said breathlessly.

He groaned and it sent a bolt of lust through her lower body. "Does it feel good?"

"Yes," she said. "I want you to touch yourself too."

She heard the sound of his zipper and then he made another low groan into the phone.

"Are you hard, Edward?"

"Christ, yes," he muttered.

"Good," she said. "Stroke your cock slowly for me."

He groaned again and she rubbed at her clit before making a low gasp of pleasure.

"Slide your finger into your pussy," he said.

She did what he asked, moaning loudly, and he made a low murmur of approval.

"That's my good girl, Katie. I keep thinking about how wet and tight you were. How good it felt to be in your pussy. I wish I was there to watch you come."

"Me too," she gasped.

"You make me – "

He stopped abruptly and she heard the faint sound of knocking through the phone.

"Edward? What's wrong?"

"Shit!" He muttered. "My friends are here early. I'm sorry, Katie. I have to go."

"It's okay. This was probably a bad idea anyway," she said.

"Yeah," he said. "Good night, Kate. I'll see you when I get back."

"Good night, Edward."

She dropped her phone on the floor and stared up at the ceiling. Her body was still aching for release but she climbed out of the tub and towelled dry. She didn't want her fingers anyway, she wanted Edward's cock.

"Oh, Chicken," she said. "I am in so much trouble."

Chapter 8

"I know what you're thinking, Chicken," Kate said as she yanked another armload of books from her bookshelf. "Only losers spend their Saturday reorganizing their bookshelf. But I'm just super organized."

She dropped the load of books on the couch and stared out the window. It had been a ridiculously long week without Edward in the office. She had received a few work-related emails from him that were short and to the point and that was it.

"I am not lonely, Chicken," Kate sighed. "I don't miss him and I didn't stay home every night this week just hoping he would call so we could have phone sex."

She checked her cell phone for about the hundredth time and reminded herself that it wasn't professional to text Edward. If he had wanted to talk to her, he would have called or texted. An hour later, finished with the bookshelf reorganization, she yanked on a pair of old shorts and t-shirt.

"It's better that he hasn't called, Chicken," she said as she rooted in the hallway closet for her gardening gloves. "It's much easier to remember it was a one night only kind of deal when I'm not hearing his sexy voice every day. It's given me time to distance myself and I've done a remarkable job. I'm not even remotely interested in having sex with Edward anymore."

Chicken stared unblinkingly at her and then growled when Kate stroked her back. She pulled her hand back when the old cat swiped at her and stuck her tongue out at her. "You'd better be nicer to me, Chicken, or I'll send you to live with your new best friend Edward."

She headed to her back yard to weed her flower beds. She had neglected them for almost two weeks and as she yanked out the weeds, she thought about Edward. According to his schedule, he was flying back home tomorrow and would be back to work on Monday. A little thrill of excitement went through her and she immediately tamped it down before yanking viciously at a particularly stubborn weed. She was not excited about seeing him on Monday. It would just be like any other normal Monday.

* * *

Kate stepped out of the shower and towelled dry before pulling on her pajama bottoms and a tank top. She had weeded for over two hours and had been sweaty and covered with dirt by the time she was finished. The shower had made her feel a little more human and she decided she would make stir-fry for supper before calling Olivia. She couldn't sit around in her house any longer. Edward wasn't going to call and she was a fool for thinking he might.

The doorbell rang and she frowned before heading down the hallway. She checked the peephole and her mouth dropped open. Her fingers tugging nervously at her wet hair, she unlocked the door and opened it. Edward, wearing a white t-shirt and a worn pair of jeans, gave her a slow smile.

"Hello, Katie."

"Wh-what are you doing here?" She stammered.

"I was in the neighbourhood and thought I'd drop by. Mind if I come in?"

He shouldered past her without waiting for an answer and Kate stared blankly at her front lawn for a moment before shutting the door.

"Edward, I thought you were in – "

She was cut off when Edward pulled her forward and took her mouth in a hard and possessive kiss. At the taste of his mouth, desire flared in her, and she rubbed against him eagerly. He wrapped his hand around her wet hair and tugged her head back before pressing wet, open-mouthed kisses against her neck.

"I thought you weren't back until tomorrow," she gasped as his tongue flicked gently against the hollow of her throat.

"I took an early flight," he muttered against her throat.

"Edward," she moaned as he lifted her and carried her down the hallway, "we said only one night."

He pushed open the door to her bedroom and dropped her on the bed. "True. But on the flight back I was thinking about your hot pussy and how much I wanted to taste it. So, here I am."

"This isn't a good idea."

"Stop talking, Kate." He grabbed the waistband of her pajamas and yanked them down her legs, growling his approval when he saw her naked pussy. He dropped to his knees, wrapping his hands around her smooth thighs, and pulled her toward his mouth.

"Edward! We can't!"

He buried his face in her pussy in reply, his hot tongue seeking out her clit and she screamed breathlessly and arched her hips into his mouth. He sucked at her clit, flicking his tongue over it in a rapid rhythm that made her toes curl into the bed.

"Oh my God!" She threaded her fingers through his hair, holding his head tightly as he licked and sucked at her clit. He nibbled at the wet lips of her pussy before licking them clean and she rocked her pussy against his mouth as she pleaded loudly for more.

He gave her what she wanted, not teasing or taking it slow. He buried his face between her legs and ate her pussy with a single-minded determinedness that had her shrieking his name and coming all over his face in less than five minutes.

She fell back against the bed, panting loudly, as Edward stood and stripped off his clothes. He slipped on a condom before flipping her roughly to her stomach and pulling her to her hands and knees. His hand fisted in her hair and he held her tightly as he slammed his cock deep into her aching pussy. She cried out with pleasure, clenching her inner muscles around his dick until he moaned her name. His fingers bit into her hip as he pounded in and out. Moaning and pleading, she met each of his thrusts with utter abandonment.

"Fuck, Katie, you're going to make me come," he moaned.

"Yes," she said. "Please, Edward."

He changed the angle of his strokes just slightly and she jerked and shivered around him when the blunt head of his cock brushed against the front wall of her pussy.

"Oh God!"

He pressed one large hand on her lower back, pushing her downward and she raised her hips and buried her face in the bed, her hands clenching helplessly in the sheets as he drove her toward the relief she was aching for.

When she climaxed, her entire body shaking and her pussy squeezing him tightly, he shouted her name and thrust a final time. Her pussy gripped him tightly, her muscles rippling around his dick as he came, and he muttered her name again before pulling out of her and collapsing on the bed beside her.

Panting lightly, she rolled over and removed the condom, tossing it in the wastebasket before lying on her side next to him and propping her head up with her hand.

"So, you took an early flight," she said.

He gave her a weak grin. "Yeah."

"We broke our one-night rule."

He shrugged. "I was thinking maybe we could amend it. It could be the one weekend rule. And since we only had one night last weekend, tonight equals our second night of the weekend."

She sat up and looked at him soberly. He reached out and brushed a stray piece of hair from her cheek as she sighed and said "Edward, this has to be the last night we spend together. You know that, right?"

He nodded and pulled her into his embrace. "I know."

"If we get caught, I'll lose my job," she said.

"I know," he repeated "and after tonight I promise I'll stay away from you."

The thought sent a wave of depression through her and he cupped her face. "What's wrong?"

"Nothing," she said. "Are you hungry? I was just going to make some supper when you dropped by."

"Sure. Do you mind if I have a quick shower?"

She shook her head and he kissed her lightly before disappearing into the bathroom.

* * *

"That smells delicious. Can I help with anything?"

Edward, barefoot and wearing just his jeans, strolled into the kitchen. Kate tried not to stare at his naked upper body. God, he looked good. She was already tempted to just say screw supper and take him back to bed.

"Kate? What can I do to help?"

She pointed to the fridge. "There are some fresh veggies in the fridge, mushrooms and broccoli, carrots and snow peas. You can start washing and cutting those up. There's another cutting board in the drawer to the left of the fridge."

As Kate took the wok out of the cupboard and plugged it in, Edward looked curiously around the kitchen. It was painted a bright yellow with white cupboards and trim. Sheer curtains hung at the window above the sink that overlooked her back yard and she had some plants in small pots growing on the window ledge. Kate cut the chicken into small pieces and add it to the wok as he rinsed the vegetables.

"I hope you like chicken stir fry," she said as she stirred the rice that was cooking on the stove.

"I do," Edward said. "But I do have a nut allergy."

"So no peanut sauce in the stir-fry," she said.

"Not unless you want to stick an epi-pen in my thigh," he replied with a grin. "How about you? You allergic to anything?"

"Penicillin," she replied.

He washed and chopped the vegetables as she stirred the chicken before smiling at her. "Do you have any siblings?"

"I have a younger sister, Lina. My parents live about two hours from here but she lives out of state so I don't see her as often as I'd like. She just moved in with her millionaire boyfriend."

"Really?"

"Well, maybe he's not a millionaire," Kate said, "but he's pretty rich. It's quick but she seems really happy so I'm happy for her. Do you only have one brother?"

"Yes. His name is Jason. He's younger than me by a few years but we're pretty close. I miss him."

"Why did you move from New York?" She asked.

He hesitated and she gave him a curious look. "Edward?"

Edward stared at the vegetables. He didn't think telling Kate he had moved to get away from the memories of his dead wife was the best idea so instead he said, "I'd been wanting a change for a while so when this opportunity came up, I took it."

Kate studied him carefully before nodding. "Are you happy that you did?"

"Yes," he said. It was true. He was enjoying the work and the opportunity to be a partner in a firm was life-long dream. There were too many partners at his old firm and it would have been years before he'd become one.

And that's all it is, he told himself. *It's not because you've met Kate. You love Tabitha and two years isn't long enough to mourn her.*

It's long enough, my love.

He didn't want to hear Tabitha's voice in his head when he was with Kate so he shoved her voice out and smiled at Kate. "Ready for the vegetables?"

She nodded and he handed them to her as Chicken wandered into the kitchen and leaped up on to a chair. When Edward picked her up to move her so he could sit down, Kate cringed but the old cat just purred loudly and weaved around his feet.

"Unbelievable," she said under her breath.

"What?"

"Chicken being so nice to you. She doesn't like me that much and I rescued her from death row at the shelter," Kate replied as she scooped stir fry onto their plates.

Edward grinned and grabbed the jug of water from the fridge. "What can I say – I'm great with pussies."

"Cheeseball," Kate laughed and continued to divvy up the food on to their plates. As Edward hunted through the cupboards for glasses, she tried not to think about how right it felt to be in her tiny kitchen cooking dinner with him. It persisted and she pushed the dangerous thought aside as Edward set their drinks on the table.

"There's beer in the bottom shelf of the fridge if you would prefer that."

"Water is fine with me," he replied.

They sat down and Edward inhaled deeply. "It smells really good, Katie."

"Hopefully it tastes as good as it smells," Kate said with a laugh. "I'm not much of a cook."

* * *

"So, let me get this straight," Kate set her fork on her empty plate, "you're twelve years old and you tell your eight-year-old brother that if he jumps from the tree you'll make him fly using the power of your mind?"

Edward shrugged sheepishly and put the last forkful of food into his mouth. "Yeah."

Kate stood and began to clear the dishes from the table. "What happened?"

"He jumped from the tree. Broke his arm in two places when he landed." Edward carried his plate to the sink as Kate rinsed the dishes and handed them to him to load the dishwasher.

"Edward!" Kate gave him a horrified look.

Edward laughed and put up his hands in defense. "Hell, at eight years old he should have known better. I know it was a stupid thing to do and in my defense it was the only time I ever did anything like that. And if it makes you feel better, my dad spanked me so hard I couldn't sit down for a week and I had to do all of my brother's chores for six months."

Kate filled the wok with warm soapy water and set it in the sink to soak. "I would have made you do them for a year," she said.

"I bet you would have." Edward laughed and stood behind her, wrapping his arms around her waist and giving her a squeeze.

"Do you want kids, Katie?" He asked.

"Yes," she replied, "When I've found the right person to have kids with." She turned and gave him a quick kiss on the jaw. "Let's go sit in the living room, it's more comfortable."

He followed her down the hall and into the living room. She curled up on the couch, tucking her legs beneath her and he sat down close beside her, resting one warm hand on her bare thigh.

"Why aren't you in a relationship?" He asked suddenly.

"Well, about five years ago I was engaged to a very nice man named Cory. At least I thought he was a very nice man."

Edward gave her thigh a quick squeeze. "I'm sorry, I'm being nosy. You don't have to tell me."

"I don't mind," Kate said. "It's a simple enough story. I wasn't feeling well, came home early from work and caught him in our bed with one of his coworkers."

"Jesus, what an asshole."

"Yes, that's what I thought too. Anyway, I threw him out of our apartment, pawned the ring, and gave all of his stuff to Goodwill."

She surprised him by laughing. "God, he was so mad when he came to the apartment to get his stuff and discovered it gone. He deserved it though. He ended up marrying his co-worker and the last I heard they were very happy and have two kids."

"I'm sorry, Kate. He was an idiot," Edward said.

She shrugged. "At least I found out he was a cheating bastard before we got married."

They sat silently for a moment before she smiled at him. "What about you? Ever been married?"

He hesitated before nodding. "Yes. My wife, Tabitha, died of a brain tumour two years ago."

"Oh God," she said. "Edward, I am so sorry."

"Thank you. She was a lawyer too. We met when we were articling for the same law firm. She was much smarter than me and she had this ability to make people feel at ease around her, you know? Everyone loved her."

"She sounds lovely," Kate said softly.

"She really was. She did a lot of pro bono work for single moms – tried to help them get alimony or child support. One time she – "

My love, stop. Talking about your dead wife to your current lover is weird.

He stopped abruptly and grimaced. Tabitha was right – he was being weird.

"I'm sorry," he said.

"For what?"

"I, uh, I shouldn't be talking about Tabitha."

"I don't mind," Kate said. "It's obvious you love her very much."

"Yes," he said.

They sat awkwardly on the couch as Kate stared silently at her hands. Edward's love for his wife had been obvious in his voice and a thin thread of jealousy went through her. She cursed inwardly. It was stupid of her to be jealous. Edward had been a widower for only two years and even if they could have dated, it obviously wasn't a good idea. He wasn't over the loss of his wife and she suspected that he never fully would be. She felt a pang of sadness for Edward and she took his hand and squeezed it gently.

"I really am very sorry, Edward."

He shook his head. "No, I'm sorry. I shouldn't have brought it up."

He hesitated and gave her an oddly vulnerable look. "Should I go, Kate?"

"No. Not unless you want to," she said.

"I don't," he replied.

There were a few more moments of awkward silence before Kate stood and held out her hand. "I know it's early, but let's go to bed."

He stood before taking her hand and following her to the bedroom.

* * *

"Wake up, Katie-did."

Kate blinked rapidly before squinting at the alarm clock. It was just after six and she made a soft groan before rubbing her eyes.

"I have to go," Edward said softly, brushing her hair back from her face. "I need to catch up with some work at the office today."

She stared at him. She wasn't a morning person and it was much too early for her to even try to form a coherent thought so she only nodded and yawned. He laughed quietly and as he leaned down to kiss her on the mouth, she realized with a sudden pang of sorrow that this was it. She threw her arms around him and hugged him tightly. He returned her hug, his warm hands stroking her bare back and she blinked rapidly to keep the tears at bay.

He kissed her quickly on the throat before whispering, "See you tomorrow, Katie."

He left the bedroom without looking back and she rolled to her side as tears dripped down her cheeks. Chicken was sitting on the pillow beside her and as Kate stared miserably at her, she licked Kate's forehead once with her rough, scratchy tongue before leaping off the bed and strolling out of the bedroom.

* * *

"Hello, Edward."

Edward looked up from his computer, groaning inwardly. "Melissa," he said shortly.

"How was New York?"

"Fine," he said briefly. "What can I help you with?"

She shook her head and sat down. Like him, she was wearing a t-shirt and jeans, and she crossed her legs before giving him a brittle smile. "I just came in to get caught up on some files."

"Then go do that," he said bluntly.

"We need to talk about Kate."

"There's nothing to talk about," he said. "Leave, Melissa."

"I know you're fucking her."

"I'm not," he lied. "I've been in New York all week, remember?"

She just shrugged. "It's inappropriate, Edward."

"Inappropriate?" He gave her a look of fury. "That's interesting talk coming from the woman who tried to seduce me in this very office last week."

"If I go to Arthur with this, she'll be fired."

"Arthur's not going to just take your word for it. You have no proof that I'm sleeping with Kate because I'm not," he said angrily. "And if you even think about telling Arthur that I am, I'll tell him about you coming on to me."

She actually laughed and his blood boiled at the smug look on her face. "I already told you, Arthur doesn't care if the lawyers sleep together. Partners sleeping with their assistants on the other hand…"

She trailed off and Edward glared at her. "What the hell is your problem with Kate? She's a hard worker and she doesn't – "

"She's a snotty little bitch who thinks she runs this office," Melissa interrupted furiously. "She thinks she can say or do whatever she wants just because she was Gerald's little pet and now she has you wrapped around her finger as well."

"Jesus," he said with a shake of his head, "you're doing this because you're jealous of her?"

"I'm not jealous of her," Melissa snapped. "By all means, go ahead and keep fucking her. It'll make it much easier for me to get the proof I need to have Kate fired."

"Get out," he said.

She stood and gave him an angry look before stalking from his office and slamming the door behind her.

He swore under his breath and stared out the window. His hands were shaking and a combination of worry, anger and guilt was gnawing at his stomach. If Arthur found out he was sleeping with Kate and she was fired, he'd never forgive himself.

He rubbed wearily at his temples. He needed to forget his attraction to Kate but fuck, it was easier said than done. The entire time in New York she hadn't been far from his thoughts and he had fought the urge to call her every evening just to hear her voice. And although he had told his parents and brother that he was leaving a day early because he needed to get caught up on some of the files here, it had only been a half truth. He had rebooked his flight Saturday with every intention of being back in Kate's bed by that evening, her warm body pressed against him, listening to her soft cries as he fucked her.

Enough was enough, he told himself grimly. He couldn't keep thinking about sleeping with Kate. Besides, he had seen the look on her face when he talked about Tabitha. He should never have fucking talked about her. He couldn't hide his love for her or how much he missed her – even with Kate – and that had been a shitty thing to do to her.

It really was, Tabitha piped up disapprovingly in his head.

Thanks.

Just being honest. There's something special between the two of you, my love, and you know it.

No, there was something special between us.

Yes, well, I'm dead and you can't mope around forever, can you?

He winced at the no-nonsense tone in his dead wife's voice.

I'm sorry, my love. But don't ruin a future with Kate because you're stuck in the past.

There's no future for us. She'll lose her job and I'm not ready.

You are.

I'm not! Leave me be, Tabitha. Please.

To his relief, her voice in his head remained silent and he rubbed at his temples again. It had been a terrible mistake to sleep with Kate and the only thing he could do now was try to repair the damage. He would keep things professional between them and Melissa would have no reason to go to Arthur.

Chapter 9

Kate shifted in her seat as an elderly lady sat down beside her. The train rumbled forward and she gave the woman a vague smile before looking out the window. After Edward had left yesterday morning, she had spent most of the day sitting on the couch, watching TV and feeling lonely and blue. By mid-afternoon she had decided it was time to stop feeling sorry for herself and went to the bedroom to strip the sheets and throw them in the wash. But when she had reached for the pillow Edward had slept on, she hadn't been able to stop herself from pressing her face into it and inhaling deeply. It had smelled like Edward and even though she knew it was silly, she couldn't bring herself to put the pillow case in the laundry. Like a love-struck teenager, she had carefully placed the pillow back on the bed, leaving it behind when she carried the rest of the bedding to the laundry room.

No regrets, she told herself firmly as the train jostled its way down the track. *Go to work, be professional, and stop thinking about Edward naked and in your bed.*

* * *

Edward stood and stretched briefly before walking to the office window and staring out at the sky. He had been here since six but by seven-thirty he had stopped concentrating on his work and was listening for the sound of Kate's voice. He crossed his arms over his chest and stared moodily out the window. Aching to see Kate and hear her warm voice was a very bad idea

"Good morning, Edward."

His heart thumping madly, he turned to see Kate standing in the doorway of his office. She was dressed in a knee-length black skirt with a white blouse and her hair was up in its customary clip. She looked crisp and professional but it didn't stop the fleeting image crossing his mind of her naked under him, her long hair free of the clip, her mouth red and swollen from his kisses and her soft voice saying his name in breathless little moans.

Frustrated, he gave her a clipped greeting in return before striding to his desk.

She frowned slightly before smiling cheerfully and asking how his weekend was.

"Fine and yours?" He said shortly.

The smile dropping from her face, Kate said, "Very well, thank you."

"Good. Can you pull all of the Yang files from the filing room and bring them to my office? It's urgent so I'd appreciate if you do it before you have your morning chat with Olivia."

"Of course," Kate replied briefly. She turned and left his office but not before he saw the hurt look on her face.

It's better this way. If you make her angry and distant with you – no one will confuse that for affection.

Feeling a little sick to his stomach, he stared blankly at his computer screen.

Kate walked rapidly to the file room and stared blindly at the files. Her throat was aching and her eyes were burning and she felt incredibly stupid.

What did you think would happen? We agreed it was over after last night.

That was true but she hadn't expected him to be the cold and distant Edward she had first met. She had thought they would at least be friends.

Why? He doesn't want a friendship with you. You're his assistant and nothing more. He wanted sex and you gave it to him willingly so stop being a crybaby and live with the damn consequences of fucking your boss.

* * *

"Honey, I'm worried about you."

"I'm fine, Olivia. Just tired," Kate said as they sat together in the lunch room. It was filled with their coworkers and she lowered her voice when Rose and Sheila glanced at them curiously. "I haven't been sleeping well."

"Is Edward still being a dick?" Olivia asked in a low voice.

"He never was. He's just very...distant," she said. She pushed her salad around with her fork before closing the lid of the container and tucking it into her lunch bag. She'd had zero appetite this week and she was tired of forcing herself to eat.

"You didn't eat anything," Olivia said worriedly.

"I could stand to lose a couple pounds," Kate replied.

"It looks like you've lost ten," Olivia said. When Kate didn't answer, she squeezed her hand. "Why don't you come by the house tonight? We'll have a barbeque and some drinks and just relax on the deck."

Kate shook her head. "I think I'll just go home. It's been a long week and I'm really tired."

"It's Friday, honey," Olivia said gently. "You need to get out and have some fun."

"No, I need to try and get some sleep," Kate said. "I'll call you on Saturday and maybe we can, I don't know, go to a movie or something."

She glanced at her cell phone. "I should get back to my desk. Edward's waiting for some documents."

She was just finishing up the document when her phone rang. She took a deep breath and forcing herself to sound cheerful, picked it up and said, "Hi, Edward."

"Mrs. Yang is going to be here in fifteen minutes. Can you bring the document to me and I'll review it before we finalize it?"

"Of course, I'm just printing it now," Kate replied. She hung up the phone and, grabbing the letter from the printer, knocked lightly on Edward's door before entering the room. Edward didn't look up as she placed the document on his desk.

As she turned to leave, he said gruffly "You might as well have a seat. It'll only take me a minute to review it."

She sat down in the chair across from his desk, crossing her legs and folding her hands neatly in her lap. As he studied the letter, making occasional changes with a pen, she studied him. It was the first time all week that she had spent more than a few seconds in his presence and she thought he looked tired and cross. There were dark circles under his eyes and he hadn't shaved this morning. Not that she looked much better, she supposed.

She was sleeping maybe three hours a night and what sleep she did get was filled with dreams of Edward. She watched as he idly drummed his fingers on the desk and was mortified when a stray memory of those long fingers caressing her breasts made her nipples harden under her shirt. She folded her arms across her chest and looked out the window before sighing quietly. She gave Edward a polite smile when he handed the letter to her and quickly escaped.

Edward took a deep breath once Kate had left. The scent of her perfume still lingered in his office and it brought forth images of her naked and willing. He had spent the entire week making sure to have as little contact with her as possible and Kate had responded in kind. He had even been borderline rude with her on a few occasions but she had displayed none of her characteristic fiery temper. God, he had fucked up so badly.

It had been a mistake to ask her to stay in his office while he looked over the letter. He had been distracted by the mere presence of her, entirely conscious of every little move she made, from crossing her legs to the small sigh that had made him look briefly at her. She had her arms crossed over her chest and was staring out the window. She had looked so tired and miserable that he wanted to pull her into his arms, rest her head on his chest and tell her everything would be okay. Instead he had finished the letter and handed it to her, giving her another brief look. The look of misery was gone and she even managed a polite smile as she took the letter from. She was one hell of an actress - he'd give her that much.

* * *

"Oh my God, this is insanity," Olivia muttered under her breath. "No one can plan this type of event in a week. Arthur's really lost it this time."

She blew out her breath in a frustrated rush as she scanned the papers in front of her. "Okay, you've got the email list of invites, yeah?"

"I do. And you're going to see about the venue and the caterer, right?" Kate replied.

Olivia cursed under her breath again as she shuffled the papers. Twenty minutes ago, Arthur had called both of them into his office and asked them to arrange for a welcome party for Edward for the following Friday. The event would serve as both a welcome to the firm of Harper and Thompson, and introduce Edward to the other professionals that the firm worked with on a regular basis.

"Yes. I might be able to book the Ruger Hotel, maybe. I've got a connection there and he owes me a favour but I have no idea how we're going to find caterers on such short notice," Olivia said. "Have I mentioned this is absolute insanity?"

Kate laughed. "You know Arthur, Olivia. He's a short notice kind of guy. We should have expected he would do something like this."

"I know," Olivia said crankily as Kate scanned the guest list, "but I repeat – no one can plan this type of event in a week."

"I'm going to go back to my desk and start emailing the invites," Kate said. "We'll just do the best we can and you know Arthur will be appreciative."

"True," Olivia sighed. "But if we can't find a caterer, it's going to be you and me cooking the night before."

Kate smiled to herself as she walked towards her desk. Arthur was always planning something or other last minute and as much as Olivia pretended to hate it, Kate knew she secretly thrived on it.

There was a slender, dark-haired woman standing tentatively by her desk and Kate smiled at her. "Can I help you?"

"I'm looking for Edward," she said. "The receptionist sent me back but I'm not sure I'm in the right spot?"

Kate jerked in surprise when Edward brushed past her and swept the woman into his arms. He embraced her firmly and she returned his hug enthusiastically as he lifted her off her feet.

"Tory, what are you doing here?" Edward said.

"I had to come here for business and thought it would be a fun surprise," she said.

"I'm so glad to see you. Come into my office."

Kate's insides churned with jealousy as she watched Edward place a kiss on the woman's cheek before taking her by the hand and leading her towards his office.

She smiled at Kate as they walked by and Edward said distractedly, "Tory, this is my assistant, Kate. Kate, this is Tory."

"Nice to meet you," Kate said.

Edward was still staring delightedly at the woman and as he ushered her into his office and shut the door, Kate sat down behind her desk. She felt ill and was dismayed to realize how close she was to tears.

What does it matter who Edward is affectionate with, she lectured silently. *You are not his friend or his lover. You're his assistant and nothing more. Get that through your thick skull.*

* * *

Kate unlocked her front door and stepped into the dark hallway. She flipped on the light and kicked off her shoes with a sigh of relief. Chicken weaved anxiously around her legs and she petted her gently before dropping her laptop bag in the living room. She changed into her pajamas and fed Chicken before pulling the bottle of tequila out from the side cupboard. She dusted it off, wondering if tequila went bad.

"I'm getting drunk tonight, Chicken," she said. "It's been a long day and an even longer week."

She rummaged through the cupboards until she found a shot glass and poured herself a shot, humming softly to herself. As Chicken ate her supper, Kate wandered into the living room and sat down in the overstuffed chair, still holding her shot glass and staring moodily at the file she had brought home.

Twenty minutes after Edward had disappeared into his office with Tory, they had reappeared. To her shock, he had taken the rest of the day off, mentioning almost absently that she and Doug could text him if they had questions about the Yang file. Kate had barely managed to nod before they were walking away. Edward's arm was curved familiarly around Tory's waist and her stomach twisted again with jealousy but when Edward had glanced over his shoulder at her she had plastered a smile on her face.

The rest of the afternoon has crept by. Images of what Edward might be doing with Tory kept flashing into her brain and she had been frustrated and feeling sick to her stomach by the end of the day. Before she could leave, Doug had appeared at her desk looking flustered.

"Kate, I need your help. I was supposed to have you type this hand-written information from Mrs. Yang for our meeting with her accountants on Monday morning at eight." He had given her a pleading look. "Is there anyway you can come in this weekend and type it?"

Kate had nodded. "Sure, but you owe me a lunch, Doug."

"No problem. Monday's lunch is on me," Doug had said happily. He had cocked his head at her. "Actually, why don't you just take the file home and work on it there? We won't need it until Monday so as long as you're in the office before eight, it'll be fine."

Deciding that was a much better idea then coming back to the office, she had packed up the Yang file and her laptop and brought them home.

"I'm a very dedicated employee, Chicky-Chick Chicken," Kate said as the old cat wandered into the living room and sat on top of her computer bag. "Taking work home when my boss isn't even working this weekend. In fact, at this very moment he's probably banging a disgustingly cute woman named Tory."

She lifted the shot glass and stared at the amber liquid that glowed in the faint light from the kitchen as Chicken leaped on to the arm of the chair beside her.

"To you, Chicken." Kate solemnly tipped the glass toward the old cat before downing the drink in one quick gulp. She gasped and wheezed as the fiery liquid burned its way down her throat.

"That? Tasted like another," she said and headed towards the kitchen for the bottle, determined to drink away the memory of Edward and his kisses.

* * *

Edward hurried up the sidewalk to Kate's house. He rang the doorbell and waited patiently. After dropping Tory at her hotel, he had returned to the office to pick up the Yang file. He had planned on working on the file over the weekend and he had searched his entire office and Kate's desk before finally texting Doug.

Doug had called him immediately, nervously confessing both his mistake and his suggestion that Kate take the file home to work on over the weekend. At Edward's sigh of frustration, Doug had quickly offered to go to Kate's and pick up the file. He had declined Doug's help, partly because the thought of another man in Kate's house, even a happily married one, made his stomach twist and partly because he would take any excuse to see Kate.

He rang the doorbell again, frowning when he didn't hear her footsteps. It was only nine thirty and the house glowed softly with lights so he was confident that she wasn't in bed. Maybe she was in the tub?

His cock reacted instantly to the thought of her naked and wet and he rearranged himself with a grimace. Before he could ring the doorbell again, the door swung open and Kate, weaving slightly, stared up at him.

"Hello, Kate," he said.

Kate stared blearily at Edward. She was drunker than she thought - she was having Edward visions. The Edward vision took a step forward and spoke again. "Are you okay?"

"What are you doing here?" She asked rudely. Before he could answer, she decided she didn't care what he was doing at her house. She had more important things to take care of - like finishing off that bottle of tequila. Leaving Edward standing in the doorway, she turned and staggered her way down the hallway toward the kitchen.

Edward stared in disbelief as Kate wandered away from him, holding on to the wall for support as she walked. He closed the door and followed her into the kitchen. She was wearing her bunny pajama bottoms and tank top and he tried not to stare at her breasts.

"Kate, are you sick?" He asked.

"Nope," she said happily as she lifted a bottle from the counter. "I am a-okay."

She took another swig of the amber liquid from the bottle in her hand.

"Hoowah!" She said loudly and slammed her hand down on the counter. Chicken, who had darted into the kitchen to greet Edward, hissed and fled the room.

"Are you drunk?" Edward asked.

"I dare say you are no gentleman, sir!" Kate said indignantly. She weaved her way toward him and took a deep breath. It pushed her full breasts out and Edward groaned to himself before forcing his gaze to her face.

"That is not a question you ask a proper lady," she said before tapping him lightly on the chest. "And despite the rumour to the contrary, sir, I am a proper lady and should be treated as such."

She staggered back a step, smiling happily to herself, and would have fallen if he hadn't reached out and caught her about the waist.

"A thousand pardons, m'lady," he said dryly as she giggled and relaxed against him.

"S'no problem, Edward, Ed...Eddie." She snickered and tipped the bottle to her mouth.

"Whoa, I think you've had enough, Katie." Edward pulled the bottle from her hand and placed it on the kitchen table behind him. "It's time for bed."

"I'm not tired," she pouted.

"Are you sure?" He asked. "You look pretty tired to me."

"Nope, I'm good. I could go dancing," she said and wrapped her arms around his waist, before leaning her head on his chest. "Dancing all night."

Edward stroked her long hair, pressing a kiss against the top of her head as she melted against him like a boneless kitten. Just as he decided he would have to carry her to her bed she jerked and pulled away from him. "How did you get into my house? Did you find the key under the flower pot out front?"

She lowered her voice conspiratorially. "Olivia says that's the worse place in the world to keep a hidden house key. She says that every thief in the world will look there first. She says I'm going to come home one day and find all my stuff gone. Just poof! Out the front door. La-dee-da. I say I'm going to come home one day and find a would-be thief torn and bleeding from multiple claw wounds courtesy of my Chicken."

She giggled quietly at the thought before giving him a scowl. "Of course, it's not a problem for you. Chicken likes you. You apparently can just walk right in the front door."

She scoffed lightly. "Dumb cat. Doesn't even like me."

She quieted for a moment before staring at him again with narrowed eyes. "What are you doing here, Edward? It's Friday night and I'm in my pajamas. I may be a little tipsy but that doesn't seem professional to me."

"I came to pick up the Yang file that you took home. I need to work on it this weekend."

Kate squinted at him. "Really? Or did you drop by to take advantage of me in my inebriated state? Because I don't know what kind of girl you think I am, but I'm not the type who just goes around all willy-nilly boinking her boss."

She paused. "Oh wait, I totally am."

She burst into laughter, leaning against him once more for support as a small smile crossed his face.

She stared slyly at him. "Be honest with me, Eddie. Are you trying to take advantage of me in my inebriated state?"

"No. I had no idea you were drunk," Edward said. "And I did try texting you first."

"I turned off my cell phone," she said. "I waited all week, checked the stupid thing every hour because I was secretly hoping you would text me, secretly hoping you might ask to come over again so we could have sex but I knew that tonight you wouldn't. Why would you call me for a quick fuck when you had that super cute Tory chick to bang?"

"I'm not sleeping with Tory," Edward said quickly. "She's Tabitha's sister."

"Oh." She gave him a look of shame. "I'm sorry, that was a horrible thing for me to say."

"It's fine."

"Fuck, I'm a mean drunk," Kate said.

Edward laughed. "You're not. And I should have told you who Tory was when I introduced you."

"It was none of my business. Besides, I've had a great Friday night. Chicken and I have been partying all night." She abruptly pushed away from him.

"I forgot to feed Chicken! Here Chicky-Chick Chicken! Come to mama."

She staggered her way to the cupboard as Edward followed her, steadying her from behind.

"Kate, honey, you did feed her. I can see food in her dish," he said. "I really think you should just go to bed. C'mon, Katie-did."

Before she could protest he scooped her up in his arms and carried her toward the bedroom. She stiffened for a moment before relaxing against him, wrapping her arms around his shoulders and pressing her face into his neck.

"I am tired all of a sudden," she whispered.

The feel of her lips moving against his throat, her warm breath tickling his skin, gave Edward an immediate erection. He grunted softly in response and gently sat her down on the bed. She sat quietly for a moment and he was about to coax her into lying down so he could tuck the covers over her when she stood up suddenly, almost hitting her head against his.

"Katie, honey, you need to go to sleep," he said.

"Katie honey doesn't sleep in pajamas," she replied indignantly. "Only weenies sleep in pajamas."

She grabbed the bottom of her tank top, pulled it up over her head and tossed it at the bottom of the bed. Edward looked away immediately. He was aching to cup her breasts in his hands and run his tongue over them. He clenched his hands into fists as Kate hooked her thumbs into the waistband of her pajamas and pushed them down. She was wearing a pair of white cotton panties with small yellow daisies on them and she laughed a little self-consciously

"If I had known you were coming over I would have worn a silk thong. Much sexier," she said as he jerked his gaze away from her perfect body and looked over her shoulder at the far wall. He didn't dare tell her the sight of her in the cotton panties turned him on as much as the idea of her in silk did.

He groaned harshly when she leaned against him and whispered, "Help me with my pajama bottoms, Edward."

She lifted her feet one at a time and he steadied her with a hand at her hip while using the other to pull off her pajamas. He could feel her breasts pushing against him, the nipples hard points against his chest, and he grimly ignored her warm hands that were currently sliding up and down his back. She snuggled up against him and placed soft kisses on his neck. He moaned low in this throat when she stood on her tip-toes and let her small pink tongue flick lightly up his neck and trace the outline of his ear.

"I like you, Edward," she breathed softly into his ear

"I like you too, Katie," he replied unsteadily.

"I can tell." She laughed and cupped his erection in her hand. "This part of you particularly likes me."

He gasped when she squeezed lightly for a moment and then began to rub him slowly and firmly. She tilted her head and kissed him, pushing her tongue into his mouth so she could explore the warmth and stroke his tongue lightly. Edward groaned and pulled her against him, cupping her ass through her panties, before kissing her deeply. He slid his tongue into her mouth and tasted tequila. He tore his mouth from hers, forcing a whimper of need from her throat.

"Not a good idea, Katie," he rasped.

She wiggled her eyebrows at him. "I think it's a great idea. In fact, it's the best idea I've had all week." She leaned in to kiss him again but he shook his head.

"I know, Katie, but the best idea is you going to sleep."

"Fine," she sighed softly and turned away from him, crawling into bed but not bothering to pull up the quilt. He tucked the sheet and quilt around her and pulled the clip from her hair as she curled up on to her side and tucked her hand under her pillow. He sat on the bed beside her as Chicken leaped silently onto the bed and draped herself across Kate's hip. She stared sleepily at him and he couldn't resist smoothing her hair from her face or leaning down to place a soft kiss on her forehead.

"Sleep sweet, Edward," she murmured softly.

"Sleep sweet, Katie-did."

Chapter 10

Kate woke late Saturday morning to a pounding headache and a bad taste in her mouth. She sat up in her bed, groaning softly and holding her aching head in her hands. Chicken sat next to her purring loudly and Kate frowned in irritation.

"Please stop purring, Chicken. It sounds like a truck is being driven through the bedroom."

She stumbled her way to the bathroom and stared into the mirror. Her hair was a ratty looking mess and her eyes were rimmed red and bloodshot. Moving slowly, she brushed her teeth and started the shower. While the water warmed she quickly took some Advil and then stepped into the shower. The hot spray of water felt good and she stood there for nearly ten minutes, letting the water ease away her aches and pains before washing and conditioning her hair and soaping her body. By the time she stepped out of the shower, the Advil had started to kick in and she felt semi-normal. She would have some dry toast, she decided, and then type up the work from the Yang file and have the rest of the day to relax. If she felt better in the afternoon she might even do some gard —"

She broke off in mid-thought, staring uneasily at herself in the bathroom mirror.

The Yang File. Oh God. Everything that had happened last night came back in one big rush and she sat down on the side of the tub and slumped over, her head in her hands. Edward had come by to pick up the file and she had been a complete idiot. She had called him Eddie. Even worse she had stripped in front of him and then tried to drunkenly seduce him.

She groaned and walked naked into the bedroom, running a comb through her hair before pulling out a pair of yoga pants and a t-shirt from the closet. He had come over on a work-related issue and she had thrown herself at him, forcing him to kindly, but firmly rebuke her. She sighed miserably as she pulled on her clothes. She would never be able to look him in the eye again.

Her headache reduced to a dull throb, Kate made some toast and fed Chicken. A piece of paper was stuck to the fridge and she squinted at Edward's handwriting.

Kate, I've taken the Yang file but left the notes to be typed for my Monday meeting in your laptop bag. Please type them asap on Saturday and email them to me.

Thanks,

Edward

She left the note on the table as she headed to the living room to grab the computer bag. An hour later, she had attached the typed document to an email and was nervously trying to compose a short message to Edward.

"Do I mention last night, Chicken or don't I?" She stared blankly at the cat before sighing and typing a quick note.

Edward,

Please find attached the documents you requested. As well, please accept my sincerest apologies for last night.

Enjoy your weekend.

Kate

It would have to do. It was better to keep it short and simple and hope for the best. She emptied the dishwasher, swept the kitchen floor and made herself a cup of tea before checking her email again. There was an email from Edward and she clicked it open.

156

Kate,

Thanks for the document.   No worries about last night.

E.

She let her breath out in a whoosh and rubbed absently at her temples as she re-read his brief email.

"Well, at least I'm not going to be fired, Chicken." She drank her tea and stared moodily out the window. She needed to get out of the house and do something or she would spend the entire weekend thinking about Edward.

* * *

"Thanks again for working on the weekend, Kate," Doug said as he opened the office door for her.

"You're welcome. Thanks for lunch," she replied.

He followed her into reception and she smiled at him. They had spent the entire lunch talking about Doug's wife, Anne, who was pregnant with their first child. Doug's enthusiasm for the upcoming birth had cheered her up considerably.

"Doug," Rose said as they walked by her, "Edward was looking for you when he got back from his meeting, I told him you were out for lunch with Kate and he said to have you come to his office when you were back."

"Thanks, Rose," Doug said.

He followed Kate to Edward's office and knocked on the open door.

"Come in and close the door," Edward said curtly.

Twenty minutes later, an ashen-faced Doug left Edward's office.

"Doug, what's wrong?" Kate asked.

"Nothing," he said and headed towards his own office. Kate left her desk and chased after him.

"Doug? What happened? Did something go wrong with the Yang file?"

"Sort of. I made a mistake, not a really big one, but Edward ripped me a new one for it. He's in a terrible mood."

He paused and gave her an odd look. "He seemed kind of angry that we went for lunch together."

"What do you mean?"

"I don't know," Doug said. "He just seemed pissed about it. Reminded me that there were no romantic relationships allowed between coworkers. Frankly it was a bit insulting since he knows I'm married."

"Sorry, Doug," Kate said. "I, uh, I think Edward is just really strict about the rules."

"Sure, that's it," Doug said. "Although it came across more like jealousy."

Kate's stomach dropped and she kept a polite smile plastered on her face as Doug stared thoughtfully at her. "Sleeping with your boss will get you fired, Kate."

"I'm not sleeping with Edward," Kate said shortly.

Doug studied her for a moment longer. "Sorry, that was rude of me. It's just – he was pretty upset that we went for lunch."

"I'll speak to him about it," Kate said. "He was probably angry because I haven't finished my work on the Henderson file and he wanted me to work through lunch."

She left Doug's office. Her good mood had dissipated and her stomach was churning with anger and anxiety. She wasn't entirely certain that Doug had believed her and if he said anything to anyone...

She took a deep breath as Edward barked her name and walked into his office.

"Yes?"

"I need you to make the changes to this letter, have Sheila run this document to the courthouse immediately, and call Mrs. Yang and set up a meeting for Thursday here at the office," he snapped.

Without replying she held out her hands for the file. He handed it to her and gave her an angry look. "Enjoy your lunch?"

"Yes," she said briefly.

"Shut the door, Ms. Jones. We need to talk."

She closed his door and shook her head when he started to talk.

"No, I'm talking first," she said.

He sat back in his chair and glared at her as she clutched the file tightly.

"Don't you glare at me, Edward Turner," she said angrily. "I just came back from a conversation with Doug where he asked me if I was sleeping with you. Do you know why? Because you yelled at him about having lunch with me and felt the need to remind him, a married man, that he can't sleep with me. Your stupid comments gave him the idea that maybe you were jealous because I'm fucking you."

"Maybe you shouldn't be going for lunch alone with male co-workers," Edward said.

"Oh you did not just say that to me," she snarled. "Sharing my bed for two nights does not give you the right to interfere in my personal life. I will go for lunch with whomever I damn well please. Is that clear?"

He continued to glare at her and she scowled at him. "Is that clear, Edward?"

"Yes," he bit out.

"Good."

* * *

By Thursday evening, Kate was exhausted from lack of sleep and pretending to be cheerful when she was completely miserable. After their fight on Monday, she and Edward had developed an unspoken truce and were walking on eggshells around each other all week while maintaining an image of polite professionalism around their co-workers.

"Katie?" Olivia said. "I'm worried about you."

"I'm fine," Kate replied.

Olivia had insisted that Kate go for dinner with her after work and as she watched Kate push the food around on her plate, she said, "You're not fine. You're not eating, you've lost weight, and you look kind of terrible."

"Thanks," Kate said with a forced grin.

"Are you sleeping at all?"

"Some," Kate said. "I – I dream a lot."

"About Edward?"

Kate nodded and pushed her plate away. "I made a stupid mistake, Olivia. I was a fool to think I could sleep with him and then just walk away."

"I'm sorry, honey," Olivia said. "Maybe if you talked to Edward – "

"No. Things are still tense between us and besides, what good would it do? I'm not going to quit my job to try and have a relationship with a man who's still in love with his dead wife."

"Just because he's still in love with her doesn't mean he isn't ready for a new relationship," Olivia said. "If God forbid something happened to Jon, I'd never stop loving him but I wouldn't shut out the idea of finding someone new. It's been two years."

"He isn't ready," Kate said flatly. "You didn't see the look on his face when he talked about her. He isn't over her loss and I understand that but I should never have agreed to casual sex with him."

"Maybe you should talk to Lina. Didn't you say she was sleeping with her boss?"

Kate nodded. "Yes. And it's all worked out for her. They're living together now."

She took a drink of water. "Can we talk about something else? I'm so tired of talking and thinking about Edward."

"Of course," Olivia said immediately. "We need to start making birthday plans for you. Since it falls on Thursday this year, I was thinking we'd have a bit of a birthday bash on the Saturday after."

"That's sweet, but I'm not sure I'm up to a party," Kate said.

"It'll be good for you. We'll keep it on the small side. We'll invite a few people from the office, Leslie and Angela from the book club, your parents and maybe my parents. Do you think Lina could come out?"

Kate shrugged. "I don't know. It's next week and the flight would be super expensive. Of course, her new boyfriend is on the wealthy side."

"I'll send her an invitation," Olivia said. "We'll have a barbeque at our place and have some beers and birthday cake."

"I don't want you making a fuss," Kate said.

"Oh please, you know I love a good party," Olivia replied. "Besides, Jon bought a new, larger grill and he's dying to try it out. Hey, speaking of parties – did you get a final list of attendees for the party tomorrow?"

Kate nodded. "Yes. Just over a hundred."

"Well, I told the caterer that it would be one-twenty-five so that works perfectly," Olivia said. "Are you going to be there?"

"Yeah, it'll look weird if I'm not. I don't think I'll stay long though. My plan is to try and slip out early."

She took another drink of water before reaching across the table and squeezing Olivia's hand. "Thanks, Olivia. I'd be lost without you."

"What are best friends for?" Olivia replied. "Besides, it'll all work out – I promise you."

* * *

Kate checked the time before cursing under her breath and hurrying to the bathroom. It was late Friday afternoon and the office was quiet. Edward had been out all afternoon at meetings and Arthur had closed the office an hour early so her co-workers could get to the welcome party. She had volunteered to answer phones so Rose could leave early and if she didn't move her ass, she was going to be late.

She absentmindedly adjusted her skirt as she headed back to her desk. Olivia was right, she had lost weight – almost ten pounds in the last two weeks – and her clothes were a little too loose. She checked her texts as she walked back to her desk. She was taking a cab to the party and she needed to call and –

She yelped surprise when she ran into something solid and warm and stumbled back, clutching her phone tightly. She tripped over her own feet and hit the floor with a hard thud, wincing when her elbow banged on the floor.

"Shit! Kate, are you okay?"

Edward picked her up from the floor and set her on her feet, keeping his hands around her waist for a moment too long before releasing her.

"I'm good," she said as she rubbed her elbow. "Just clumsy."

"I'm sorry. I wasn't watching where I was going," he said.

"Neither was I. What are you doing here? Aren't you supposed to be at your party?"

"I needed to drop off a file. What about you? Aren't you supposed to be there?"

"I was just on my way," she replied.

"Do you need a ride?"

"No," she said a little too quickly.

"You drove your car to work today?" Edward asked.

"Uh, no," Kate said. "I'm calling a cab."

"You can ride with me. You'll be late if you don't," Edward said.

When she didn't move, he gave her a slightly impatient look. "Ready, Kate?"

"Yes."

Bad idea, Kate! Very bad idea!

* * *

Kate stared silently out the car window at the passing scenery as Edward drove. He was a fast driver and weaved the powerful car quickly and confidently in and out of traffic. She stared at his long tanned fingers as they gripped the steering wheel, idly remembering how it felt to have those same fingers gripping her thighs, gently urging her to open them so he could settle his body between them.

She flushed and cursed to herself, forcing her gaze away from Edward's hands. She was acutely aware of his very male presence beside her and she wished that she had just taken a damn cab. She was pretty sure she wouldn't have been trying not to drool on a cab driver.

Edward gripped the steering wheel and did his best to concentrate on the road in front of him. It had been a mistake to give Kate a ride to the party, especially given the anger and awkwardness between them, but he couldn't resist the urge to be alone with her. He stole a quick glance at her. She was sitting quietly in the seat beside him with her hands folded in her lap as she stared out the windshield. Her face was pale and thinner and he had felt her ribs when he had picked her up off the floor at the office.

Say something, my love. Tell her you're sorry for being such a jackass on Monday, Tabitha whispered in his head.

"Kate – "

"Edward, I – "

They smiled awkwardly at each other and he said, "You first."

Kate cleared her throat. "I like your car."

He flashed a boyish grin that made her pulse rise. "Thanks. I've had her almost two years now. I have to admit I'm pretty fond of her myself."

"Her?"

For the first time in a week, Kate gave him a genuine smile and he returned her smile with a mixture of relief and embarrassment.

"All my cars have been women," he said.

"Of course they have been. Does she have a name?"

"Uh…"

"She does!" Kate laughed. "Tell me."

"Nope. I can tell when you're making fun of us." Edward gave her a mock scowl.

"Oh c'mon, I have to know. Give me just the first letter - maybe I can guess," Kate said.

"If I tell you, you have to promise not to tell anyone else at the office. I can't have them knowing I've named my car. It would seriously undermine my position as an authority figure in the office."

"No problem," Kate said.

"Promise?"

"I will take it to my grave. Hand to God," Kate said solemnly.

Edward burst out laughing as he stopped the car for a red light.

"Her name is," he paused for dramatic effect, "Matilda."

"Matilda?" Kate stared at him, "You named your car Matilda?"

"Matilda was my grandmother's name," he said.

"You named you car after your grandma?" Kate laughed. "I'm sure she loved that."

"My mom says she would have approved. Apparently I got my love for fast cars from her."

"Your family sounds interesting," Kate said. She relaxed against the seat, looking out the window. This was the best she'd felt all week. It seemed right to be sitting in Edward's car, laughing and joking with him. She smiled as they passed a mini-van full of kids and a frazzled looking woman.

"Kate, I want to apologize for what I said and did on Monday. I was a complete – "

Jackass, Tabitha prompted in his head.

"I was a complete jackass and your personal life isn't any of my business."

"I'm not the type of woman to sleep with a married man, Edward," she said.

"I know you're not. I have no excuse for my behaviour and I'm sorry."

She studied him for a moment before nodding. "Apology accepted."

She hesitated before blushing a little. "I should probably apologize in person for the night you came by to pick up the Yang file. I had too much to drink and I acted really inappropriately with you."

Edward turned into the hotel parking lot. "Don't worry about it, Katie. It's already forgotten," he lied. Every moment with Kate was burned into his brain. Especially the moments where she ended up half-naked and in his arms.

She gave him an uneasy smile as he parked and shut off the car. He returned her smile before opening his car door.

"Ready for the party, Katie-did?" He asked.

"Yes. But you need to remember to call me Kate - not Katie or Katie-did. Okay?"

"Right. Sorry," he muttered. Kate stepped out of the car and the two of them walked across the parking lot in silence.

* * *

"The food is delicious, Katie. You should try some." Olivia said as she took a sip of wine.

"I will," Kate said. "I'm just waiting for the crowd to thin out a bit around the buffet table."

They stood silently in the large conference room, watching the crowd of people milling around, before Olivia smiled at her.

"I think we've outdone ourselves this time."

Kate laughed. "All I did was email people. This success is all on you, Olivia."

"Thanks, honey. Although I couldn't have done it without you."

Olivia took another sip of wine as she stared over Kate's shoulder. Her eyes widened and she grabbed Kate's arm. "Shit. Henry Dobson has spotted you and is moving across the room. I repeat, Henry Dobson is on the move."

"Ugh, I need to hide," Kate muttered.

"Too late," Olivia murmured before smiling politely. "Henry. How are you? It's so good to see you again."

"Hello, Olivia!" Henry shouted. His round face was beet red and, instead of the usual overpowering scent of cologne, he smelled of garlic and wine. Kate wasn't sure which smell was worse. He staggered a bit as he turned to Kate and reached for her hand.

"Henry," Kate said as he grinned greasily at her and took her hand in his, planting a loud kiss on her knuckles."

"Kate, you're looking as lovely as ever, my dear." His eyes skimmed down her body, pausing at her breasts, and Kate grimaced inwardly before yanking her hand free.

"Thank you, Henry. Enjoying the party?"

"Now that I've found you, my dear, absolutely."

He smiled again and weaving a little on his feet, crept closer to her.

"If you'll excuse us, I need to use the ladies room and I was just telling Olivia that Arthur was looking for her," Kate said quickly.

She grabbed Olivia's arm and, giving Henry another polite smile, steered her to the opposite side of the room. They squeezed through a couple of large groups of people and slowed their pace.

"Yuck," Olivia said. "That man is nasty."

"You're telling me," Kate replied, "It's only two hours into the party and he's plastered. At least he didn't have time to offer me a different *position* at his firm."

"Kate?"

She turned to see Josh standing behind her.

"Josh! It's good to see you," she said.

"You too," he said and after a brief moment of awkwardness, gave her a hug.

She returned his hug, patting his back gently, before stepping away. "Olivia, this is Josh Dumont. Josh, this is Olivia Stafford. She's Arthur Harper's personal assistant."

"Nice to meet you, Ms. Stafford," Josh said and shook her hand. "If your office is anything like mine, you're responsible for this fantastic party. The food is unbelievable."

Olivia grinned at him. "Well, Kate and I both worked on it but thank you. And please, call me Olivia."

"You both did a wonderful job." He grinned at them again, the dimples in his cheeks deepening.

"If you'll excuse me," Olivia said, "I need to speak with Arthur."

She disappeared into the crowd and Josh smiled again at Kate. "How have you been?"

"Good, thank you. And you?"

"Not bad," he replied.

"I haven't seen you on the train lately."

"I've been taking the earlier train," Josh said. "It's been super busy at work."

Across the room, Edward watched as Kate and Josh talked animatedly. His eyes narrowed when Josh leaned forward and whispered something in her ear and Kate laughed up at him. His stomach tightened when Josh offered his arm to her and they headed to the buffet table. He unclenched his fists and took a few deep breaths. Kate had said that she and Josh were just friends and even if that had changed, it was none of his business. Which was why his urge to stalk across the room and punch Josh in the face was completely irrational.

You know, my love, I always thought your jealousy was adorable but you should probably reign it in a bit.

I am not jealous.

Do you forget who you're speaking to, my love?

No. I know exactly who I'm speaking to and I'm starting to wonder if maybe having conversations with my dead wife is a sign that I need therapy.

Therapy is always a good idea. You can talk to them about why you won't admit you want to move on with Kate.

He grimaced and shoved Tabitha's voice out of his head as Melissa approached him.

"Hello, Edward."

"Melissa."

He stared silently at her. She had been avoiding him and Kate for the last two weeks but he wasn't sure if it was because he had piled enough case files on her to keep her busy for months or if she had decided it wasn't worth her time to try and get Kate fired.

"I was thinking we should meet first thing Monday to go over the Martin file. It's got – "

"I'm in New York next week," he interrupted her. "And you've been moved off the Martin file."

She frowned at him. "Are you really going to keep switching me off of files just to avoid working with me?"

"In a word – yes," he said bluntly. "Excuse me."

He walked away, forcing himself to smile politely when Arthur waved him over to introduce him to yet another person.

* * *

Kate washed her hands and checked her reflection in the bathroom mirror. The party was starting to wind down, although there were still plenty of people drinking and mingling, and she was tired and ready to leave. She had spent most of the night with Olivia and Josh and when Josh had offered to give her a ride home she had accepted.

She left the ladies' room, groaning inwardly when Henry Dobson stepped out of the men's room at the same time. The hallway was empty and she wrinkled her nose at the smell of garlic and booze emanating from him.

"Hello, Kate," he said before stumbling toward her.

"Henry," she replied briefly and tried to slip around him. He grabbed her wrist in one beefy hand and forced her to a stop.

"Leaving the party so soon?"

"Yes."

"Let me give you a ride home," he slurred.

"No. You're drunk." Kate tried to pull her wrist free but Henry squeezed her wrist, grinding the bones together. She gasped in pain and glared at him.

"Let me go. Right now."

"Just give me one little kiss and I'll let you go."

He leaned toward her and Kate pushed him in the chest. He stumbled, his hand tightening painfully around her wrist and she made a low curse of pain.

"You're hurting me," she gritted out between clenched teeth.

"Just one little kiss," he mumbled. "That's all I want."

He leaned forward breathing wine and garlic in her face and her temper got the best of her. She had spent the last two weeks in a constant state of emotional turmoil, she couldn't sleep, she couldn't eat, and now she was being attacked by a slob of a man who wore too much cheap cologne, had questionable personal hygienic routines and drank too much at business functions.

She gave him a look of pure fury. "Let go of me now, Henry, before you get hurt."

Henry snorted laughter before squeezing her wrist and pulling her toward him.

"Kate?"

She breathed a sigh of relief at the sound of Josh's voice and as Henry glanced over his shoulder, she slammed her knee into his crotch. He made a harsh groan, his face turning the colour of old linen and collapsed to the floor. His hands cupped his crotch as he wheezed and groaned.

"I told you to stay away from me," she said before stepping over him and striding down the hall.

"Jesus, Kate, what happened?" Josh said.

"Henry was being an ass," she said.

She rubbed her wrist gingerly as Josh took her hand and led her down the hallway. She spared a glance at Henry as they turned the corner. He was sitting up and he continued to rub his crotch as she gave him a frosty look.

"Come in here." Josh led her into an empty conference room and examined her wrist. It was bright red and she made a hiss of pain when he touched it lightly.

"Fuck. I think we need to call the police," he said.

"No," Kate said immediately. "That asshole learned his lesson."

She laughed shakily, feeling a little sick to her stomach, and Josh pulled her into his embrace.

"Are you sure?" He asked as he rubbed her back.

She nodded and leaned against him. "I'm sure. I just want to go home."

Tears were starting to drip down her face and she cleared her throat before stepping out of his embrace. He cupped her face and wiped at her face with his thumbs.

"Thanks," she said.

He gave her a solemn look. "Are you sure you're okay?"

"Yes."

"Okay." He dropped a brief kiss on her forehead. "C'mon let's get you home and -

"Am I interrupting?" Edward's voice, full of anger, spoke behind them and Kate stared guiltily over Josh's shoulder.

"I was just taking Kate home," Josh said.

"Are you?" Edward said stiffly. "I need to speak with Ms. Jones about a work-related matter."

Josh frowned at him. "She's had a rough night and – "

"It's fine, Josh," Kate said. "Just give us a minute, okay? I'll meet you out front."

He nodded and ignored the angry look Edward gave him as he left the room.

Kate folded her hands behind her back and waited. When Edward didn't say anything, just stared at her angrily, she sighed loudly. "What can I help you with, Edward?"

"I'll be in New York for the week," he said.

"What? Why didn't you tell me?" She said.

"I just found out this morning. There are issues with a few of my old files and they need my help. I'll be emailing you some documents to work on and there may be a couple days where you'll have to work some overtime," he said tersely.

"That's fine. Have a safe trip." She scooted past him and into the hallway.

"I thought you and Josh had decided to just be friends." He had followed her out into the hallway and when she didn't reply he reached out and took her wrist, swinging her around to face him.

She made a low hiss of pain and yanked her wrist free.

"What's wrong with your wrist?" He asked.

"Nothing. Good night, Edward."

He grabbed her forearm, holding her steady as he examined her wrist before cursing loudly. "What the hell happened?"

"It doesn't matter. I'm fine, I just want to go home."

"You're not fine. Tell me what happened?" Edward demanded before taking her cold hands and holding them tightly.

"What happened?" Kate whispered raggedly. "What happened is that for the past two weeks I've spent every waking moment trying not to think about you or be alone with you and trying to understand how you can be so distant one moment and then so sweet the next. I have to go to a stupid party in your honour when all I really want to do is go home, and then I get sexually harassed at your stupid party."

She glared angrily at him. "I thought after driving over here with you that maybe we could be friends again but now you're angry with me over something that wasn't even my fault. I'm tired, I'm upset and I want to go home."

"Sexually harassed?" Edward said in a dangerously soft voice. "Who, Kate? Was it Josh?"

"No," she said. "It doesn't matter who it was. I have to go – Josh is waiting to give me a ride home."

He let go of her hands but before she could walk away, he pulled her into his embrace and rested his forehead against hers. His big hands rubbed her back and he pressed a light kiss against her mouth.

"Tell me who did this to you, Katie," he said.

"Edward, I – "

"Tell me. I'm not letting you go until you do."

"You have to promise not to do something stupid," she said.

"I won't do something stupid," he said. "Who hurt you?"

"Henry Dobson," she said. "He grabbed my wrist and tried to kiss me because he's completely plastered. Josh showed up, I kneed Henry in the groin, and we left him on the floor outside the men's room."

"Okay," he said.

He stepped away from her and she grabbed him by the arm. "Edward, where are you going?"

"To find Henry. I'm going to teach him to pick on someone his own size," he said with an odd calmness that frightened her badly.

She stepped in front of him and pressed her hands against his chest. "He was drunk. He probably won't even remember it in the morning. I don't want you going near him, okay?"

He glanced at her and she could tell by the blank look in his eyes that he was only partially listening.

"Edward, please." She gave him a little shake. "Don't do this. Please."

The blank look in his eyes disappeared and Kate breathed a sigh of relief as he glanced over her shoulder. His nostrils flared and he gave her a brief smile before cupping the nape of her neck with his hand and slanting his mouth over hers. He kissed her deeply, sliding his tongue into her mouth, as she moaned and clung tightly to him. It was a mistake to kiss him but after nearly two weeks of dreaming about him, she couldn't help herself. He pulled her closer, his hand rubbing the small of her back as their tongues tasted and teased. Much too quickly, he released her and she touched his jaw lightly.

"Everything's good, right?" She asked.

"It's good," he replied before stepping around her. She turned to see Josh and Olivia standing at the end of the hallway staring wide-eyed at them and she closed her eyes for a moment.

"In fact, everything will be more than good as soon as I have a brief chat with Henry," Edward said in a low voice as he strode down the hallway toward Josh and Olivia.

"Josh, Olivia, stop him. He's going after Henry," she said as she chased after him.

Josh put a hand on Edward's arm and pulled him to a stop. "He's not worth it. Besides, I just saw one of his colleagues loading him into a cab a few minutes ago. He's gone."

Kate caught up to them and placed a hand on Edward's back. "I really want to forget this happened and just go home. Please, Edward. We'll talk more about it when you're back from New York."

He reached for her, but she stepped back with a warning glance and a little shake of her head.

"I'll drive you home," he said roughly, "Just give me a minute to talk to Arthur."

"No, I'll be fine. You can't leave your own party. Josh has offered to see me home and you know how it will look if we leave the party together," she said softly.

Edward's eyes narrowed and he glared at Josh. "Get her home safely."

"I will," Josh replied.

"Don't touch her. Do you understand?"

"Edward," Kate said. "Enough, please."

"Don't touch her," Edward repeated.

"I heard you the first time," Josh said.

Edward scowled but before he could say anything, Kate took his hand and squeezed it tightly. "I'll talk to you later, Edward."

"It should be me driving you home," he said bitterly before walking away without looking back.

Olivia leaned against the wall. "Please remind me never to make Edward angry."

"No kidding," Josh replied.

"Katie, are you okay?" Olivia asked.

Kate nodded. "Yes. I just really want to go home."

"Let's get you home then," Josh said. He reached for her hand before hesitating and dropping his hand to his side.

"Probably a smart idea," Olivia said solemnly. "Hell, at this point, even *I'm* afraid to touch her."

A grin crossed Josh's face and even Kate managed a small smile.

"Good night, Olivia. I'll call you tomorrow, okay?"

"Sounds good. Get my Katie home safe, Josh."

"I will," Josh promised.

* * *

Josh pulled into her driveway and shut off the car before smiling at her. "So, you and Edward huh?"

"Um, I'm not sure what you mean," Kate said nervously.

"Please." Josh gave her a wry look. "I'm not a stupid guy. The guy had murder in his eyes when he found out what Henry did to you. And I was there when he kissed you in the hallway remember? I don't kiss any of the admin staff in my office like that. And if I did I'd probably end up with a knee to the groin like Henry back there."

Kate sighed before unclicking her seatbelt. "There's – there's an attraction between us but if we act on it, I'll definitely lose my job and Edward might too. I'd appreciate it if you kept what you saw tonight to yourself."

"I will," Josh said. "But the way he looks at you, especially when you're around other men, are you sure he knows you're trying not to act on it? He saw both Olivia and me standing there before he kissed you. And he was pretty clear with his 'don't touch her' demand."

"He knows. It's just been a difficult few weeks. We'll get it sorted out. Thank you again for the ride home and for helping me this evening. I really appreciate it." She smiled wearily at him as she opened the car door.

"You're welcome. Take care of yourself and I'll see you on the train, okay?"

"Yes. Good night, Josh."

She closed the car door and walked slowly to the front door. She let herself in and closed it behind her before sliding down the wall and sitting on the floor. Chicken appeared in the darkness to weave around her legs and she scooped her up, ignoring the way the old cat stiffened against her, and buried her face in Chicken's soft fur.

"I want to be with Edward, Chicken," she whispered. "I want to be with him so much it hurts."

Chapter 11

She wasn't surprised when Olivia showed up at her doorstep the next morning. She let her in and took the cup of coffee with a grateful smile.

"How did you sleep?" Olivia asked.

"Terrible," Kate admitted.

"You look like you didn't sleep at all. How is your wrist?"

"Fine."

"Let me see it." Olivia pushed up Kate's sleeve and muttered a curse. "Fuck, it's swollen and bruised."

"It doesn't feel as bad as it looks," Kate said. She tugged her arm free and pushed down her sleeve.

"You should at least tell David what Henry did last night. David's a good guy and I doubt he wants to have a partner in his law firm who attacks women," Olivia said.

"I already did," Kate replied. "I emailed him earlier this morning and he called me right away. I thought about it all night and decided I couldn't keep quiet."

"What did David say?"

"He's going to speak to Henry about the incident. He asked if I was pressing charges and I said no but that I thought he should know. He thanked me for telling him but whether anything comes of it – I don't know. I'm pretty confident that Henry won't do it again but..."

She trailed off and Olivia gave her an evil little grin. "Probably not. Especially since his left testicle is probably still up somewhere around his liver."

"I told him not to touch me," Kate said.

Olivia laughed and took a sip of coffee. "From what Josh told me, you really nailed him. Little fucker deserves to be singing soprano for the rest of his life."

She tapped one long nail on the kitchen table. "I was looking for you when Josh pulled me aside and told me what happened. Next thing I know we're in the hallway watching Edward give you one hell of a kiss. Fuck, it made me hot just watching it."

Kate shook her head. "He shouldn't have done that. He only did it to keep Josh away."

"Well there was certainly no doubt that it was a 'this is my woman' kind of kiss. And if Josh did have any doubt, Edward telling him not to touch you would have ended it," Olivia said.

She paused and gave Kate a thoughtful look. "Did it bother you that Edward practically claimed you in the hallway in front of Josh?"

"Well, the method was a little too caveman for me but I wasn't exactly bothered by it," Kate said before dropping her head into her hands. "I'm an idiot."

"No, you're not. I get it, really I do, but just make sure you're not missing out on a possible relationship with someone else just because Edward goes all caveman when another guy looks at you."

"I know." Kate stood and paced back and forth. "I need to speak to Edward about his behaviour and I will. I just − it felt stupidly good to have him be so − so protective. Like, maybe for just a minute, he actually cared about me. That it wasn't just sex he wanted."

"I think it's more than that," Olivia said. "I know you think he's still carrying a torch for his dead wife, but I have a feeling that torch is getting dimmer by the day."

"I don't think so," Kate said moodily. "Why the hell couldn't I just be attracted to Josh? He's a nice guy."

Olivia sat back and sipped at her coffee. "That's why. He's way too nice. You like your boys rough and tough. I'm going to invite Josh to your birthday party and set him up with Sheila."

Kate laughed. "And does Sheila know you're doing this?"

"Not yet," Olivia said cheerfully. "I'll let her know on Monday."

"You won't be happy until everyone's married off, will you?" Kate laughed.

"Trust me," Olivia said, "Josh and Sheila are going to be a perfect match."

* * *

Monday afternoon Kate was reviewing a document that Edward had emailed to her when her phone rang. She answered it, her stomach twisting when she heard Edward's familiar voice.

"Kate, it's Edward." He still sounded angry and she sighed to herself.

"Hi, how's New York?"

"Fine," he replied. "I'm calling because it looks like I have a lot more work here then I originally thought."

"Okay," Kate said. "I can reschedule your appointments for next week if you're going to be staying later."

"No," Edward replied. "I've arranged for you to come to New York and help me."

Kate pulled the phone away from her and looked at it for a moment before slowly replacing it against her ear.

"Did you hear me, Kate?" Edward said impatiently.

"Yes, but what possible help could I give you to shorten your time there?" Kate said. "I can just as easily type letters and documentation here, as I would there."

"The firm here has had a sudden shortage in admin staff and it'll be easier and faster to have you working directly with me."

"I – how long will I be there?" Kate asked.

"Just until Friday. We'll fly home Friday evening."

"But, Thursday - "

Kate paused. Edward wouldn't care that it was her birthday.

"What about Thursday?" Edward asked impatiently.

"Nothing," Kate said. "But is this really necessary? I mean, couldn't you work something out there with a temp?"

"This isn't a request, Kate. You're my assistant and I need your help. Your flight is booked for early tomorrow morning," Edward snapped.

"Fine," Kate said. "Do you have the information for my flight?"

"I'll have travel services email you the itinerary and I'll arrange for a car to pick you up at the airport tomorrow. See you then."

Edward hung up the phone without waiting for her reply. Feeling a little like she'd been run over by a very large truck, Kate slowly hung up and stared blindly at her computer screen. She was going to New York – tomorrow. She stood up abruptly and headed down the hall to Olivia's desk.

"Kate? Why do you look like that?" Olivia asked.

"I'm going to New York."

"What?"

"I'm going to New York," Kate repeated. "Edward just phoned, they have a shortage of admin staff at his old firm, he needs my help, it's not a request, I have no choice, and I'll be there until Friday."

"Are you kidding me? You're going to New York because Edward wants a secretary?" Olivia said in disbelief. "Why not just hire a temp?"

"I suggested that and he just cut me off and said it wasn't a request and that I was flying to New York. The man's lost his mind."

"No doubt," Olivia said with a small grin. "But hey, you get to spend your birthday in New York City. That's quite the birthday present."

"Sure, except I'll be sitting alone in a hotel room with nothing to do," Kate said.

"Don't be silly," Olivia replied. "Just pick the most outgoing person at Edward's old firm, make friends with her and get her to take you dancing on your birthday. It'll be a blast. You can do some tourist stuff, go shopping, and then hit the bars and French kiss some guy you'll never see again."

Kate laughed, "Yes, because making out with random guys is totally my thing."

Olivia shrugged. "Maybe it should be. It might help you get over a certain someone."

"Maybe," Kate said. "Hey, can you stop in once a day and feed Chicken while I'm gone?"

"Sure," Olivia replied. "Honestly, Katie, I think going to New York will be good for you. Just don't do something you shouldn't with," she glanced around before lowering her voice, "Edward."

"Trust me, I've learned my lesson," Kate replied.

* * *

Kate searched anxiously through the crowd of people at the airport for a sign with her name on it. The flight to New York had been long but uneventful and after retrieving her luggage she had begun to look for the driver that Edward had promised her would be there. Just as she was starting to panic, she saw a young man in a dark coloured suit and cap near the large automatic doors holding a sign with her name on it. She made her way over to him, smiling gratefully when he took her suitcase and said, "Ms. Jones?"

"Yes," she replied.

"Please follow me." He turned and led her out the doors and across the busy street, weaving his way through the crowds of people with ease. He held open the door to a dark-coloured town car and Kate climbed in and relaxed against the leather seats. The driver stowed her luggage in the trunk before starting the car and taking his place in the line-up of cars leaving the airport.

"Am I going to the hotel first?" She asked.

"No, ma'am. Mr. Turner asked that I take you directly to the office. I'll take your things to the hotel and arrange to have them placed in your room for you."

"Thank you very much. I'm Kate."

"Jeffrey, ma'am," he replied.

"Nice to meet you, Jeffrey." She leaned forward and held out her hand as they stopped at a red light. He shook it firmly.

"Nice to meet you as well."

"So do you work for Lenkman, Samson and Company?" She asked politely.

"Not really," Jeffrey replied as he shoulder-checked and squeezed into the right lane. "I work for a car service that Lenkman, Samson and Company uses on a regular basis."

Her cell phone buzzed and she replied to Olivia's text as Jeffrey drove silently. An hour later, they were parked in front of a massive skyscraper. She stared up at it as Jeffrey opened the car door for her.

"This is the office building?" Kate asked.

Jeffrey nodded. "Wait until you see the inside – it's even more impressive. Just go to the front lobby and let security know who you are. They'll direct you to the right floor."

"Thank you so much, Jeffrey," Kate said.

"You're welcome, Kate. Enjoy your stay." He nodded to her, one hand touched the bill of his cap briefly, before sliding behind the wheel and merging into the honking mass of traffic. Kate took a deep breath and walked into the building.

* * *

"Excuse me?" Kate smiled at the receptionist sitting behind the desk.

"Hi, how can I help you?"

"My name is Kate Jones. I'll be working with Edward Turner?"

"Right." The receptionist smiled at her. "I'm Alison. Let me call Bev and she can get you set up. Edward's out at a client meeting right now."

After a quick phone call, a small, grey haired woman came hurtling into reception, making a beeline for Kate. "Hello, Kate. I'm Bev, so nice to meet you."

She shook Kate's hand distractedly before turning to Alison. "Allie, can you call Hank and let him know that the document he requested has been typed and emailed to him? You know he never checks his email. Follow me, Kate. I'll show you your office and get you started on some work."

"Office?" Kate asked.

"Well, more of a cubby hole really," Bev laughed as she quickly led Kate through a maze of cubicles. "Each of the partner's offices has a small adjoining room. I think originally they were more of a filing storage area, but I arranged to have them turned into small offices for the partner's assistants. We're here so much, we deserve a small space to call our own don't you think?"

Kate nodded as she hurried to keep up with Bev.

"Edward's original assistant is on maternity leave and Kendra, one of our general admin people is out sick with a bad case of food poisoning. That reminds me - don't eat at Paul's Pizzeria down on the corner. Alison, Shannon and I were very happy when Edward told us he had arranged to bring you down for the week. Being this short-staffed, we just couldn't afford to delegate one person to Edward. We offered to bring in a temp but Edward insisted on flying you in. Frankly, I'm not that surprised. He's very particular about who he works with."

Kate didn't think Bev had taken a single breath since leading her out of reception. She followed the woman into a large office as Bev hurried to the far side of the room.

"This is Edward's office when he's here, and here's your office," she said brightly.

Kate peered inside the room. Bev hadn't been kidding when she said it was more like a cubby hole. The room was so tiny that she could barely squeeze past the desk to sit down in the chair.

"So, this is it. There's not much of a view but there's lots of privacy. Oh and it's so hot because the heating system went on the fritz two days ago. Middle of January and we've got people wearing tank tops in the office. The repair guys are here today so expect to hear some banging around in the ducts," Bev said cheerfully

"Thank you, Bev," Kate said.

"You're welcome. I've arranged to give you temporary access to our system. Your login password is written on the notepad in the top drawer. Don't worry about trying to navigate our computer system. Just create a folder on your desktop and save all of your work there. We'll move it on to the system later. I've also set up a temporary email for you and the address and password is written on the notepad as well. Give me half an hour and I'll have a temporary security clearance badge and an office access card for you."

She pointed to a large stack of documents perched precariously on the edge of the desk. "Edward left that for you. He said he emailed you instructions and to text him if you need clarification. The copy room is down the hall. Take your second left, then your first right and then your first left. The washrooms are five doors down on the right and the staff lunch room is three doors down on the left. Got it?"

Kate nodded and Bev checked her watch. "Edward should be back in the office around three-thirty. If you need any help or have any questions, give me a call. There's a piece of paper with a list of extensions just under the phone. My last name is Smith."

She scurried out of the room and Kate, feeling a little overwhelmed, logged into the computer and opened her email.

* * *

Edward stood in the doorway of the small room and stared at Kate. She was staring intently at a piece of paper in front of her, trying to decipher something he had written. The small room was explosively hot and she had taken an elastic band from his desk and put her hair up in a pony tail. He could see her suit jacket draped over the chair behind her and she had unbuttoned the top two buttons of her shirt. A light sheen of perspiration covered her face and he watched fascinated as a drop of moisture rolled down her collarbone. He was struck with the sudden urge to lick the drop of moisture off her skin before it could disappear into her shirt.

He watched silently as Kate sighed and closed her eyes, leaning back in her chair and rubbing at her temples. She looked pale and unwell and the bruise on her wrist stood out in stark contrast against her pale skin. Anger flared inside of him at the sight of the bruise.

"Hello, Kate," he said in a low voice.

She jumped a little and sat up quickly, opening her eyes and smiling tentatively at him. "Hi, Edward."

"How was your flight?"

"It was good, thanks."

"Are you feeling okay?"

"Yes." Kate stood and squeezed past the desk. "I have a few questions about some of the work you left for me. I've put it on your desk."

As they reviewed the documents, Kate took shallow breaths and tried to ignore the throbbing pain in her head. She had been too keyed up about the trip to sleep last night and her flight had left at four this morning. The lack of sleep combined with the heat in the small office had given her a pounding headache. As she tried to concentrate on what Edward was saying she thought longingly of a nice cool shower and a dark room. She had taken some Advil a couple hours ago but her head was still throbbing and aching. At this point, nothing would help but lying down and trying to sleep.

"Kate?"

She realized Edward was staring expectantly at her and she forced herself to smile at him and take the papers he was holding. "Thanks. I'll get this finished up."

She returned to the small and stuffy office and stared blearily at her computer screen. Just another couple of hours and she would be in her hotel room and lying down. She squinted at the papers, rubbing absentmindedly at her temples as her head throbbed.

* * *

Edward closed his laptop and stuffed it into the bag. It was almost six and he was starving. He glanced at the open doorway to Kate's office. She had been strangely quiet the last half hour or so and he decided he would invite her to have dinner with him. There was nothing improper about that. They both needed to eat and it was the least he could do for dragging her out to New York on short notice. She had looked tired and unwell earlier and he felt a moment of guilt. He should have just let Bev bring in a temp but he had wanted to see Kate. The thought of going an entire week without seeing her made him weirdly unsettled.

He stood and walked over to Kate's office. They would have dinner and go back to the hotel. He had booked her a room next to his, not because he was imagining how easy it would be for them to slip back and forth to each other's room, but because if he needed her help with work in the evening, it was much more convenient. He hadn't spent any time at all last night picturing how good Kate would look sprawled naked across the king size bed in his room.

He stuck his head into the small office. "Kate, let me take you to dinner. It's the least I can…:"

He trailed off. Kate was sitting in her chair taking slow, deep breaths and she was very pale with dark circles under her eyes. He squeezed past the desk and crouched beside her, knocking his knee against the chair and cursing under his breath.

"Kate? Honey, what's wrong?" He asked before taking her hand. Despite the warmth of the room it was cold and he rubbed it between his, being careful to avoid the bruise on her wrist.

Without opening her eyes she murmured, "I have a really bad headache. I'll be fine but I need to lie down. Are we done for the day? I'd like to go back to my hotel room, if that's okay."

"Of course," he said. "Let me help you."

"Thanks."

He stood and helped her to her feet, frowning when she swayed a little, and she smiled wanly at him. "I'll be fine."

"You look like you're going to throw up," he said.

"Truthfully, I might. Maybe I should take my own cab to the hotel," she said. "I'd rather not vomit in front of my boss."

"I don't care," he said. He helped her into her jacket before he took her hand and led her out of the office and through the cubicles. It was quiet, most of the employees had already left, and Kate shaded her eyes with her hand as she followed Edward to the elevators. He was still holding her hand and he squeezed it reassuringly as they stepped into the elevator.

"Lean against me," he said.

"It's fine. I think it's getting a little better," Kate said. She craned her head to look at him and groaned loudly when a fresh bolt of pain ripped through her head. She pressed her fingers against her temple as she staggered back against the elevator wall.

"Jesus, Kate. Come here." Edward pulled her into his embrace and she leaned her head against his chest as he rubbed her back lightly. She couldn't remember the last time she'd had a headache this bad and she swallowed thickly as her stomach rolled with nausea. The vision in her right eye had gone blurry and she massaged her temple lightly as the elevator carried them down to the lobby. It made her feel even more nauseous and she groaned softly, praying like hell she didn't vomit all over Edward.

She put her head down and kept her eyes closed as Edward led her out of the lobby. The frigid air washed over her and her teeth chattered as Edward quickly hailed a cab. She climbed into the cab and leaned against Edward's solid warmth. He put his arm around her and kissed the top of her head gently. She listened to the solid beat of his heart, blocking everything else out as she concentrated fiercely on controlling the nausea that was rolling through her stomach.

At the hotel, Edward kept his arm around her, leading her through the lobby and stopping to pick up her room cardkey. He opened the door to her room and, before she could protest, picked her up and carried her into the room. He set her down on the bed and she collapsed on her back, throwing her arm over her face to block the light.

"Can you shut off the light?" She mumbled.

He clicked it off and sat quietly on the bed beside her. She was hot and her clothes were sticking to her with sweat but she rested for ten minutes, waiting for the pain to ease a little, before sitting up.

"Katie, you should just lie down," Edward protested.

"I want a cool shower," she mumbled. "It'll help the headache."

"Stay there. I'll turn on the shower."

She waited obediently until she heard the spray of the shower. She kicked off her boots and shrugged out of her suit jacket, leaving them both on the floor, before stumbling to the bathroom.

"Thank you, Edward" she said. "I appreciate your help."

She squinted at him when, instead of leaving, he quickly stripped off his shirt and then unbuttoned hers.

"What are you doing?"

"Helping you," he replied. He removed her shirt and unbuttoned and unzipped her pants, tugging them down over her hips.

"I'm fine, Edward." Kate said.

"You don't look fine," he said. "He helped her take off her pants. "In fact, you look worse."

"This is really inappropriate," she protested weakly.

"I've seen you naked before, Katie," he reminded her before unclasping her bra.

She gave up, allowing him to remove her bra and panties before he stripped off the rest of his clothes and reached for the elastic band in her hair.

"Hold on," he said. "This will probably hurt."

Despite his gentleness, the plain rubber band still caught on a few strands and pulled sharply. She groaned in pain and blinked back the tears.

"Sorry, honey," he said before pressing a light kiss on her mouth.

They stepped into the shower together and Kate stood under the cool spray of water. She was starting to shiver but she stopped Edward when he reached to turn up the hot water.

"Cool is better," she said through chattering teeth.

"Do you want me to wash your hair?" He asked.

"No. I don't want my head touched at all," she said.

She reached for the soap but Edward took it from her and quickly and efficiently washed her body before rinsing her clean. He shut off the shower and wrapped a bath towel around her before drying his own body. He used a fresh towel to blot the water from her pale skin and carried her to the bed, setting her down next to it. He pulled back the covers and frowned when Kate stumbled toward her suitcase.

"What are you doing?" He asked.

"Advil," she said hoarsely. "There's Advil in my suitcase."

"I'll get it. Lie down, honey."

He steered her back to the bed and she dropped the towel on the floor and slid between the sheets with a sigh of relief. She rested her head carefully on the pillow, covering her face with her arm again.

She listened to Edward rustle in her suitcase before he poured her a glass of water and sat on the side of the bed. "Here, take these."

"Thank you," she whispered. She swallowed the pills and drank the rest of the water before lying down again. Edward crossed the room and pulled the drapes closed. The room was plunged into darkness and Kate turned on to her side, tucking her hand under her pillow and closing her eyes. The bed shifted with Edward's weight as he sat down beside her.

"Can I do anything else for you?" He asked.

Her skull thudding painfully, she blurted out, "Will you stay with me for a while?"

He immediately climbed into the bed behind her and spooned her. He kissed her on the back of her shoulder and nuzzled the nape of her neck. "Sleep, Katie-did."

* * *

She woke around midnight, Edward's body still plastered against hers and his soft snoring reverberating against her back. Her headache was better, although there was still a dull throb in her temples, and she tried to ease her body away from Edward.

His grip tightened around her and she inhaled sharply when his hand cupped her naked breast. He mumbled something in his sleep before squeezing her breast and brushing his mouth against the back of her neck. Lust, warm and sweet, threaded through her and she made a soft moan when his fingers tugged her nipple into an aching hardness.

"Kate," he muttered before pushing her on to her back. He stared sleepily at her before dipping his head and sucking on her nipple. She moaned again, fisting her hands in his hair as he pulled on her nipple with his teeth.

"Edward," she whispered.

He froze and lifted his head, blinking the drowsiness away, before he pushed away from her and gave her a look of regret.

"Jesus, I'm sorry, Kate. I shouldn't have done that. How's your headache?"

"It's not completely gone," she admitted.

"Do you want some more Advil?" He asked.

She shook her head and grabbed his arm when he started to get out of bed.

"I should go," he said. "You need sleep and if I stay I'm going to..."

He trailed off and jerked in surprise when she pushed him down on to the bed and straddled him. She rubbed her pussy against his erection and he groaned harshly as he gripped her hips.

"Kate, what are you doing?"

"Did you know," she said as she traced her fingers over his broad chest, "that orgasms can help headaches?"

"I didn't know that," he muttered. His hand wandered from her hip, tracing across her flat abdomen before dipping between her thighs. He rubbed her clit lightly and she ground her pussy against his hand.

"It's true," she said. "I read it on the internet."

He laughed softly and she smiled at him. "I think it's worth trying, don't you?"

"Yes," he said immediately. "Fuck, yes."

He cupped her breasts and teased her nipples as she rubbed her pussy over the thick length of his cock.

"I want to be inside you, Kate," he rasped.

"I want that too," she panted.

"I don't have any condoms."

She leaned over him, letting her breasts brush against his chest and he muttered another low curse before cupping her ass and kneading it roughly.

"I'm disease free. You?" She said.

"Yes."

"Good. I'm on the pill." She kissed him, teasing the seam of his mouth with her tongue until he parted them, and she slid her tongue between his lips and licked lightly. He sucked on her tongue and she thrust her pelvis against him. They kissed for long moments, their tongues battling for control, before he broke away from her and gripped the back of her neck.

"Fuck me. Right now," he demanded.

"Whatever you say, Mr. Turner," she whispered.

She held the base of his cock and rubbed the head of it against her swollen clit. They both moaned and she rocked against him until he made a low snarl.

"Kate, now."

She pushed herself down on to his cock, making a breathless little moan as she stretched around him. He watched his cock slide into her, the lips of her pussy stretching around him, and wrapped his hands around her waist and pushed fully into her.

"Oh God!" She cried and he grinned up at her.

"Your pussy is so pretty, Katie-did. Ride me - I want to watch you take my cock in your tight little pussy."

She braced her hands on his chest and rode him slowly, rocking against him so that it put pressure on her aching clit. She was so close and she cried out with frustration when Edward sat up and flipped her on to her back. He pushed her thighs apart and entered her again, pushing into the hilt, and pinning her arms over her head.

"Edward," she squirmed under him. "I want to come."

"I know, Katie," he said. "Soon."

"Now!" She tried to free her arms but he was holding her forearms firmly and she twisted helplessly in his grip. A new trickle of lust was growing in her belly and she glanced up at his hands.

"Be good," he said, "or I'll tie you to the bed."

Her pussy clenched around him and he groaned before giving her a wicked grin. "My Katie likes that idea."

She glared at him and squeezed her legs against his hips. "Edward, fuck me."

He made two short, hard thrusts and stopped. She whimpered loudly and then lifted her head and nipped him hard on the throat.

He grunted with pain. "Be nice, Katie-did."

She squeezed her pussy around him again before giving him a pleading look. "Please, Edward."

He kissed her, sucking lightly on her bottom lip, before releasing her arms. She dropped her hands to his waist, clutching tightly as he propped himself above her and moved with long, slow strokes. She slipped her hand between them and rubbed at her clit."

"Don't come yet, Katie."

"I have to," she moaned.

"Not yet, honey," he whispered.

She moved her hand, pouting at him, and he grinned before resting on his forearms above her. It pressed his chest against her breasts and he kissed her slowly and thoroughly as he moved faster. His pelvic bone rubbed against her clit, sending bolts of lightning through her nervous system, and she groaned before digging her nails into his back.

"Edward, I can't wait. I can't."

She gasped and moaned as he moved faster. His low grunts of pleasure as he fucked her only intensified her lust and she kissed him desperately as she rocked her hips against his.

He fisted his hand in her amazing hair and pulled her head back. "Look at me, Katie."

She stared obediently at him and he groaned and pumped faster at the look of naked desire in her gaze. She suddenly stiffened beneath him, her back arching and her mouth dropping open, and she made a low keening noise of pleasure as her body shuddered and her pussy clamped around his cock with exquisite tightness.

He thrust rapidly in and out, her pussy pulsing and squeezing around him, until he climaxed deep inside of her with a harsh shout. Her pussy squeezed him compulsively as his hot seed coated her insides and he rested his forehead against hers as she clung to him.

"Jesus, Kate," he mumbled. "That was amazing."

"Yes," she said breathlessly.

He rolled off of her and put his arm around her when she curled up against him. He kissed her damp forehead. "How's your headache?"

"Better."

"Really?"

"Really, really," she said with a small smile.

They laid silently for a few moments before she sat up. "Thank you for staying with me and for..."

She trailed off and he grinned wickedly. "Fucking your headache away?"

She snickered before rubbing her hand across his chest. "Crude but accurate."

"Are you hungry?"

She shook her head. "Not really. It's a little too late for me to eat."

She glanced at the alarm clock before clearing her throat. It was obvious what she wanted and, a weird tingle of dismay going through him, he sat up and pushed back the covers.

"I'll get out of your space. My room is, uh, right next to yours so if your headache comes back, just let me know."

He grimaced inwardly at how stupid and pathetic he sounded. He wanted to spend the night with Kate, not because he wanted more sex but the thought of going back to his empty bed knowing that Kate was only a few feet away, made him miserable.

"Edward," she caught his hand before he could climb out of the bed, "I don't want you to go."

He hesitated and she gave him a tentative smile. "I mean, if you want to go I'll understand but I'd like you to stay. I know we had an agreement but you're, um, already here and we're both naked so... will you stay?"

He stared silently at her and she flushed. "We can go back to the way it was tomorrow. Right?"

"Are you sure?" He said. "I know you're tired and it's going to be a busy day."

He desperately wanted to stay with her but she still looked exhausted and he gave her a worried look.

"I'm sure," she said. She suddenly smiled saucily at him before rubbing at her temples. "I think my headache is coming back."

He laughed and she squealed softly when he pushed her back on to the bed and covered her body with his. "I've heard that multiple orgasms are required to help cure a headache."

"Oh yeah?"

He nodded. "I read it on the internet."

"It must be true then," she said.

"I don't know," he said before licking her throat, "I think we need to do our own research just to be on the safe side."

"Whatever you say, Mr. Turner," she said breathlessly.

Chapter 12

Kate added the folder to the stack that was sitting on Edward's desk. It was close to four, he had left for a meeting at one and she was finally caught up on the files he had left for her. She stared out the window of his office. It had started to snow an hour ago and the streets were covered in a light dusting of it.

She sighed and rested her forehead against the cold glass. Edward had been up at six this morning. She had sat up in bed, yawning and blinking, while he dressed quickly and there had been a few moments of awkwardness between them before he kissed her lightly.

"I have an early morning meeting," he had said. "I've arranged for a car to pick you up at eight and bring you to the office."

She had nodded blearily and he had kissed her again before resting his forehead against hers. "Thank you, Katie-did."

He had left before she could do something stupid like ask him if he wanted to keep fucking while they were in New York.

The phone in her small office rang and she hurried to answer it.

"Edward Turner's office, Kate speaking."

"Kate, it's Alison at reception. Edward's four o'clock appointment is here. Do you know when he'll be back?"

"He should be back any time now," Kate said.

"Can you do me a favour and show Mr. Mitchens to the small boardroom that's down the hall from Edward's office?" Alison asked.

"Of course."

Kate squeezed out of her office and walked toward reception. It was only her second day here but she had already figured out the layout of the office and navigated her way through the maze of cubicles with ease.

She smiled brightly at the tall, blonde man standing by the elevator.

"Mr. Mitchens?"

She held out her hand and he shook it firmly.

"My name is Kate. I'm Mr. Turner's assistant."

"Nice to meet you, Kate. Call me Tom," he replied.

"Mr. Turner is running a little late, but I'm sure he won't be long so if you'll follow me, I'll show you to the boardroom where you'll be meeting," Kate said.

"So I haven't seen you in the office before, Kate. Are you new here?" Tom asked curiously as he sat down at the glossy table in the boardroom.

Kate poured him a glass of water. "Actually, I'm Edward's assistant in his new firm. They were short staffed in this office so I'm here for the week to help out."

"Have you been to New York before?" Tom asked leaning forward and resting his hands on the table in front of him.

"I haven't," Kate replied.

"Are you planning on checking out the tourist side of New York?" Tom asked.

"I'm going to try and do a few things," Kate said.

"You have to at least do some," Tom said. He suddenly grinned at her, revealing even white teeth. "What you really need is someone local to be your tour guide."

"That's a good idea," Kate said.

"I'm full of good ideas," Tom replied with a boyish smile. "Have a seat, Kate. I'd love some company while I'm waiting for Edward."

* * *

Edward hurried toward the boardroom. He was late for his meeting and he hated keeping clients waiting. He heard Tom laugh loudly and he frowned when he ducked into the room and saw Kate sitting with him. Tom leaned forward and touched her hand and jealousy spiked through him.

"I swear it's the truth. Some naked guy was riding a donkey through Times Square," Tom said.

"I don't believe you," Kate laughed.

"Swear to God," he said solemnly. "You see all sorts of crazy things in Times Square, Kate,"

He glanced up to see Edward standing in the doorway.

"Edward! How are you?" He shook Edward's hand as Kate stood gracefully and headed toward the door.

"Sorry I'm late, Tom," Edward said as Kate brushed past him.

"No problem," Tom replied. "Kate was gracious enough to keep me company. Besides, Bonnie is running late as well."

"Kate, could you grab the file from my desk?" Edward asked.

"Of course," she said.

She snagged the folder from his desk and returned to the boardroom, setting it on the table in front of Edward.

"Thank you for keeping me company," Tom said.

He held out his hand and she shook it, her cheeks flushing slightly when Tom refused to let go of her hand.

"Remember what I said. If you get the chance be a tourist and want some company, give me a call." He handed her his business card.

"Thank you, Tom. It was nice to meet you," Kate replied and hurried out of the boardroom without looking at Edward.

She was barely back to her desk when the phone rang again.

"Ms. McKenzie is here for the meeting with Mr. Turner and Mr. Mitchens," Alison said.

"Thank you, Alison."

She made her way to reception again to greet the attractive older woman with the bleached blonde hair standing by Alison's desk. She was very tiny and slender and she stared up at Kate with bland disinterest.

"Hello, Ms. McKenzie. I'm Kate, Mr. Turner's assistant. Can I get you a cup of coffee or glass of water before you join them in the boardroom?" She asked.

"No, thank you," she replied tersely.

Kate led her to the boardroom. She knocked lightly and opened the door, stepping aside so Ms. McKenzie could sweep into the room.

"Hello, Bonnie," Tom said cheerfully.

Bonnie gave him a distracted nod before smiling at Edward.

"Edward, good to see you again," she said before hugging him tightly.

Kate bit her inner cheek to keep from laughing at the look on Edward's face as he patted the woman's back before squirming out of her embrace.

Bonnie grabbed both of Edward's hands and squeezed them firmly. "You look wonderful."

"Thank you, Bonnie," Edward said before tugging his hands free and pulling out the chair beside Tom. "Please, have a seat."

She ignored the chair and took the one next to him. Edward, his face carefully blank, said, "Would you like something to drink?"

"Yes." She turned to Kate and barked, "I'll take a glass of water," before smiling at Edward. "Sorry I'm late, traffic was terrible."

Kate poured two glasses of water as Edward sat next to Bonnie and set them in front of Bonnie and Edward. Before she could leave, Edward cleared his throat and said, "Could you stay and take some notes please, Kate."

He had the strangest expression on his face and she studied him briefly before nodding and taking a pen and pad of paper from the small side table. She sat across from Tom as Edward, his cheeks red, cleared his throat again and said, "Let's get started."

* * *

An hour later, Kate was back in her office. She started to type up her notes and when Edward stuck his head into her office, she dissolved into laughter.

With a mock sigh of exasperation, Edward said, "It's not funny."

"It's sort of funny," Kate said. "Bonnie is an interesting woman."

"Interesting is a polite way to put it," Edward said in a low voice.

"She certainly is very fond of you," Kate said. When Edward only grunted in reply, she said, "Why don't you ask her out? She's an attractive lady and she can't be that much older than you."

"She's had extensive work," Edward said solemnly as Kate grinned at him.

"And now I get to go to dinner with her and Tom," he sighed dramatically.

Kate laughed harder. "Just fend off her advances politely. You'll be fine."

"Sure, easy for you to say," Edward snorted. "You won't have handsy McKenzie feeling up your leg during dinner tonight."

"It's a shame I'm going to miss it," Kate said teasingly. "I rather enjoyed watching you do a statue impression in the meeting."

"She had her hand on my leg the entire meeting. I was afraid to move in case she thought I was encouraging her," Edward said.

Kate laughed again as Edward shoved his hands into his pockets. "That's why you're coming to dinner with us."

"What?"

"Dinner. You're coming with us. I can't be alone with Bonnie. I need someone to protect me from her." He gave her a boyish grin.

"Edward, I can't go to a client dinner. Besides, Tom will be there too. There's no need for me to - "

"You're coming to dinner, Kate," Edward said. "I've already told Tom and Bonnie that you'll be joining us"

A scowl crossed his face. "Tom was thrilled."

"But I still need to type up the notes and – "

"They can wait until tomorrow," he said. "I'm not kidding about needing protection from Bonnie. I met with her the last time I was in New York and she insisted on driving me back to the hotel after dinner. If Jason hadn't been waiting for me in the hotel lobby for drinks, I'm positive she would have thrown me over her shoulder and carried me off to my room."

"Fine, but you owe me, Edward Turner."

He gave her a delighted look. "I'll make it up to you, Katie, I promise."

His gaze drifted down her body, lingering between her thighs, and heat swept through her. She could think of all sorts of ways Edward could repay her for going to dinner with them – none of them at all appropriate.

"Ready, Katie?" He asked hoarsely. Now his eyes were on her breasts and she could feel her nipples hardening in response.

"Yes," she said as she grabbed her purse. "I'm ready, Edward."

* * *

Tom smiled at Kate as they left the elevator and walked through the lobby. "I'm so glad you could join us, Kate."

She returned his smile as Bonnie tucked her hand into the crook of Edward's elbow and pulled him closer to her.

"Do you need a ride, Edward?" Tom asked.

"No, I've arranged for a car to pick us up. We'll meet you at the restaurant."

"I have a better idea," Bonnie said. "Why don't all of us take the car together? It'll give us more time together."

She trailed one perfectly manicured finger down Edward's arm and marched toward the main doors, dragging him with her. Kate pressed her lips together in an effort to stop the laughter bubbling up inside of her. Tom make a weird coughing noise and she realized he was trying madly to keep a straight face. She grinned at him as he offered her his arm.

"I'll bet you fifty bucks that Bonnie gropes Edward during dinner," he said in a low voice.

"Like I want to lose fifty bucks tonight," she said.

He laughed. "Poor Edward. I keep thinking he'll just give in and sleep with her – what Bonnie wants, Bonnie gets – but he's been remarkably resilient to her advances."

They followed Bonnie and Edward outside and as the driver stepped from the car, Kate smiled at him.

"Hello, Jeffrey."

"Hi, Kate. It's nice to see you again," he said politely.

He opened the front passenger door and Bonnie said, "Why don't you sit up front, Tom?"

"Would love to, Bonnie," Tom replied with a grin.

Jeffrey opened the back door and Bonnie slid into the car, patting the middle seat. "Sit beside me, please, Edward."

Edward gave Kate a decidedly panicked look and, taking pity on him, she said brightly, "Edward's legs are so long, it'll be more comfortable for him if I sit in the middle."

She climbed into the car and smiled cheerfully at Bonnie as Edward squeezed in beside her.

As they drove to the restaurant, Bonnie gave her a shark-like smile. "It's so crowded back here that I suppose we should have taken two cars. Your outfit is so slimming, I forgot you were one of those big girls, Kate."

"I do have a set of hips on me," Kate said agreeably. She shifted closer to Edward. He laid his arm across the back of the seat and she tucked her body up against him. She suppressed the urge to rest her hand on his thigh.

"So, how long have you been a secretary?" Bonnie asked.

"About eight years," Kate replied.

Bonnie studied her in the dim light. "I hope you don't mind me asking, but how old are you?"

"I'm twenty-seven," Kate said.

Bonnie blinked at her. "Really? You should try moisturizing on a regular basis, it can do wonders for your skin."

"Thanks for the tip," Kate said before putting her head down and staring at the floor.

Edward groaned inwardly and discreetly rubbed Kate's thigh with his, hoping like hell her temper wouldn't get the best of her. She was trembling with anger and the last thing he needed was Kate tearing one of the firm's most loyal clients a new one. Her trembling increased and he nudged her leg with his. She gave him a quick sideways glance and he realized that what he had mistaken for anger was barely contained laughter.

Kate stole a quick glance at Edward when he nudged her thigh and, at the look on his face, the laughter threatened to bubble to the surface again. She quickly returned her gaze to her knees, struggling for control as Bonnie prattled on about the cold weather.

It was the day before her birthday and she was in New York City, crammed into the back seat of a car between her boss/lover and a cranky old woman who had just called her fat and old. The absurdity of it struck her funny bone again and a giggle escaped. She covered her mouth with her hand and manufactured a coughing fit.

"That's quite the cough. I do hope you're not coming down with something and infecting the rest of us," Bonnie said icily.

Kate shook her head as Jeffrey parked in front of a brightly-lit restaurant. "Should I arrange for a car to bring you to the hotel after dinner, Mr. Turner?"

"Yes, please, around eight," Edward said before opening the door and climbing out of the car. He helped Kate and Bonnie from the car, scowling slightly when Tom immediately offered his arm to Kate, and the four of them walked into the restaurant.

* * *

"You've really never been to Paris, Kate?" Tom said as the server cleared away their empty plates.

"I haven't," Kate replied.

Tom placed his arm across the back of her chair, letting his fingertips stroke her shoulder lightly. Across the table, Edward was noticeably glowering at him and she was just about to try and kick him under the table when his eyes widened. Bonnie had insisted on sitting next to him and while she had seemed rather well-behaved during dinner, one hand was now under the table. Edward shifted uncomfortably in his chair and Kate smiled sweetly at him. He gave her a pointed look and she looked away before she burst into laughter.

"Everyone has to go to Paris at least once in their life," Tom said. "It's beautiful there. Such a rich history of culture and the people are so interesting."

"It smells bad, the buildings are old and the weather is atrocious," Bonnie sniffed. "I don't plan on ever returning to Paris. Besides, Paris is a place for lovers. Didn't you mention you were single, Kate?"

Kate nodded as Tom shrugged and casually squeezed her shoulder. "If you ever want to go to Paris, Katie, just give me a call. I'll gladly escort you."

Tom perused the dessert menu as Edward gave him a smoking look of anger. Kate kicked his shin under the table. He flinched before glancing at her and she gave him an almost imperceptible head shake. Having Edward ruin a long-standing relationship with a client because he couldn't keep his caveman behaviour under wraps was not her idea of a successful client dinner. She stared pointedly at him until he relaxed slightly.

"What are you lovely ladies having for dessert?" Tom asked.

"The cheesecake looks good," Kate said.

"Oh, I couldn't possible have another bite," Bonnie said. "I'm so full. I swear, Kate, you must have a hollow leg. I have never seen a lady eat so much."

"My mom says the same thing," Kate said cheerfully. "I wish I could introduce you to her. You're close to the same age and I bet would have a lot in common."

Bonnie stiffened and scowled at her as Tom made an odd snorting noise before coughing loudly into his closed fist. Kate patted him gently on the back and held out his water glass. He took a sip before grinning at her.

"Have we made a decision on dessert?" The tension was broken by the server and Kate smiled at him.

"I'll have the cheesecake, please."

* * *

"You know she's asking him to go home with her, right?" Tom murmured into Kate's ear.

They were standing in front of the office building and Kate shivered as the snow fell. She wasn't used to the cold weather and her feet felt like frozen blocks of ice in their thin boots.

"Probably," Kate said in a low voice.

They watched as Bonnie hugged Edward again before whispering into his ear. He gave her an apologetic look and shook his head before glancing at his watch.

"He's giving her the 'it's really late excuse'," Tom said. "Rookie mistake. It's only eight thirty."

Kate laughed and Tom threw his arm around her shoulders. "You're shaking, Kate."

"Wimpy California girl," she said through chattering teeth.

Tom rubbed her arm. "Would you like to have drinks with me tonight?"

She blinked at him and he laughed. "Don't look so surprised, Kate. I've been flirting with you all night. I know a quiet little pub not too far from here. I can drive you back to the hotel after."

Kate shook her head. "I really can't, Tom. I'm here for work reasons not pleasure."

"So having drinks with me *would* be pleasing. Good to know," he said happily.

She laughed. "You're somewhat charming."

"I am, aren't I?" He said. "What about tomorrow night? We could go for dinner, and I could show you a few tourist things. I'll have you back at your hotel by nine at the latest, I promise."

She hesitated, glancing at Edward as he untangled himself from Bonnie's grip and started toward them. "I'd really better not. Like I said, Edward flew me out here to work not socialize."

"It'll be after work," Tom said. "You need to have some fun while you're here."

He pulled her a little tighter against him and studied her mouth before smiling. "Have dinner with me tomorrow night. Edward won't mind."

"Actually Edward does mind."

Edward pulled Kate away from Tom and wrapped his arm around her waist, tucking her firmly against his body and gripping her hip possessively. "I already have plans for Ms. Turner tomorrow evening."

Tom studied Edward carefully before smiling at Kate. "It was nice to meet you, Kate."

"Nice to meet you too, Tom," Kate said. She tried to step away from Edward and was rewarded with his arm pulling her even closer.

"Good night, Edward," Tom said.

"Good night," Edward replied stiffly. Tom held out his hand and after a moment, Edward shook it firmly.

Tom smiled at Kate again before shoving his hands into his coat pocket and, whistling softly, joined Bonnie by the parking garage. The blonde woman was glaring at them, Kate could practically feel her hot rage, and she pushed lightly at Edward's arm.

"Edward, let go," she said under her breath. "Bonnie's about to come over here and murder me."

He ignored her and, keeping one arm firmly around her waist, led her to the car. They climbed into the back seat and she gave him a curious look as he leaned forward and said curtly, "Close the partition, please."

The driver nodded and the tinted glass rose with a soft whir. When it was closed completely, he leaned back in his seat and glared at Kate. "I don't want you having dinner with Tom tomorrow night."

"That's obvious," Kate said.

He continued to scowl at her and she sighed loudly. "What's the problem, Edward?"

"Stay away from Tom," he snapped.

"I'm not having dinner with him," she retorted. "Your jealous caveman act back there worked. You need to control your jealousy, Edward. What if Tom decides to drop the law firm because you were being a dick?"

"I wasn't being a dick," Edward protested. "You're here to work, not socialize."

"That's what I told him," she said angrily. "I don't need you turning down dates on my behalf, Edward. I can do that perfectly fine on my own."

"So you do want to date him," he said in a sulky voice.

"Oh my God," she said in exasperation. "I don't even know him."

"Which is why you shouldn't be going on a date with him!" He shouted.

"I'm not!" She said. "Now stop shouting at me or I'll punch you in the face."

He blinked in surprise before suddenly grinning. "Did you just threaten to punch me in the face?"

"Yes," she said. "If you keep shouting and acting like a jealous little boy, you deserve a punch in the face."

He suddenly slid across the seat and yanked her into his embrace. He threaded his fingers through her hair, holding her immobile, and gave her a look of apology. "I'm sorry, Katie-did. I was being a jealous dick. You have every right to go to dinner with Tom tomorrow night and I'm sorry I said you couldn't. If you want to have dinner with him, I won't try and stop you."

"I don't want to have dinner with him," she said.

"Why not?"

She sighed. "Can we just drop it, Edward? I'm cold and I'm tired and I want to get back to the hotel room and have a hot bath."

He studied her mouth in the light from the street lamps flashing by. "Your lips are blue, Katie."

"I'm cold," she reminded him.

He dipped his head and pressed his mouth against hers. His lips were warm and firm and she moaned happily when he slipped his tongue into her mouth. He tasted like the chocolate cake he'd eaten for dessert and she didn't object when he pushed her back against the seat and kissed her hungrily. He cupped her breast through her jacket, muttering under his breath at the bulkiness of it, and she kissed him again. He groaned into her mouth, his hand tightening on her breast when she sucked at his tongue.

"Katie," he rasped, "Will you – "

They jerked apart when the back door opened and the driver leaned his head in. "We're here, sir – oh, sorry."

Kate, blushing, glanced out the window. They were parked in front of the hotel – she hadn't even noticed the car stopping – and she climbed out of the car, smiling distractedly at the driver before following Edward into the hotel.

They rode the elevator silently, walked down the hallway silently, and stood in front of their respective doors in silence. Edward opened his door and, without looking at her, said, "Good night, Kate. The car will be downstairs at eight."

He stepped into his room and shut the door before she could reply. She opened her own door and slammed it shut a little harder then necessary before kicking off her shoes and dropping her purse on the bed. The clasp popped open and the contents spilled on to the bed. With a sigh of frustration, she stuffed the various items back into her purse.

She lingered on Tom's business card, running her fingers lightly over the raised letters, before sitting on the bed and staring at the phone. Maybe she should call him. She wasn't in a relationship with Edward and he had just said he didn't have a problem with her having dinner with Tom.

Is that what he actually said?

She ignored her inner voice and stared at Tom's business card again. It was her birthday tomorrow – did she really want to tour New York on her own or worse, spend it alone in her hotel room? No, she decided, she really didn't.

She picked up the phone, dialed nine and then punched in the first three numbers before cursing under her breath and dropping the phone back into its cradle.

"You are fucking losing it, Kate," she muttered to herself. "You are not in a relationship with Edward and having dinner with Tom is not cheating on him."

No, it wasn't. So why did she feel like it was?

She paced the room agitatedly, staring at the wall that separated her from Edward, and tried to resist the urge to go to him. She really should have a hot bath and just forget that Edward was in the next room, possibly naked.

Why?

What?

Why do you have to forget that? Why can't you just go over there and take what you want?

Because I'll get fired, remember?

Only if someone finds out.

He's still in love with his dead wife.

Yes, but he does want you. That can be enough. Now's your chance to fuck his brains out without worrying about someone from the office catching you. Why the hell are you just standing here wasting all this perfectly good fucking time?

The thought made her grin and, before she could lose her nerve, she grabbed her cardkey off the table, took a quick peek into the hallway, and walked quickly to Edward's room. She knocked and waited patiently. After a minute she was about to knock again when the door opened. Edward was shirtless and bare foot and at the sight of his tanned upper body, her mouth went dry. She stared mutely at him as he gave her an uncertain look.

"Kate? Is there something wrong?"

"No, may I come in?"

He stepped back and she brushed past him, resisting the urge to trail her hand across his bare chest as she walked by. He shut the door and she stared at the large muscles in his back as the familiar aching need started up inside of her.

"Kate, what are you doing here?" He asked quietly.

She took a deep breath and smiled at him. "I was sitting in my hotel room thinking about your big cock and how much I wanted to taste it. So, here I am."

"Fuck," he muttered. "This is a very bad idea."

She placed her hands on his chest and pushed him back toward the bed until he was standing in front of it. She unbuckled his belt and unbuttoned his pants as he cleared his throat.

"Kate, are you sure – "

"Stop talking, Edward." She pushed his pants and his briefs down his legs and smiled with satisfaction at his erect cock. "You like the idea of me sucking on your cock."

"Of course I do," he muttered.

"Good."

She pushed him into a sitting position on the bed and knelt on the floor between his legs before taking him in her hand and stroking firmly. He moaned, his hands tightening on the bedcover, as she stroked him until a bead of precum appeared on the head of his cock. She licked it away, smiling at the way he gasped, before suckling firmly on the head. His hands immediately twisted in her hair, holding her head tightly as she sucked. She glanced up at him, all of the muscles in her lower abdomen tightening at the look of lust on his face.

"You look so pretty with my cock in your mouth, Katie," he said hoarsely.

She licked him again from the base of his shaft to the head and he moaned her name as his hips bucked. She held the base of him, sliding her mouth up and down as she varied the pressure of her mouth, and he groaned harshly.

She released him with a soft pop and smiled up at him. "You taste good, Edward."

"Keep sucking. Please, Katie," he begged quietly.

He tugged on her hair, urging her mouth back over him and she traced the head with her tongue before taking over half of him in her mouth. He cried out and she made a muffled gasp when he thrust his hips upwards. She sucked steadily as his hands stroked her hair and he made whispered pleas that were half compliments and half begging for more.

His cock was swelling in her mouth, more of his slightly salty taste coating her tongue, and she released him again before smiling.

"Do you want to come in my mouth, Edward?"

"Yes," he rasped. "But I also want to fuck you."

She stroked and caressed his cock with her warm hands. "You choose."

He hesitated only a second before saying, "I want to fuck you."

She stood and quickly stripped off her clothes. Edward reached for her, wrapping his hands around her waist and dragging her forward until he could nuzzle her ribcage.

"You taste so good, Katie," he muttered. "You feel good, you smell good – I can't get enough of you."

He cupped her breasts, teasing her nipples until they had stiffened into tight peaks before sucking on them. She clutched his head, her back arching, as his hands kneaded her naked ass. He slipped one hand between her legs, stroking her swollen clit until she was moaning loudly.

He pulled her down on to the bed, nudging her thighs apart and wedging his big body between them. His cock grazed her clit and she arched beneath him. He grinned at her and reached between them to guide his cock into her wet and aching entrance. As he filled her completely, he studied her face in the dim light before brushing a lock of her hair back.

"You feel so good, Katie. So warm and wet."

"Edward," she whispered, "fuck me."

He straightened to his knees and lifted her legs until they were draped over his shoulders. He fucked her with hard, deep strokes, watching his cock slide in and out of her wet pussy before whispering, "Touch yourself, Katie."

She rubbed at her clit, the look on Edward's face as he watched sending waves of trembling lust from her core to her toes. He pushed her hand away and touched her with rough fingers as he slowed the rhythm of his thrusts.

"Come for me, Katie. I want to feel your pussy squeezing my cock."

He tugged on her clit, pinching it lightly between his fingers, and she bucked against him before her body arched and she came with a hoarse cry. He groaned at the increased pressure and thrust wildly back and forth.

"Fuck! So fucking tight!" He groaned as her pussy rippled around him. He rubbed her clit again. She cried out and tried to push his hand away and he captured her wrists with one big hand and held her firmly as he stroked her clit.

"Edward! Wait! I can't have another – "

She shuddered all over and made another ragged cry as a second orgasm rocketed through her. She writhed under him and he drove back and forth, thrusting his cock deep inside of her and shouting her name when his orgasm raced through him. He dropped her legs, his big body shuddering with pleasure and his chest heaving for air, as she sprawled beneath him, her pussy still squeezing him rhythmically.

He collapsed on his side next to her and she rolled to face him, rubbing her fingers along his jawline as he shuddered again before opening his eyes.

"Jesus, that was so good," he muttered.

He cupped her face and kissed her lightly on the mouth. "Thank you, Katie."

"No, thank you," she said cheekily. "I've never had back-to-back orgasms before."

He grinned smugly at her and she poked him in the stomach before sitting up. He frowned and wrapped his fingers around her wrist.

"Don't leave."

"I'm not," she said. "I was just going to have a hot bath."

He relaxed and released his grip as she slid off the bed and walked to the bathroom. She turned on the light and made a soft gasp before sticking her head back out into the room.

"You have a soaker tub! I don't have a soaker tub in my room."

He laughed and put his hands behind his bed. "You didn't request one when I booked your hotel room."

She wrinkled her nose at him before disappearing into the bathroom. He waited fifteen minutes before tugging on a pair of shorts and opening the bathroom door. Kate was chin-deep in bubbles and she smiled happily at him as he sat on the side of the tub.

"I could stay here all night," she said.

He leaned over and kissed her on the forehead. "While you're enjoying the tub I'm going to do a bit of work."

She nodded and sunk lower into the tub. "As long as you don't ask me to type anything when I get out of the tub, I'm happy."

"No typing," he promised.

"Fucking?" She cracked open one eye and gave him a hopeful look.

He laughed and slipped his hand under the water, cupping her full breast and running his thumb over her nipple before kissing her roughly.

"Definitely," he murmured before leaving her to her bath.

* * *

Edward smiled when a pale foot with pink painted toenails wiggled its way on to his lap. He sat back in the chair as Kate, wearing one of his t-shirts, slid her leg over his lap and sat down. He put his hands on her hips as she leaned forward and nuzzled his neck.

"You've been working for almost two hours. Don't you think it's time you came to bed?"

She sucked briefly on his ear lobe as he slipped his hands under her shirt and stroked her bare back. He buried his face in her neck and breathed deeply. The sent of her skin intoxicated him and he kissed her neck with warm, wet brushes of his mouth as she sighed happily.

"Will you stay the night with me, Katie?" He asked almost hesitantly.

She nodded. "Yes."

"Why?" He asked and she made a careless little shrug.

"Why not? No one from the office will find out. Why shouldn't I stay with you? We're having fun, right?"

Stung by her words, he just nodded, and she ran her hand over his face. "We can go back to the way it was when we go home, okay?"

"Is that what you really want?" He asked.

"Does it matter? Can't we just enjoy ourselves without having to worry that we're going to be caught by our co-workers?"

"I don't want to hurt you, Kate," he said quietly.

"You won't. I know what this is and it's fine. Now, take me to bed and fuck me – unless you've changed your mind? I can go back to my room if you have."

"No," he said as he stroked her bare thighs. "I want you in my bed."

"Then stop talking, Mr. Turner, and take me to your bed," she breathed into his ear.

"Yes, Ms. Jones."

Chapter 13

"Wake up, Katie."

Kate groaned loudly and buried her head in the pillow as the smell of coffee filled the air.

Warm hands reached under the covers and lightly stroked her back. "Time to wake up."

Kate squinted at the clock on the bedside table beside her. It was just after six and she sighed grumpily and yanked the covers over her head.

Edward laughed and pulled down the covers. "You're really not a morning person, are you?"

"I'm tired," she griped. "You kept me up all night."

"You shouldn't have been rubbing your naked body against me all night," he said.

"I did no such thing," she muttered and pulled the covers over her head again as he sat down on the bed beside her.

"I have something for you."

She blinked rapidly. Did Edward somehow know it was her birthday?"

"C'mon, Katie," Edward coaxed. "Sit up."

She pushed back the covers and stared at the cup of coffee in his hand. He grinned at her, "Cream only, right?"

He frowned at the look on her face. "Kate? What's wrong?"

"Nothing," she said. It was stupid of her to think that Edward would one – know it was her birthday and two – get her a gift. They were having sex not a relationship.

She struggled into a sitting position, wrapping the sheet around her and taking the cup of coffee from him. "Thank you, Edward. Coffee in bed is the only thing that makes mornings bearable."

He laughed and kissed her forehead. "I'm going to have a shower. Are you showering here or going back to your room?"

"I'll go back to my room," she said as she sipped at the coffee. "Mind if I take this with me? I think I'm going to need an extra-long shower to wake up and I don't want to be late for work. My boss will freak out."

"Just tell him you were having sex all night with an extremely handsome, extremely well-hung, stud of a man. He'll understand."

"I can't lie to my boss like that."

"Ouch," he said before kissing her on the forehead again. "You're a mean little thing in the morning, huh?"

"Two more cups of coffee and I'll be my usual sweet self," she promised.

He squeezed her leg and stood. "I'll see you downstairs at eight?"

"You will," she said.

She dressed quickly as he went into the bathroom, and then grabbed her cardkey and her cup of coffee. The hallway was empty and she scurried to her own room. She checked her phone as she finished her coffee. There were already texts from Lina and her parents wishing her a happy birthday and she quickly texted back before finishing her coffee and brushing her teeth. As she stepped into the shower and let the hot water soothe her aching muscles, she decided that having sex with Edward and waking up to coffee in bed wasn't a bad way to start her birthday.

* * *

"Kate?" Alison knocked on the door of her office before setting the flowers on her desk. "These came for you."

"Thank you, Alison," Kate replied. She plucked the envelope from the arrangement as Alison left and read the enclosed card.

Happy Birthday, Katie-pie!

Love,

Olivia and Jon

She smiled and then nearly dropped the card on the floor when Edward cleared his throat. He was standing in the doorway with a scowl on his face as he stared at the flowers.

"From Tom?" He asked.

"No," she said before tucking the card into her purse.

"Who are the flowers from?" He asked immediately.

She arched her eyebrow at him and he shrugged. "I want to know, Katie."

"Olivia and Jon," she said. "This file is almost done and I – "

"Why are Olivia and Jon sending you flowers?" He interrupted.

"Because I'm awesome?"

"Tell me, Katie."

"It's my birthday."

His eyes widened. "Your birthday is today? Why didn't you tell me?"

"Why would I?" She asked.

Before he could reply, Bev appeared. "Nice flowers, Kate. Edward, can you meet with Mr. Baker for ten minutes? He heard you were in town and dropped by the office insisting he needed to speak with you."

Edward glanced at his watch. "Yes, but if I'm not done in twenty minutes, come into the boardroom and tell me I have a phone call. If you don't, I'll be with him all day."

Bev laughed. "I can do that. Thanks, Edward."

* * *

Kate placed the file folder on Edward's desk. He had left over an hour ago without giving her any details and she wondered briefly what he was doing. He didn't have a meeting scheduled on his calendar and he hadn't told Alison at reception what he was doing either. She hurried back to her office when her cell phone rang and snagged it from the desk.

"Hi, Olivia."

"Happy Birthday, Katie-pie!"

"Thank you, honey," Kate said. "I got your flowers — thank you. How's Chicken?"

"Chicken is just fine," Olivia laughed. "I go over every day after work and every day she faithfully ignores me from the top of the kitchen cupboards and pretends she's not interested in me or eating. But the food keeps disappearing." She laughed again. "Actually, last night she ignored me from the top of the kitchen counter instead of the cupboards so I think we're making progress. How's New York?"

"It's good. Really busy," Kate replied. "Edward wasn't kidding when he said there was a lot of work to do."

"Did you meet anyone interesting to take you touring on your birthday?"

"No. But I've decided to take myself sight-seeing this evening. I'll bring you back a cheesy tourist gift."

"Super," Olivia said. "How are things with Edward? Still tense?"

"No," Kate replied. "It's going fine. How are things at Harper and Thompson?"

"Going fine?" Olivia repeated. "Is that code for 'we're barely speaking' or 'we can't keep our hands off of each other'?"

"Well..."

"You're sleeping with him."

"I might be."

Olivia sighed. "Well, it's your birthday so I'll give you a pass but Katie, be careful, okay? Don't like, fall in love with him or something."

"I'm not," Kate said. "Don't worry, Olivia, I know what I'm doing. How are things at the office?"

"Busy as usual," Olivia said. "Only, it's no longer Harper and Thompson. Our new sign was put up yesterday and Arthur had me send formal notices to all of our clients and associates the last few days. We're now officially 'Harper, Thompson and Turner'."

"Does Edward know yet?" Kate asked.

"No, not yet. Arthur said he was going to email him, but you know Arthur, he'll never get around to it. I figured I would send him a quick email, unless you want to do the honour?"

"I'll let him know," Kate said. "I'd better get back to work. Thank you for the flowers and for looking after Chicken."

"You're welcome, Katie. I hope you have a wonderful birthday. Love you."

"Love you too. Bye, Olivia."

She set her cell phone on the desk as Edward, his cheeks red from the cold, stepped into her office. He squeezed to the side and shut the door as she smiled at him.

"You're back."

"Just got back," he said.

"I've got good news. Olivia called me – we have a new sign at the office. It now says Harper, Thompson and Turner."

"That's great. We'll have to go for lunch to celebrate both the new sign and your birthday."

She laughed. "That's a nice offer but you don't have to take me for lunch, Edward."

"I insist," he replied.

He stood next to her desk, suddenly looking hesitant and unsure and she gave him a curious look. "What's wrong?"

"Nothing's wrong. I just – I have something for you."

He pulled a small flat box from the inner pocket of his jacket. It was wrapped in blue ribbon and she stared in surprise at it as he handed it to her. "Happy Birthday, Katie."

"You bought me a present?"

"Yes," he replied. "Open it."

She untied the ribbon and lifted the lid from the box. Inside, nestled in blue velvet was a silver chained necklace. A silver heart with her birthstone dangled from the chain and she touched it lightly before glancing up at him. "Edward, I – I love it."

"Good." He gave her a pleased smile.

She lifted it from the box before standing and squeezing around the desk. "Will you help me with the clasp?"

He nodded and took the necklace from her as she turned and lifted her hair. He clasped it around her neck and she shivered when he placed a gentle kiss on the back of her neck.

"Happy Birthday, Katie."

She turned to face him, touching the necklace around her throat. "Thank you, Edward. I'd say you shouldn't have but I love presents and I really love jewelry."

He laughed and slipped his arm around her waist. "You deserve it, Kate."

She stood on her tiptoes and brushed her mouth against his. "Thank you again."

"You're welcome," he said before taking her mouth in a harder, more thorough kiss.

She returned his kiss eagerly, nipping at his lower lip with her teeth, and he groaned softly and cupped her breast through her shirt. "I have one more birthday gift for you, Katie."

"Oh yeah? What's that?" She asked breathlessly as his hand squeezed and kneaded.

He shrugged out of his suit jacket and tossed it on the desk before crowding her up against the wall. He reached for her skirt, tugging it up around her hips, and she gave him an alarmed look.

"Edward, what are you doing?"

"Fucking you," he said as his hand slipped into her panties.

"We're in the office!" She hissed at him as he rubbed at her clit.

She tried to tug his hand away and he pinned both of her hands above her head. "I know. So we'll have to be quick and quiet."

"We can't do this here," she said. "We're going to get caught."

"Not if we're very quiet," he said before kissing her neck.

She moaned and he nipped at her collarbone. "That's not being quiet, Katie-did."

"Edward, please," she whispered as his fingers pulled at her clit.

He kissed her again, taking control of her mouth as he dipped his tongue between her lips and stroked her tongue roughly. His fingers continued to dance over her clit and when she was rubbing her body against his, he released her mouth.

"Please what, Katie?"

"Please fuck me," she said immediately. It was madness but she was aching for him and the thought of having to wait until tonight to have his cock made her feel nearly crazy.

"Well, it is your birthday and your pretty little pussy is delightfully wet," he said with a small grin.

He slid his middle finger into her and she clamped her mouth shut against her cry of pleasure.

"Good girl," he breathed into her ear. "I can only fuck you if you promise not to make a sound. Do you promise, Katie?"

"I promise," she whispered. "Please, Edward."

He released her hands and fumbled at his belt with his left hand as he continued to fuck her with his fingers. She made an impatient sound and unbuckled his belt before unbuttoning his pants and shoving them and his briefs down to his feet.

He helped her shimmy out of her panties before pulling her skirt up around her waist. They were nearly frantic with desire, their mingled panting the only sound in the tiny office, as he put his arm around her and lifted her. She squeaked softly in surprise before wrapping her legs around his hips and pulling up his dress shirt. His cock rubbed against her lower abdomen and he made a low groan before pressing her against the wall and whispering into her ear.

"Put me inside you, Katie."

She wiggled her hand between their naked lower bodies and, as he shifted her a little higher, guided his cock to her pussy. He pushed inside of her, both of them moaning quietly as he did, and made a few light thrusts.

"Harder," she whispered. "I need you, Edward."

"Yes," he said before trailing a path of wet kisses down her throat.

He moved with short, hard thrusts as they kissed with frantic need. He sucked at her lower lip, worrying it with his teeth, as her soft gasps grew louder.

"Quiet, Katie," he growled against her mouth.

"I'm trying," she muttered.

He gave her a cocky grin before thrusting harder. Each stroke sent a delicious wave of pleasure through her body and she clung helplessly to him as he moved in and out of her.

"Fuck, you feel so good, Katie," he whispered into her ear. He thrust repeatedly as she made low whimpers of pleasure.

"I'm going to come," she gasped into his ear.

"Yes," he groaned. "Fuck, yes. Come all over my cock, Katie."

His hot words, his hard cock ramming into her, sent her over the edge and she buried her face in his neck to muffle her loud cry of pleasure. He groaned and plunged into her twice more before stiffening and pinning her against the wall as his big body trembled. His groan of pleasure was very loud in the small space and she slapped her hand over his mouth in a frantic bid to stifle it.

He kissed her palm and she dropped her hand before giving him a look of disapproval. "You weren't quiet, Edward."

"Your fault," he said cheerfully. "Do you have any idea how tight your pussy gets when you're coming?"

She blushed and he laughed before easing out of her and setting her on her feet. They hurriedly pulled on their discarded clothing and she smoothed her hair before giving him a self-conscious look.

"How do I look?"

"Like you've just been fucked."

"Edward!"

He grinned at her and pressed a kiss against her mouth. "Your lips are red and swollen, you have marks on your neck from my stubble and your cheeks are adorably flushed. Sorry, Katie-did, but it's the truth. You should probably stay in your office for a little while."

"I need to use the ladies room," she protested.

"Keep your head down and don't stop to chat to anyone," he suggested with a wicked grin as he opened the door to her office.

"Very helpful, Edward," she grumbled as she slid by him. He grabbed her ass and squeezed it and she jumped and slapped him lightly on the chest before marching out of the office.

"Hands to yourself from this moment on, Mr. Turner. We're very lucky we didn't get caught by…"

She trailed off and Edward touched her back lightly as he followed her into his office. "Kate, what's wrong?"

"Hello, Edward!"

Beside him, Kate made a small gasp of dismay and he took a step away from her as he forced a smile to his face.

"Tory, what – what are you doing here?"

"Your mom told me you were in the city and I had an appointment a few blocks away. I thought I would stop in and see if you wanted to have lunch. Alison sent me back to your office. I didn't mean to," she paused and he could feel his cheeks turning red, "interrupt your meeting."

"Oh, um…"

Tory grinned like a maniac at him before holding out her hand to Kate. "Hi, you're Kate right?"

"Yes," Kate said faintly. "It's nice to see you again, Tory."

"It's lovely to see you too."

"We're short-staffed here in New York so I flew Kate in to help me with some, um, work stuff," Edward said.

"How nice," Tory said. She was still grinning at him and he knew without a doubt that she had heard them in Kate's office. His cheeks flushed again and Tory's grin widened before she turned back to Kate.

"Have you been to New York before, Kate?"

"Uh, no, first time." Kate was studying the carpet in the office with great interest and Edward silently applauded her when she raised her head and smiled at Tory.

"How nice. I only come to the city for business or to visit Edward when he's in town, I kind of hate how crowded and noisy it is, but I know a lot of people love the crazy vibe here."

She paused before giving Edward a look of disapproval. "Jason had to find out from mom that you were here, why didn't you call us?"

"It's been busy," Edward said apologetically. "I'm only here until tomorrow so I figured I'd catch up with you the next time I'm here."

"Well, lucky for you, your mom has arranged for us to all have dinner tonight. You're supposed to be there promptly at six."

At Kate's look of confusion, Tory raised her eyebrows at Edward. "Didn't you tell Kate I was engaged to your brother?"

Edward shook his head as Kate said, "Oh, uh, congratulations."

"Thank you, Kate," Tory said. "So, we'll see you at six, Edward?"

"I have plans already," Edward said. "I told mom I wouldn't have a chance to see her on this visit."

Tory laughed. "You know your mom - she won't take no for an answer. Jason and I had plans this evening too and we had to change them. What plans do you have for tonight? Maybe your mom can work around it."

"Well," Edward glanced quickly at Kate, "today is Kate's birthday and since it's my fault she's away from family and friends on her birthday, I'm taking her out for supper."

"Not a problem," Tory said. "Kate can come for dinner with us."

"Oh no," Kate said, "I can't intrude on a family dinner. Edward, go for dinner with your family – I can grab a bite at the restaurant at the hotel."

Edward shook his head stubbornly. "No, I'm not leaving you alone on your birthday."

"I'll be fine," she said. "I don't mind."

"No," Edward repeated.

Tory, an impish grin on her face, said, "This is easily solved by having Kate join us for dinner, Edward."

"Kate does not want to hang out with my entire family on her birthday. It's one thing to subject us to Mom's grilling about our personal lives but why would we force that on her?"

"It'll be fine," Tory said airily. "Kate, you must come for dinner. Mom's motto is 'the more the merrier', and I know she'd love to meet Edward's," she paused, "assistant. And Edward, you know that mom will never forgive you if you don't come for dinner tonight. If you don't bring Kate with you, I'll tell her how you left her alone on her birthday in a strange city. What do you think she'll say to you then?"

Edward visibly shuddered and Tory laughed again. "We'll see you both at six. Edward, we'll have lunch the next time you're in town. Take Kate out – it's her birthday."

She squeezed Kate's arm. "Happy Birthday, Kate. And don't worry – our family isn't nearly as bad as Edward is making it sound."

She kissed Edward on the cheek and left the office as Edward and Kate stared blankly at each other.

"I'm sorry, Kate." Edward grimaced and rubbed his hand across his face.

"She heard us, Edward," Kate said miserably. "You know she did."

"It's fine."

"It's not fine! She – she's Tabitha's sister and she's engaged to your brother! What if she says something to your family?"

"She won't say anything."

Kate rubbed at her forehead. "I can't go to your family dinner. Just tell them I had a headache or something, okay?"

He shook his head. "No. I already told you – I'm not leaving you alone on your birthday. Either we both go tonight or neither of us do."

"Edward…"

"It'll be fine. Well, other than my mom asking way too many personal questions and my grandfather," he hesitated, "I don't even know how to explain my grandfather."

He checked his watch. "It's almost lunch. I just need to talk to Phil for a minute but grab your coat and I'll meet you at reception."

Chapter 14

"Did you get enough to eat, Kate?" Edward asked as they left the restaurant.

"More than enough," Kate replied before rubbing her flat abdomen. "In fact, I may never eat again."

Edward laughed. "My mom's a great cook. Trust me, you won't be able to resist eating again."

Kate groaned. "Can we stop talking about food and eating? I should never have let you talk me into sharing a dessert."

Edward took her hand and squeezed it. "Sounds to me like you need to walk off that meal. Some exercise will have you ready to eat by dinner."

"Is that your way of telling me I'm walking back to the office?" She said. "Are you taking the car and leaving for a meeting or something?"

He shook his head as the driver opened the door and they climbed into the back seat.

"No, there aren't any meetings this afternoon. In fact, we've done a great job getting caught up this week. You really were a big help, Kate, so thank you for coming out here. Phil was impressed at how many of the files we got cleaned up."

"Does this mean you're done in New York now?" Kate asked.

"For the most part. I may have to go back another couple of times but most of the files are finished and I can concentrate solely on the Harper, Thompson clients."

"Harper, Thompson and Turner clients," she reminded him.

She stared out the window for a few minutes before frowning at Edward. "Isn't this the direction of the hotel, not the office?"

He nodded. "It is."

"Why aren't we going to the office?"

"Well, I thought since it's your birthday and I'm taking up your last free evening in New York, we should do some tourist stuff this afternoon. We're stopping at the hotel to change clothes and put on comfortable shoes and then I'll take you to Times Square and we'll go from there."

Kate gaped at him. "But what about work?"

He shrugged. "I told you - Phil was really happy with what we accomplished this week and since technically I'm doing him a huge favour by helping clean up these files, he didn't have a problem with it when I told him I was taking the afternoon off."

"Edward, I don't − I mean, I feel really guilty playing hooky when you flew me out here to work."

He laughed. "We'll finish up the rest of it tomorrow morning before we leave for the airport. Relax, Kate, and let me show you the city. Okay? Think of it as another birthday gift."

"Are you sure?" She asked. "I can do some tourist stuff on my own, it's not that big of a deal."

"I want to go with you," he said. "Unless you don't want me to?"

"No, I do," she said.

"Then it's settled," he said happily.

* * *

"Tired, Katie?" Edward asked as he put his arm around her and pulled her close.

"Hmm, a little," she said.

"Maybe we should cancel dinner with my family and just go back to the hotel instead," he said.

She laughed. "Nice try."

"What was your favourite place this afternoon?" He asked.

She thought briefly. Edward had taken her to Times Square and the Empire State Building before they made a quick tour of the Museum of Modern Art. They had finished with a short walk in Central Park – it had started snowing again and Kate was freezing by the time they were done – before the car service had picked them up.

"Times Square, I think," she said. "Although I think I would have enjoyed Central Park more if it wasn't so cold."

"You'll have to go back in the summer," he said.

"Maybe," she replied.

"I'm sorry we didn't get to see very many spots," Edward said.

"Don't be. I really enjoyed what we did and it was nice to have company," she said. "Thank you. It's been a great birthday."

Edward stroked her arm as they stared out the window. They had left the city and she stared delightedly at the small town they were driving through. "Is this where your parents live?"

Edward nodded. "Yes, it's called Scarsdale."

"It's very pretty," she said. "Did you grow up here?"

He nodded again. "My parents have been in the same house since I was a baby. I moved to the city when I was in my early twenties and going to school. I had planned to move back to Scarsdale, it's only about half an hour or so by the Metro-North to get to Manhattan and I like the small town feel, but then I met Tabitha in law school and she loved the city so we rented a place in Manhattan. Expensive as hell but it made her happy."

"Why did you leave New York, Edward?" Kate asked. "Was it because..."

She trailed off and Edward gave her an uncomfortable smile. "If I'm honest, it was partly because Tabitha died and there were too many painful memories and partly because I wanted to be a partner and was too impatient to wait for a position to open at Lenkman. I'm already thirty-four and didn't want to wait until I was in my forties to make partner."

She wanted to say how glad she was that he had moved to California but it seemed like a terrible thing to say when the man had just finished telling her he'd moved because he missed his dead wife.

Sudden guilt flooded through her. She couldn't do this. She couldn't meet Edward's family when he was still in love with his wife. No doubt they knew how much Edward missed her and what would they think when she showed up with him. What kind of woman tried to date a man who wasn't over the loss of his wife?

You're not dating. You're fucking.

That was true and it made the whole damn thing that much worse. If Edward's family found out that they were just having a fling, they'd really think she was horrible.

She shifted in the seat, trying to move away from Edward, and he clutched her tighter against him. "Kate, what's wrong?"

"Um, nothing," she said. "But I think this was a mist –"

The car stopped and Edward smiled hesitantly at her. "We're here."

Her stomach churning, she followed him out of the car and stared at his childhood home. It was on the small side with dark green siding. A short chain-link fence enclosed the front yard and the sidewalk leading to the front porch had been cleared of snow.

Edward opened the small metal gate and ushered her down the sidewalk. Her hands were freezing from a combination of the cold and her nerves and she shoved them into her pockets, jumping when a loud, rough voice barked, "About time you got here, Eddie. Supper's getting cold because of your tardiness."

An old man, wearing a thick jacket and a wool cap, heaved his body up from the wicker chair on the porch. He was tall with large bushy eyebrows, dark brown eyes and broad cheekbones. He leaned heavily on his cane as they climbed the stairs.

"Sorry, Grandpa Joe. Traffic was bad," Edward said as they joined him on the porch.

"Ayuh," the old man muttered grumpily as he stared suspiciously at Kate. "Who's this then? You bringing some tart home to meet your mother, are you?"

"Grandpa Joe!" Edward snapped. "Be polite! This is Kate Jones. She's a work colleague."

"It's nice to meet you," Kate said and held out her hand.

Grandpa Joe shook her hand and gave her a cool and appraising look. As the seconds ticked by, she grew more and more apprehensive but she kept her back straight and refused to look away.

"You can call me Grandpa Joe," he said gruffly.

"Only if you call me Kate," she said.

"Well don't just stand there with your mouth open, I told you supper was waiting for you," he growled in his raspy old man voice before opening the door. Kate's nerves were slightly overshadowed by her amusement when she realized that Edward was indeed, standing there with his mouth slightly ajar. She nudged him, giving him a quizzical look, and he stared blankly at her as Grandpa Joe waved his arm irritably.

"After you, Kate."

"Thank you, Grandpa Joe," Kate replied politely and entered the warm front hallway. She could feel Edward's reassuring bulk behind her as he helped her out of her jacket and hung it on the hook. Grandpa Joe let the door slam shut behind him and squeezed his way past them, his cane making a hollow thumping sound against the linoleum-covered floor.

As Grandpa Joe turned the corner and disappeared from view, a large silver-haired man popped his head around the corner.

"Hello, Edward." He had a loud, booming voice and as he strode towards them, the pictures hanging in the hallway shook minutely. He gave Edward a brief hug before turning to Kate.

His resemblance to Edward was so strong that Kate was not surprised when Edward said "Kate, this is my father, Jacob. Dad, this is Kate Jones, a work colleague."

"Nice to meet you, Kate," Jacob said, his large, rough hand swallowing her small one. "I hope you're hungry, Barb's cooked up a huge feast for us."

She gave him a nervous and shaky smile before following him down the hall and into the living room where Tory and a blond-haired man were sitting on a small love seat. Grandpa Joe sat next to them in an ancient rocking chair, talking loudly about how hungry he was.

"Yes, dad." Jacob brushed off his grumbling with a small shake of his head. "Dinner's almost ready."

The blond man stood and hugged Edward before smiling at her. "Hi, I'm Jason."

"Hi, Jason. I'm Kate," she said.

She shook his hand as Tory gave Edward a quick peck on the cheek. The two brothers were so different looking it would have been impossible to tell they were related. Where Edward was tall and dark with broad shoulders and a lean waist, Jason was short, fair-skinned and stocky. Only their eyes were the same - that brilliant shade of dark blue that made Kate think of the lake at her parents' home.

A tiny, blonde woman came hurtling into the room, her eyes as blue as her sons.

"Soup's on!" She hollered cheerfully as she zoomed across the room to where Kate was standing.

"You must be Edward's Kate." She beamed happily at Kate. "Don't you have the prettiest coloured hair. You're as beautiful as Tory said you were."

"Oh, I um…"

Kate turned a bright shade of red as Edward groaned and Tory had the good grace to blush a little as well.

"Mom, this is Kate Jones, a work colleague. Kate, my mother Barb." Edward gave his mom a fierce glare that would have wilted Kate on the spot. Barb, however, only reached up and patted his cheek lovingly.

"You look tired, dear. Have you been getting enough sleep?"

"Yes, mom," Edward said as Barb took both of Kate's hands in a warm grasp.

"It's so lovely to meet you, Kate. You'll have to forgive me - I'm a bit excited to meet Edward's lady friend."

"Mom, Kate is not a lady friend - she's a work colleague," Edward said loudly but Barb ignored him and led Kate from the room.

"I understand it's your birthday today, dear. And that child of mine made you not only work on your birthday but took you away from your family and friends as well." She glared over her shoulder at Edward who stared back defiantly for a moment before admitting defeat and staring at the floor.

Kate, a little rattled by the woman's warmth and friendliness, said, "Well, I only had to work half a day and then he treated me to lunch and we did some tourist stuff for the rest of the afternoon so don't be too hard on him, Mrs. Turner."

"Call me Barb, dear. Do you have any siblings?" She asked as she ushered Kate into the small, warm kitchen.

"Yes. I have a younger sister."

"And your parents? Do they live near you? Are you close to them?"

"They live a few hours away and we are," Kate replied.

"Oh, that's lovely." Barb smiled at her before turning to stare at the table. "I'm afraid it's going to be a bit cozy but we'll manage."

"Honey, where are we sitting?" Jacob asked as the rest of the family crowded into the kitchen.

"You and Grandpa Joe can sit at the ends of the table and we'll put the kids on each side and I'll squeeze in between you and Edward," Barb said.

Within minutes they were sitting around the small table. Edward's large thigh brushed comfortably against hers and she gave him a nervous smile when he subtly reached under the table and rubbed her thigh with his warm hand.

"Thank you, Grandpa Joe," she murmured when the old man passed her a large steaming bowl of potatoes.

"Ayuh," he grunted softly.

Kate helped herself to some potatoes and passed them on to Edward. As Grandpa Joe passed her a platter piled high with roast beef, Barb said, "Kate, dear, take lots. You're looking a little peaked and thin."

"Mom," Edward sighed with exasperation, "How could you possibly decide she's looking thin and peaked? You haven't met her until tonight."

"A mother knows these things, Edward." She brushed off his protests with a small wave of her hand before turning to Tory.

"Dear, how did that meeting with that awful woman from the flower shop go today?"

As Tory told Barb about her meeting, Kate accepted the plate of asparagus Grandpa Joe was holding out to her and dished some out on to her plate.

"Are you a lawyer?" He asked abruptly.

"No, I'm an administrative assistant at the law firm," Kate replied.

"Good, there are too many lawyers in this family already," Grandpa Joe barked loudly. Jason snorted laughter through his nose and Edward gave him a dirty look.

"Oh, are you a lawyer as well, Jason?" Kate asked politely.

"Me? No, I'm a teacher," Jason replied, slathering butter onto a bun.

"So your parents are lawyers?" Kate said to Edward.

Edward shook his head. "Dad's an engineer and mom works part time at a fabric store. I'm the only lawyer in the family."

She glanced at Grandpa Joe who shrugged. "Like I said - too many lawyers in the family."

Kate grinned at Edward as Grandpa Joe continued. "Lawyers are crooks, you know, Kate."

"You don't have to tell me, Grandpa Joe. I've worked with them for the last five years," she replied.

The old man snorted laughter as Jason choked on a bite of bun and Tory patted him on the back. Once he had stopped coughing and taken a drink of water Kate asked, "What grade do you teach, Jason?"

"High school physics and math," Jason said.

"Do you enjoy it?"

"For the most part. I'm looking forward to summer break." He gave Tory a warm look that she returned immediately, reaching out to smooth his hair back from his forehead.

"Tory and Jason are getting married this August," Edward said.

"Congratulations," Kate said.

"Have you ever been married, Kate?" Barb asked curiously.

"Mom!" Edward gave her another of his fierce looks which Barb blithely ignored.

"I haven't," Kate replied.

"Why not?" Grandpa Joe grunted. "A pretty girl like you should be married."

"Not every woman wants to get married, Grandpa Joe," Tory chided gently.

The same thunderous look that frequently appeared on Edward's face when he was irritated now appeared on Grandpa Joe's face.

"And why not? In my day, women were proud to get married, raise babies and - "

Before he could start on what Kate was suddenly sure was a familiar rant, Barb interrupted smoothly. "Do you have any children, dear?"

"No, not yet." Kate said as Edward sighed loudly again. She took a bite of the tender roast beef. "This meal is delicious, Barb."

"Thank you. So you want children?"

"Someday," she said.

"Oh good. Did you know that Edward is wonderful with children?" Barb took a sip of water and smiled at Jacob who gave her an amused look.

At his mother's statement, Edward turned an alarming shade of red and closed his eyes.

"What are you doing, dear?" Barb asked as Edward inhaled deeply and rhythmically.

"Counting to ten," he replied through clenched teeth.

"What number are you at now?" Kate asked.

"Four."

Kate waited a few seconds. "And now?"

"Seven."

"Kate leaned forward to smile at Barb. "I've seen him do this at the office too."

"He doesn't deal well with stress," Jason announced, taking a huge bite of potatoes and roast beef.

"I deal just fine with stress," Edward retorted before opening his eyes to glare at his brother.

He closed his eyes and started to silently count again as Kate patted his arm soothingly. He sighed with relief when Kate began to question Tory about wedding details and his mother joined in.

* * *

Edward watched silently as, across the living room, his mother showed Kate the latest cross-stitch she was working on. After dinner, Barb had insisted they stay for coffee and his stomach twisted oddly when his mother smiled happily at Kate.

They like her, my love. This is a good thing.

He stared at the floor. His family did like Kate – hell, his mother was treating her like she was his girlfriend for God's sake – and as the evening wore on, his guilt was increasing. This was the first time in days he had heard Tabitha's voice in his head. The first time in days that he had even thought of her. His stomach twisted again and he continued to stare grimly at the floor.

His family had loved Tabitha and not once in the last two years had they pushed him to move on. He had thought it was because *they* weren't ready for him to find someone else but now, watching them with Kate, he suspected they had only been giving him time and space.

They love you. They want you to be happy, Tabitha said.

I was happy with you.

Was, my love. Our time is over.

He winced and stood up abruptly. Tabitha had always been blunt, it was one of the things he had loved most about her, but now it was like a stab in the back. Mumbling something about needing fresh air, he hurried out of the living room as the rest of the family stared at him.

Kate watched as Edward, his face pale, stood and muttered something before walking out of the room. She gave Barb an uncertain look and the woman patted her arm soothingly before turning to Jacob.

"Honey, go check on Edward, would you?"

He nodded and left the room. There was an awkward silence and Kate rubbed her legs nervously. "Um, may I use your bathroom, Mrs. Turner?"

"Of course, dear. And I told you to call me Barb. It's right down the hallway, third door on the left."

Kate gave her a weak smile and hurried out of the room. She found the bathroom and used it quickly before washing her hands. She thought the evening had been going well. Edward's family were obviously close and she had seen a side of Edward she didn't know existed. Gone was the rather grave and somber Edward and more than once, she had found herself smiling at the sound of his laugh. He was completely at ease, happy and relaxed, and she had loved seeing that side of him. She had been admiring Barb's elaborate cross-stitch project and hadn't noticed anything was wrong until Edward had abruptly stood up and left the room. He was obviously upset and that was upsetting her.

His family was being very kind to her and she had found it amusing at first how his mother continually referred to her as 'Edward's Kate' and acted like they were dating, but now she realized how that must have made him feel. It was obviously bothering him that his family had accepted her so readily and she hated that it did. She couldn't blame him though. He wouldn't want his family to forget about Tabitha the minute he brought a new girlfriend to meet them.

You're not his girlfriend.

No, she wasn't. And it was stupid to wish she was.

She stared at herself in the mirror. Fuck, this had been a bad idea. She really shouldn't have come here. She rubbed briefly at her temples. Okay, it had been a mistake and there was nothing to do but go forward. Maybe she could pull Edward aside and fake a headache so they could leave.

She opened the bathroom door and started down the hallway toward the living room, glancing absently at the framed photos on the wall. Her breath caught in her throat and she stopped abruptly, staring at the picture in front of her. It was Edward, at least ten years ago, looking young and impossibly happy as he sat in front of a small cabin. There was a woman sitting on his lap, small and petite with curly dark hair and warm brown eyes. She was smiling at the camera as Edward stared adoringly at her and Kate's chest suddenly started to ache with an intensity that took her breath away.

"That's Tabitha." A voice spoke into her ear and she jumped and stumbled back as Tory gave her an alarmed look.

"I'm sorry, Kate. I didn't mean to frighten you."

"Uh, you didn't. I was just um…"

She trailed off and Tory gave her an encouraging smile. "Has Edward told you about Tabitha?"

She nodded and Tory traced the picture with one finger before smiling at Kate. "Did he tell you she was my sister?"

"Yes," Kate said quietly.

"Brothers marrying sisters. Funny, huh? I actually had no interest in Jason when I first met him. I thought he was a nice guy but that was about it. Then Tabitha got sick and he was so sweet to her and his brother, did so much for them when she was in chemo and radiation and I started seeing him differently. We started dating about a month after Tabitha died. I was worried that it would upset Edward, thought maybe seeing so much of me would remind him too much of Tabitha, but he was happy for us. Falling in love with Jason helped heal the loss I felt when my sister died."

"I'm sorry," Kate said. "I couldn't even begin to understand how much you must miss her."

"I do miss her," Tory said. "She was a good person, a little too blunt from time to time perhaps, but kind-hearted. She wasn't perfect but she would have done anything for her loved ones."

Her throat burning, Kate said, "Edward still misses her."

"Yes," Tory agreed. "I imagine there will always be a part of him that misses her."

"I should go," Kate said suddenly. "I'm getting a bit of a headache and – "

"Kate," Tory grabbed her arm before she could leave, "you're good for him, you know."

"I – what?"

"You're good for Edward. We can all see it. It's one of the reasons why Barb is so taken with you. The Edward that showed up tonight is the Edward he used to be before Tabitha died. You make him happy."

"We – we're not dating, Tory. He's, um, just my boss. I'm sorry but I think your family is seeing something that isn't there."

Tory suddenly grinned and Kate flushed bright red. "What you heard in the office earlier today was, um, it was…"

"I don't need the details," Tory said with a soft laugh. "Edward likes you Kate."

"Maybe, but he isn't ready to move forward," Kate said. "He doesn't want a relationship with me."

"Have you asked him if he's ready?" Tory asked.

Kate blinked at her before shaking her head. "No, but I can see that he isn't. We talked about your sister once and the look on his face - it was easy to see he wasn't ready."

"I think you should talk to him and – "

"We can't date anyway," Kate said. "There's a no dating policy at the firm. I'm sorry, I should probably find Edward and see if he's ready to leave. It's getting late and tomorrow will be a long day.

* * *

"You okay?"

Edward nodded as his father joined him on the front porch. "Yeah, just needed some fresh air."

They stood silently for a few moments before his father said, "Kate's a nice girl."

"She is."

"Your mother really likes her. I do too."

"You barely know her."

His father laughed. "We've got good instincts when it comes to people. Are the two of you dating?"

"No."

"Why not?"

"It's complicated."

"Is it?"

"Yes."

"Because of Tabitha," his father said with a heavy sigh. "She would want you to be happy, son."

"It's only been two years, dad. I need more time."

"Kate seems to make you happy. Why not give it a chance?"

"Because I don't want to forget Tabitha," Edward snapped. "Already I close my eyes and can barely remember what she looks like. I have to look at pictures. I used to have daily conversations with her in my head and now — now I hardly think about her at all. I spent over ten years with her and now when I close my eyes, I see Kate, not her. What kind of person does that make me, that I would forget about my wife just because someone else comes along that I'm attracted to?"

"You're being too hard on yourself, Eddie," his father said. "Your mother and I have been worried about you and tonight, for the first time in a long time, we can see that you're happy. Give Kate a chance."

"I'll just end up hurting her," Edward said hoarsely. "We both know it. Right now what we're doing — no one is going to get hurt. We both know it's not going anywhere and once we go back to California we'll end it for good."

"Will you?"

"Yes. We have to. There's a no dating policy at the firm. If they find out we're sleeping together, Kate will be fired and I could lose my job as well. There's no potential for an actual relationship but we're both well aware of that and know exactly what this is."

"Do you?" His father said thoughtfully.

"Yes," Edward said firmly. "Kate isn't going to leave her job just to date me."

"Have you asked her if she would?" Jacob said.

"Well, no, but I know she won't and I wouldn't want her to anyway. I told you – I'm not ready for another relationship."

"Edward – "

"I'm sorry, dad, I should find Kate and get going. It's getting late and we have a long day tomorrow."

* * *

Kate glanced worriedly at Edward as they walked toward their rooms. He had been quiet and withdrawn the entire way to the hotel and she had no idea what to say to him. She berated herself again for agreeing to go with him to his family dinner as he stopped in front of his hotel door.

She moved past him to her room and he frowned before joining her. "My room has the tub, remember?"

"Edward, are you sure – I mean, do you want me to stay with you tonight?" She asked hesitantly.

"Yes." He took her hand and tugged her back to his door before opening it and leading her inside.

The door was barely shut before he was pushing her up against it, kissing her fiercely as his hands worked at the buttons on her shirt.

"Edward," she moaned as warmth pulsed through her lower body. "It's okay if you're not into this tonight. I know it was an awkward evening."

He pressed his erection against her belly. "Does it feel like I'm not into it, Katie?"

She shook her head and he kissed her almost angrily as he fisted his hands in her hair. "Do you want me?"

"You know I do," she whispered.

"Good," he muttered. "Because I have one last birthday gift to give you."

He stripped her naked before removing his own clothes and kneeling in front of her. She moaned when he draped one smooth thigh over his shoulder and buried his face in her pussy. She leaned against the door, her hands clutching at his dark hair, as he licked her pussy with hard, firm strokes. She gasped his name when he sucked on her clit and made a low pleading noise. He flicked his tongue rapidly before sucking again and she pushed frantically at his head.

"Edward, I'm going to come if you don't stop. Please!"

He renewed his efforts, pinning her against the door as he reached up with one hand and tweaked her nipple. He sucked harder, his tongue working feverishly over her aching clit, and she clamped her arm over her mouth as she screamed with the intensity of her orgasm. Her knees buckled and he steadied her with one big hand around her waist before standing and carrying her to the bed. She was shaking and trembling and, without speaking, he laid her on the bed, spread her thighs wide and entered her with a hard thrust.

"Look at me, Kate," he demanded.

Her eyelids fluttered open and she stared hazily at him as he plunged in and out of her. He kissed her again, pushing his tongue into her mouth until she could taste her own arousal, before biting her lower lip.

She cried out, her hands digging into his arms as he pumped his hips rapidly. He dropped to his elbows, his chest brushing against her breasts, and kissed her repeatedly. She met each of his thrusts, bracing her feet on the bed as they rocked together in a rapid rhythm that sent him over the edge quickly. She watched as his head fell back, the cords in his neck straining in stark relief, as he climaxed with a harsh shout before collapsing against her.

She rubbed his damp back as he panted and shuddered against her before kissing her throat. He rolled to his side and spooned her, cupping her breast and kissing the back of her shoulder. "Stay with me tonight, Kate."

"All right," she whispered.

He cupped her face and turned her head toward him. "Happy Birthday, Katie."

She returned his kiss before he pressed her back into the pillow. "Thank you, Edward. Good night."

"Good night, Katie," he mumbled.

She listened to his breathing slow and deepen as she laid in the darkness. She touched the necklace around her neck, tracing the heart with her fingers, and was careful not to make a sound when she started to cry.

Chapter 15

Kate stared out the small window of the plane. The captain had just announced they were making their final descent and she was beginning to see glimpses of the city beneath them through the thick layer of clouds. She had been quiet the entire flight and when Edward had questioned her about it, she had given the excuse that she was tired. She twitched when Edward took her hand in his.

"Your hand is cold, Katie," he said.

"Bit of a nervous flyer," she fibbed before squeezing his hand and giving him what she hoped was a natural smile. It must have looked more natural than it felt because he relaxed in his seat and closed his eyes. She returned her gaze to the window, knowing the rolling sensation in her stomach had nothing to do with flying and everything to do with the decision she was wrestling with.

You can't keep doing this, she reminded herself sternly as the plane descended steadily toward the ground. *"It's too dangerous to keep sleeping with Edward. Sooner or later you'll get caught and then you'll be out of a job or worse yet – you're going to fall in love with him.*

Oh, Kate, that ship has long since sailed.

Shut up! She hissed furiously at her inner voice. *I am not in love with Edward.*

Still holding her hand, Edward stroked her thumb gently with his.

"Okay?" He murmured quietly.

She nodded, giving him a pale smile as the plane landed with a gentle thud. They departed from the plane and retrieved their luggage without problems and Kate didn't protest when Edward led her to his car in the long-term parking.

Edward remained quiet on the drive to her place but Kate could feel him stealing small worried glances at her. He parked and shut off the car and as he popped the trunk, Kate gave him another pale smile. "Thank you for the ride home, Edward."

"You're welcome," he replied. He stepped out of the car and before she could stop him he was carrying her luggage to her front door, waiting patiently as she fumbled through her purse for her house key.

They stepped into the hallway and as Chicken raced down the hallway toward them with loud, insistent meows, Kate bent and scooped up the old cat before burying her face in the cat's soft fur.

"I missed you, Chicky-Chick Chicken," she mumbled. Whether she had missed her or because she had caught sight of Edward, Chicken purred softly, making no attempt to free herself from Kate's embrace.

Edward reached forward and scratched Chicken under the chin. "Glad to see us, old girl?"

Chicken kneaded the air before butting her head against Kate's chin. She set the cat on the floor and brushed the hair off the front of her shirt. "Um, did you want a drink?"

Idiot! Send him home before you do something stupid!

"I'd love one," he replied.

He carried her suitcase to her bedroom as Kate grabbed a bottle of wine and two wine glasses. He met her in the kitchen and as she poured them both a glass of wine, he snuck a look at the note taped to the fridge.

Welcome home, Katie! Drop by our place tomorrow night at six for your birthday party. Your parents will be there but Lina couldn't make it – I'm sorry! It won't be anything too crazy – just a few friends and some people from the office. Can't wait to see you! Love, Olivia.

A stupid twinge of jealousy went through him. Olivia hadn't sent him an invitation to Kate's party, but why would she? He had no right to feel hurt.

He looked away as Kate turned around, not wanting her to see him snooping, and she handed him a glass of wine. They both took a sip as Chicken weaved anxiously around Edward's feet, meowing loudly.

"Kate, I..."

"Edward, we need..."

They stopped and stared at each other.

"Ladies first," Edward said. He sat down at the table and Chicken leaped into his lap, purring loudly. He stroked the old cat's head as she placed her front paws on his chest and butted her head against his chin.

Kate leaned against the counter and gave him an uneasy smile. She was pale and ill looking and Edward stared worriedly at her.

"Katie, are you okay? Are you feeling sick? Maybe you should sit down."

"No, I'm fine, I just need a minute." She took a few deep breaths. "I guess we both know that we can't..."

She trailed to a stop as Edward stared solemnly at her.

"We can't," she paused again before suddenly shaking her head, "we can't let others know we, uh, slept together but I still wanted to invite you to my birthday party tomorrow night. Olivia's throwing a small get-together and there will be other people from the office there, including Arthur, so it won't look too odd if you're there."

"You want me to come to your birthday party?" He asked.

"Yes. If you want to," she said.

He set Chicken on the floor and put his arms around her. "I would love to. Thank you for inviting me."

She smiled shakily at him and he stroked her back. "Are you sure you're okay?"

"Yes," she said. "What were you going to say?"

"Just that I had a really great time with you in New York."

Sunday, Kate thought. *I'll end this for good on Sunday.*

Edward breathed in the sweet scent of Kate's hair as she relaxed against him. It was almost seven and he should probably leave and let her go to bed. Despite her assurances she looked tired and unwell. As she sighed and buried her face in his neck, he hugged her tightly and stared out the small window over the sink. He didn't want to leave. He didn't want to go home to his dark apartment, open the fridge and find nothing but juice and stale bread. He didn't want to wander around his empty place, thinking about Kate and what she was doing until finally going to bed alone. He wanted to stay in her warm, bright kitchen, have dinner with her and then take her to bed and make love to her, bury himself in her warmth and the sound of her soft voice crying his name.

He reluctantly let go of her as she stepped away and picked up her glass of wine.

"I should probably go," he said. "I'm sure you want to have a bite to eat and go to bed."

She smiled uncertainly. "Would you like to stay and have dinner with me? I'll understand if you'd rather go home, but I'm going to be cooking anyway and it's just as easy to cook for two."

Relief rushed through him and he grinned broadly at her. "I'd love to, Katie-did."

"Are you sure?"

"I'm positive." He leaned down and kissed her thoroughly. She groaned softly and leaned against him as he urged her mouth open with soft, gentle kisses.

"Maybe we should change into something more comfortable before we eat," he said as he cupped her breast with one large hand. His cock was pushing against her hip and she reached down and stroked him firmly.

"Sounds like a good idea to me," she whispered before he took her mouth in a hard, demanding kiss.

Neither noticed when Chicken padded from the room toward the front door. She hissed softly when it opened before racing for the bedroom, her tail stuck up stiffly behind her.

Kate moaned softly, letting her head fall back as Edward placed warm kisses on her pale throat. He reached down and cupped her ass, pulling her tightly against him. She was just reaching to pull his shirt from his jeans when someone cleared their throat loudly behind them.

They broke apart and Edward stared at the two women standing in the kitchen. One was shorter and on the chubby side with long dark hair and the other was tall and slender. Her hair was the same colour as Kate's and she was staring at them in shocked silence.

"Mom? Lina? What – what are you doing here?" Kate sputtered.

"Surprise," Lina said. "We're here for your birthday party."

"But Olivia's note said you couldn't make it," Kate said. She realized she was still standing in Edward's embrace and, blushing fiercely, she pushed away from him.

"I wanted to surprise you," Lina said.

"We picked Lina and Aiden up at the airport and then drove straight here," Kate's mother said. "Your dad and Aiden are getting the suitcases from the car. We thought we'd spend tonight and tomorrow with you because your father and I have to leave the party early. Your dad is taking your Uncle Earl on a fishing trip at the lake early Sunday morning."

She hesitated, glancing at Lina, before saying, "I'm sorry, we didn't mean to interrupt. We used our key because we thought you wouldn't be home yet."

"That's fine," Kate said.

She hugged Lina hard, blushing furiously when Lina whispered in her ear, "Holy shit, he's hot."

She hugged her mom as her dad popped his head into the doorway.

"Surprise, Katie-bear! Happy belated birthday!" He dropped the suitcase and stepped into the kitchen, giving Kate a rough one-armed hug and kissing the top of her head with a loud smacking sound. "Say, did you get a new car? It's a damn nice – "

He stopped and stared at Edward before holding out his hand. "Alvin Jones."

"Edward Turner."

"You're dating our Katie, are you?" Alvin asked as they shook hands.

"No. Dad, this is my boss," Kate said hurriedly.

Behind Alvin, Kate's mother's eyebrows rose and she stared wide-eyed at Lina. Lina grinned cheerfully at her as Edward controlled his own urge to laugh.

"You must be Kate's mother," he said before holding out his hand.

"I am. I'm Julia. It's nice to meet you, Mr. Turner."

"Edward, please," he said pleasantly.

"Hello, Edward, I'm Lina." Kate's sister gave him an impish grin and he shook her hand as another man entered the kitchen. He was tall with dark hair and he put a possessive arm around Lina's waist before kissing her on the top of her head.

"Katie, this is Aiden. Aiden, this is my sister, Kate."

"Hi, Kate. It's nice to meet you – Lina's told me a lot about you," Aiden said politely.

"It's nice to meet you as well," Kate said. "This is my boss, Edward Turner."

They shook hands and there was an awkward silence that Kate hurried to break. "Edward gave me a ride home from the airport and we were just, uh…"

She trailed off as Lina gave her an innocent look. "Just what, Katie?"

"We were just discussing dinner options," Edward said smoothly.

"Dinner?" Alvin said loudly. "We brought dinner with us didn't we, Julia?"

She nodded, grimacing slightly. "You father brought some salmon he caught yesterday, I swear I'll never get the smell out of the car."

"Katie loves my barbequed salmon," Alvin protested. "I was doing it for her, honey."

"Well, now that you have dinner plans, Kate, I'll leave you to it," Edward said.

"Nonsense!" Alvin bellowed. "There's plenty of fish for everyone. Why don't you stay and have dinner with us?"

Edward looked at Kate who said nervously, "Dad, I'm sure Edward has other things to do."

"Not at all," Edward said. "I'd love to stay for dinner."

"Excellent!" Alvin cried. "I'll just go grab the cooler from the car while you and Aiden start the barbeque."

* * *

"I like your family," Edward said as they stood on the porch.

"They like you too," Kate said. "Thank you for having dinner with us. Sorry about all the fishing talk from my father."

Edward grinned at her. "I didn't mind. I had a good time."

There was an awkward moment and then he pulled her into his embrace, stroking her hair gently as she wrapped her arms around his waist.

"I was going to ask you to stay the night," she whispered.

"I was going to say yes," he replied.

He cupped the back of her head and kissed her. It was unexpectedly warm and tender and she blinked back the sudden tears.

"I'll see you at the party tomorrow, Katie-did."

She nodded, not trusting herself to speak, and watched as he walked to his car. When he was gone she stood in the front hallway as Chicken crept down it and stood at her feet. The tears were slipping down her cheeks and she wiped them away as she crouched and petted the old cat. She could hear Aiden and Lina talking quietly in the living room and the louder voices of her parents in the kitchen.

"That Edward seems like a nice enough fellow," her father said. "Did you like him?"

"I did," Julia replied. "He's very well-spoken."

"I think he might have a bit of a crush on our Katie. Did you see the way he looked at her?"

Her mother made a small sound of agreement.

"Well, he's not big on fishing so that's against him but I suppose she could do worse," Alvin said thoughtfully.

Kate smiled and wiped her cheeks a final time before heading toward the kitchen.

* * *

"Kate, wake up."

Kate muttered and buried her face in the pillow as the side of the bed dipped. "C'mon, Katie, wake up. I have coffee."

She sighed loudly and blinked at her sister. "What time is it?"

"Just after seven."

"What are you doing in my room?"

"I wanted to talk and mom and dad are still sleeping and Aiden's gone for a run so this is the perfect time."

"No, the perfect time would be noon," Kate grumbled as she struggled into a sitting position and yawned.

She took the offered cup of coffee and sipped at it as Lina reached out and tentatively petted Chicken who was sitting on the pillow beside Kate. The cat hissed loudly and swiped at her before flouncing off the bed.

"That cat," Lina laughed, "is a menace. This is why I have dogs."

"Where are the dogs?" Kate asked. "And how is Daisy doing? I keep meaning to ask."

"They're staying with our friends Joe and Stephanie and she's doing so much better. I swear, you'd never even know she had been stabbed," Lina replied.

"You look really happy," Kate said.

"I am happy. The last few weeks have been really good."

"I'm glad, honey. Really, I am. Aiden seems like a nice man."

Lina laughed. "Nice isn't the word I would use to describe Aiden but damn if I don't love that man."

"He's very good looking."

"Isn't he? And he's an absolute rock star in bed. I thought I was terrible at sex, Kent certainly went on and on about how bad I was, but Aiden helped me see the truth. He was so patient with me and all of my sex issues. Now I can't wait to get naked with him."

Kate laughed. "Nice job, Aiden."

"Very nice," Lina said solemnly. "And he's got a lovely big dick and a wickedly talented tongue."

Kate choked on her sip of coffee and Lina grinned at her. "Too much information?"

"Maybe just a little."

"What about Edward?"

"What about him?"

"Does he have a lovely big dick?"

"Lina!"

Lina laughed loudly. "Spill it, Katie. You know you're dying to give me all the dirty details."

"Why would you think I have any dirty details to spill? He's my boss, remember? I'm not allowed to have a relationship with him."

"Oh please. The way you were practically undressing each other in the kitchen suggests you're more than just co-workers. I'm guessing the 'one night' thing didn't really work out for you?"

"I tried," Kate said. "We agreed to just one night of sex and then it just..."

She trailed off and Lina stared sympathetically at her. "You both needed more."

"Yes," Kate replied. She set her coffee cup on the bedside table and stared at her hands. "We tried to stay away from each other, really we did, but I was completely miserable and then he flew me out to New York to help him with some files and I just... there was no one there to catch us, you know?"

"I do know," Lina said solemnly.

"So I decided I would just sleep with him a few more times when there was no worry about being caught only he was so sweet to me, Lina. He bought me this necklace for my birthday, he took me sight-seeing, and then I met his family and – "

"Whoa – you met his family?" Lina interrupted. "I haven't even met Aiden's family yet."

"It just sort of happened. They wanted Edward to come for dinner and insisted he bring me along. Edward told them we were just co-workers but his brother's fiancé heard us having sex in the office so she knew we were more than that and the rest of his family totally treated me like I was his girlfriend."

She sighed loudly. "I was going to break it off the minute we returned home but instead I invited him to my birthday party *and* he met my family. And you liked him."

"We did," Lina said. "He seems perfect for you and, frankly, it's kind of obvious he's in love with you."

"He's not – "

"He is," Lina interrupted. "Maybe you can't see it or maybe you don't want to see it but the guy's in love with you. And you're in love with him."

"I've known him for a month, Lina," Kate said. "People don't fall in love in a month."

"Who says they don't?" Lina said. "I love Aiden and he loves me and we haven't known each other that long."

"You've worked for him for three years," Kate protested.

"Yeah, but I knew nothing about him other than that he was an arrogant jackass. In the entire three years, we didn't have a single personal conversation. He called me Ms. Jones for God's sake. I didn't think he even knew my first name."

Kate grinned a little and Lina snickered softly. "It's true. Turns out he did know my first name and his bad behaviour was a cover because the man was so hot for me he could barely think straight."

She paused before laughing again. "Well, most of his bad behaviour anyway. Like I said, Aiden's not known for being a 'nice' guy. But the point is – I still fell in love with him partly because after we started sleeping together I started to see a different side of him and partly because of the multiple orgasms and spankings."

"Jesus, Lina," Kate said before bursting into laughter.

"Turns out I'm kinky as hell," Lina said cheerfully. "But the point is, we're in love but we're still getting to know each other's likes and dislikes and weird little habits – I swear Aiden brushes his teeth like six times a day – and that's okay. In fact, I think it makes it a little easier for us to accept each other's idiosyncrasies because we're already in love. Who says it can't be the same for you and Edward?"

"Because he's still in love with his dead wife."

"What?" Lina stared at her in shock.

"Edward was married to a woman named Tabitha. She died two years ago of a brain tumour and he's still not over his loss. He might be starting to have some feelings for me but it isn't love. He still loves her and misses her."

"Well, shit," Lina said. "That complicates things."

"Yeah," Kate replied. "You're right, you know. I am in love with him – at least I think I am – and I'm an idiot for it."

"You're not," Lina said. "And are you absolutely certain that he isn't ready to move on? Have you talked to him about it? He looks at you like he's ready to move on, is all I'm saying."

"I haven't talked to him about it," Kate admitted. "I want to but any time he talks about her, the look on his face – it's easy to see how much he loves her still – and it makes me jealous as hell. I'm a horrible person."

"I think that's a normal reaction," Lina said thoughtfully.

Kate buried her face in her hands and Lina rubbed her back soothingly. "Katie, honey, you need to tell him how you feel. I know you believe he doesn't feel the same way but I think you're wrong. Take a chance, honey. You can't keep going the way you are – hiding your love for someone is a rotten way to live."

"I'm afraid," Kate whispered. "What if he doesn't feel the same way as I do?"

Lina took her cold hands and squeezed them. "There's only one way to find out, Katie."

* * *

"Katie!" Olivia hugged her tightly. "Did you like your surprise?"

"I did," Kate said. "Very sneaky of you."

"I know, right? I'm excellent at keeping secrets," Olivia said before hugging Lina. "Hi, sweetie. You look great."

"You do too, Olivia," Lina said.

"Where are your parents and your new man?" Olivia asked.

"Outside with Jon," Kate replied. "Dad's already talking to him about fishing."

Olivia laughed and Lina grinned at her. "Aiden's surprisingly outdoorsy so he and dad are getting along like a house on fire. They're already planning a fishing trip in the spring and I think dad's trying to convince Jon to go with them."

"It won't take much convincing," Olivia replied.

"What can I do to help?" Kate asked.

"You can take this glass of wine and go outside and relax, greet the party-goers as they arrive. Lina will help me, won't you?" Olivia said.

"Yes, go on, Kate," Lina said. "Enjoy your party."

"Olivia, I – I invited Edward, I hope that's okay," Kate said.

"Of course it is," Olivia replied before studying her carefully. "Are there some new developments I should know about?"

Kate glanced at Lina. "I'm not sure yet."

Olivia squeezed her arm lightly before handing her a glass of wine. "We'll talk later about it, okay?"

Kate nodded and, leaving Lina in the kitchen with Olivia, headed outside.

* * *

"Happy Birthday, Kate."

She turned, shivers running down her spine at his familiar voice, and smiled at the bouquet of flowers Edward was holding.

"Thank you, Edward. Those are lovely." She took them from him and inhaled their fragrant scent as Edward smiled at Josh and Lina.

"Um, you remember Josh," Kate said briefly.

"I do. Nice to see you again, Josh." Edward held out his hand and Josh shook it firmly. "I need to apologize for my behaviour the last time we met."

"No need," Josh said.

Olivia appeared and took Josh's arm, "Josh, come with me. There's someone I want you to meet. Her name's Sheila and you're going to like her, I guarantee it."

She pulled Josh away with a small wink at Kate and Edward smiled at Lina. "Hi, Lina. How are you?"

"Good, thanks," Lina said. "What's up with Olivia and her matchmaking?"

Kate laughed. "She thinks Josh and Sheila will be the perfect couple."

"They do look super cute together," Edward said solemnly. Lina burst out laughing as Aiden wandered over to them.

"I should put these in water," Kate said. "I'll be right back."

She was filling the vase she found in the kitchen cupboard with water when Edward's warm arm slid around her waist. He kissed the back of her neck and she shivered delicately as she placed the vase on the counter. He turned her and cupped her face, kissing her slowly and deliberately as the chatter of the party guests drifted through the open window.

"Edward," she whispered when he cupped her breast. "We can't do this here."

"I've missed you," he muttered.

"It's been less than a day," she said.

He just shrugged and kissed her forehead. "How was your day with your family?"

"It was good." She tried to squirm out of his embrace as she glanced at the window and he tightened his hold on her. "Uh, how was your day?"

"Fine. I sat around the apartment, did a bit of work, thought about you. Will you have your place to yourself tonight?"

She shook her head. "No. My parents are leaving today but Lina and Aiden don't fly out until tomorrow morning."

He gave her a disappointed look. "I was hoping we could spend the night together."

"I'm sorry," she said.

"Don't be. It's good that you get to spend time with your sister. I'm just being selfish," he replied.

He bent his head and kissed her again, stroking the seam of her mouth with his tongue. "Open up, Katie-did," he whispered.

"We can't," she said. "Edward, our coworkers are right outside."

He sighed loudly and stepped away from her just as Arthur and his wife wandered into the kitchen. Kate turned quickly, hoping like hell Arthur hadn't caught a glimpse of her red cheeks and swollen mouth.

"Edward! How was New York?" Arthur said as Sylvia joined Kate at the counter.

"It was good. Very busy," Edward said.

Kate, her hands shaking, tried to cut the string around the flower stems. If Arthur and Sylvia had come in a moment sooner...

Her hands trembled harder and, without speaking, Sylvia took the knife from her and cut the string.

"Thank you," Kate said.

"You're welcome, Kate. Are you enjoying your party?" Sylvia asked.

"Yes. Thanks for coming."

Sylvia leaned against the counter as Kate stuck the flowers into the vase. Behind them, Arthur was chatting about some work that was due on Monday, and Kate gave Sylvia a nervous look when the older woman stared silently at her.

"Well, I should probably get back to the party," she said quickly as she picked up the vase of flowers.

"Here, I'll carry those for you," Edward said before plucking the vase from her hands.

"Thanks," Kate mumbled. Without looking at Arthur, she hurried from the kitchen, Edward following silently behind her.

Arthur frowned at his wife. "Is it just me or is there some tension between the two of them?"

"Not just you, my darling," Sylvia said.

Arthur sighed loudly as Sylvia grabbed a few more wine glasses from the counter. "I hope they can work it out. The last thing I need is Edward to be fighting with his PA. He's really proving his worth at the office and Kate's an excellent PA. If they're fighting and butting heads, it'll spread tension through the rest of the office."

Sylvia was giving him a rather amused grin and he said, "What? Why are you looking at me like that?"

She kissed his cheek affectionately. "Nothing, my darling. I just don't think you need to worry about Edward and Kate fighting."

"You don't think so?" Arthur said with obvious relief.

Sylvia laughed and kissed his cheek again. "I really don't. But you may have to look at hiring more admin in the near future."

"What do you mean?"

She shook her head before looping her arm around his. "Never mind, darling."

* * *

"Well, that was a fun party," Lina announced as she sat down at Kate's kitchen table.

"It was," Kate replied. She added water to the teakettle and set it on the stove before turning the burner on. "Who wants tea?"

"I'll take a cup," Lina said. "Aiden, do you want a beer?"

"I can get it," he said to Kate before opening the fridge and bending down.

Lina stared appreciatively at his jean-clad ass before winking at Kate. "Did you have fun, Katie?"

"Yes. Thanks for coming to the party, honey. I know the flight must have cost you an arm and a leg."

"You're worth it," Lina said with a small grin. "So now what?"

Kate shrugged. "I'm going to have a cup of tea and go to bed."

"It's not even eight-thirty," Lina said.

"I know, but – "

The doorbell rang and she glanced down the hallway. "Who could that be?"

"No idea," Lina said innocently as Aiden grinned and joined her at the table.

Kate gave her a suspicious look before heading to the front door. She opened it and stared in surprise at Edward standing on the porch.

"Edward? Wh-what are you doing here?"

His smile faltered. "Lina – "

"I invited him," Lina said as she popped up behind Kate. She grinned at Edward. "Come in, Edward."

He stepped into the hallway and Lina took his jacket. "I wanted to play Trivial Pursuit and we needed a fourth player for partners. When we were leaving the party, I asked Edward to join us."

She smiled at Edward. "I hope you're prepared to have your ass kicked at Trivial Pursuit. I'm really good at it. Head on into the kitchen, Aiden's in there having a beer, and we'll grab the board game."

When Edward was gone, Kate grabbed Lina's arm. "What are you doing?"

"Playing Trivial Pursuit?" Lina said.

"Lina, you shouldn't have invited Edward over."

"Why not? You like him, he likes you and no one overheard me asking him to come over. Relax, Katie. I know you want to be around him and you should have seen the look on his face when I asked him to drop by. He was like a kid in a candy store, for fuck's sake. Think of this as an opportunity to get to know him outside of the bedroom – isn't that what you want?"

"Yes, but…"

"No buts," Lina said firmly. "Grab that board game and let's see if we can make those hot studs of ours beg for mercy when we destroy them at Trivial Pursuit."

* * *

"How can you not know that Kim Kardashian had a sex tape?" Lina stared in disbelief at Aiden.

"I don't even know who that is," Aiden said.

"This is why we're kicking your ass at Trivial Pursuit," Lina replied.

Aiden laughed. "You didn't mention it was Trivial Pursuit Celebrity Edition."

"Didn't I?" Lina said innocently. "I'm sure I did."

"Edward?" Aiden raised his eyebrows at him. "Did she say it was the celebrity edition?"

"She did not," Edward replied solemnly. "Nor did she mention that she and her sister were trash-talkers."

Kate downed her glass of wine. "We learned the art of trash-talking during board games from our mother. Besides, it's not our fault you don't keep up with celebrity gossip."

"I don't have time," Edward said. "I'm too busy doing important lawyer-y things."

"Lawyer-y things?" Lina snickered. "Is that an official term?"

"Yes?" Edward said and Lina laughed again before stroking Aiden's hair affectionately.

"Ready for bed, handsome?"

He nodded and Lina kissed Kate on the forehead. "Good night, honey. I'll text you when we're home."

"I can drive you to the airport," Kate said.

"No need. Aiden arranged for a car to pick us up at seven. Don't bother getting up, okay?"

"Of course I'll get up," Kate said. "I'll make us coffee and we can have one last visit before you leave."

There was silence at the table and Kate said, "What?"

"Don't take this the wrong way," Lina said,

"But you're really not a morning person," Edward finished.

They looked at each other and grinned as Kate scowled at them. "Morning people are the worst."

"We really are," Lina agreed cheerfully before standing and grabbing Aiden's hand. "Come on, you. Time for bed."

They left the kitchen and Kate added the wine glasses and the mugs to the dishwasher as Edward put away the board game. When they were finished, she smiled tentatively at him. "Thanks for stopping by, Edward. This was fun."

He put his arms around her and drew her forward. "It was fun."

He pressed a kiss against her mouth and she moaned quietly and parted her lips. He kissed her hungrily, his hands cupping her ass and pulling her up against him as she sucked on his tongue.

"Please don't ask me to leave, Katie," he muttered against her mouth. "I want to stay with you."

Her heart pounding madly, she cupped his face and smiled at him. "I want you to stay too."

He returned her smile happily and followed her to her bedroom. She closed the door and he was on her in an instant, kissing her greedily as he cupped both her breasts. They undressed each other slowly and when they were naked and lying in her bed, he started a slow exploration of her entire body with his mouth and his hands. He took his time, discovering all the hidden spots that made her squirm with need when he caressed them, and she was moaning softly and begging for him to take her by the time he was finished.

She parted her legs, smiling at the way his gaze was drawn to her pussy, and made another soft moan of need. "Please, Edward."

"I want you so much, Katie," he whispered.

"I want you too. Don't make me wait," she replied.

He knelt between her legs, burying himself deep inside of her warm body and, as he began a slow and gentle rhythm that filled her entire body with a deep, pulsating pleasure, she buried her face against his neck and mouthed the words 'I love you'.

Chapter 16

"I told you to stay in bed," Lina whispered as Kate staggered down the hall early the next morning.

"I wanted to say goodbye," Kate mumbled. She yawned and rubbed at her eyes as Aiden brought the suitcase out from the bedroom.

"Aiden, it was really nice to meet you," she said.

"Likewise," Aiden replied before smiling at Lina. "I'm going to take this out to the car."

"Thanks, honey. Give me five minutes, okay?" Lina said.

She waited until he left before grinning at Kate. "I see Edward's car is still in the driveway."

"He didn't want to leave," Kate said. "And I didn't want him to either."

"Talk to him, honey," Lina said. "The guy wants a relationship with you – I know he does."

Kate nodded. "After last night, I think so too. I'll talk to him today."

"Good." Lina kissed her cheek with a loud smacking noise. "Text me later and tell me how it went, okay?"

"I will. Bye, Lina, I love you."

"I love you too, Katie."

Kate stood on the front porch, waving at Lina as the car pulled away, before moving quietly to the bedroom. Edward was still sound asleep in her bed and she hesitated before stripping off her robe and climbing naked into the bed beside him.

He blinked sleepily at her before tucking his large body around hers and nuzzling her neck.

"Okay?" He muttered.

She kissed his chest before resting her head on it and closing her eyes. "Yes. Go back to sleep."

"Kay," he mumbled. "Love you, Katie."

She froze against him, her eyelids flying open as her heart pounded in her chest. She lifted her head, staring wide-eyed at him, but he was already asleep again, his chest moving in slow, rhythmic inhales and exhales. She returned her head to his chest, wide awake and trembling with excitement and happiness.

* * *

"Good morning."

Kate flipped the French toast before smiling at Edward. He had dressed but he was looking adorably sleepy and rumpled and he kissed her warmly before collapsing in the kitchen chair. Chicken weaved around his legs and he petted her roughly as he glanced at the clock. It was after ten and he studied Kate carefully as she added the French toast to the pile and shut off the stove. There was something different about her this morning – she was positively beaming with happiness – and he smiled at her as she set the French toast on the table and joined him.

"How long have you been up?" He asked.

She shrugged. "I got up around seven thirty. I couldn't sleep after Lina and Aiden left."

"You should have woken me," he said. "I could have helped you fall back asleep." He grinned wickedly at her and she laughed before pouring syrup on her French toast.

"I needed some time to think," she said.

"About what?" He asked curiously as he speared a piece of bread and popped it into his mouth.

"About us. About where we're going with this."

He froze and gave her a cautious look. "What do you mean?"

She took a deep breath. "I want more, Edward, and I think you do too."

"You'll lose your job, Kate," he said slowly.

"I don't care about my job. I'll quit and find another," she said. "There's something good between us and I know you can feel it too. I want to be with you. Edward, I love you."

Kate smiled at Edward, waiting for him to say he loved her too and when he gave her another one of those weirdly cautious looks, her stomach began to churn.

"Say something," she whispered.

"Kate, I – I still love Tabitha," he said.

For one brief moment, she thought she was going to vomit all over the table. She fought it bitterly, swallowing down the bile rising in her throat, before whispering, "You told me you loved me this morning."

"I – what?" He said.

"This morning when I crawled back into bed with you, you said 'love you, Katie'," she said dully.

"I'm sorry. I don't remember saying that," he said quietly.

She didn't reply and he flinched when he touched her hand and she yanked it away. "Kate, I'm so sorry. I thought I was clear that I'm not ready for a relationship right now. It's why I only wanted - "

"You only wanted one night," she interrupted before laughing bitterly and dropping her head into her hands. "What a fool I am."

"No!" He said quickly. "This is my fault. I – I encouraged this because I was lonely and you were the first woman since Tabitha who I …"

He trailed off and she raised her gaze to him, her eyes dull with pain, "Wanted to fuck."

"It was more than that," he said immediately. "Just not – "

"Love," she whispered.

"I'm so sorry," he said again. "I never meant to hurt you."

"I know," she said. She took a deep breath and wiped away the tears that were sliding down her cheeks. "You should go."

"I don't think I should leave you alone," he said.

She made another bitter little laugh that tore at his heart. "Please go. I'm not angry with you, Edward, I swear. I understand but I – I can't be around you right now, okay? I'm too embarrassed."

"Katie…"

"Don't," she said. "You love Tabitha, not me, and deep down I think I always knew that. I just got swept up by your sweetness and that's my fault for being so blind to the truth. Please leave, Edward. I swear, I'm fine."

He tried to touch her again and she shoved her chair back and stood up, staggering backwards when he stood as well. "Do you want me to beg you to leave?"

"No," he said. "I'll go. I'm sorry, Kate."

"I'm sorry too. Good bye, Edward."

* * *

"Olivia? Do you know where Kate is? It's after nine and she's still not in the office," Edward said. "Did she call in sick?"

"She's gone," Olivia said flatly as she stared at her computer screen.

Panic flared in him. "What do you mean she's gone?"

She finally looked up from her monitor and gave him an icy look. "It's personal and I'm not telling you a damn thing."

"Olivia, please. I'm worried about her and I – "

"You're worried about her?" Olivia said in a low hiss. "You broke her heart yesterday but thought what – that she would just come strolling into work this morning like nothing had happened? Leave me alone, Mr. Turner. Unless it's work related, I don't want you to speak to me."

She stared resolutely at her screen as Arthur's door opened. "Edward? Can I speak to you for a moment?"

He nodded and followed Arthur into his office. He sat down heavily in the chair as Arthur gave him a look of confusion. "Do you know what's going with Kate?"

"I – what do you mean?" He asked hoarsely.

"She called me early this morning, said she was sorry but that she needed to take an unexpected leave of absence but wouldn't tell me why. She's never done anything like that before. Did she not tell you she was taking one?"

"Yes," Edward lied. "But she wouldn't tell me anything either."

Arthur sighed. "Well, we can assign Lydia to you in her absence. Kate said she needed two weeks but she sounded so upset, I told her to take as much time as she needed."

He glanced up at Edward and frowned. "Edward, are you all right? You look quite ill. Are you coming down with the flu?"

Edward shook his head. "No, I – I'm good. I'd better get back to work. Thanks, Arthur."

* * *

You're an idiot, my love.

Give it a rest, Tabitha, he snarled.

It had been the longest fucking week of his life. On Wednesday, worried sick about Kate, he had gone to her house. He had knocked repeatedly and when she didn't come to the door, he had used the key under the flowerpot to let himself in. Chicken had greeted him enthusiastically, purring and rubbing against his pant legs, but he could tell immediately that she wasn't there. The house was empty and it hadn't taken a rocket scientist to figure out she hadn't been there for days.

"Edward?" Doug stuck his head into his office. "A bunch of us are going for drinks. You want to come with?"

He shook his head and Doug hesitated for a moment. "Are you okay, Edward? You've been off all week."

"I'm fine," he snapped. He rubbed his hand wearily through his hair. "Sorry, I didn't mean to snap. It's been a long week."

"Well, thank God it's Friday," Doug said cheerfully. "You should think about joining us for drinks. You look like you could use one."

"Next time," Edward said distractedly.

He stared blankly out his office window. He had fucked up so badly and he didn't have a clue how to fix it.

You do, my love. Why are you being so stubborn?

I'm not. I'm not ready for a relationship.

Bullshit, Tabitha said dryly in his head. *I never expected you to stay single for the rest of your life. You love Kate.*

I love you.

And I'm dead and you're going to spend the rest of your life alone because you can't accept that.

I have accepted it, I just —

You just what?

I don't want Kate to be some type of replacement for you. I can't do that to her.

We both know you don't think of her as a replacement. Stop being such an asshole.

He sighed and rubbed again at his forehead. *I do love her, Tabitha. I'm sorry.*

There's nothing to be sorry for. Tell Kate you love her.

I don't know where she is, he thought petulantly.

Then find her, my love.

* * *

"I've made a terrible mistake, Olivia, and I need your help," Edward said in a low voice.

She gave him a frosty glare before starting to stand. "If it's not work-related, I'm not interested."

"Please, just sit down and hear me out," Edward said as she started to leave his office. "Please, Olivia."

She sighed and returned to her seat.

"I love her," he said hoarsely. "I love her and I need to tell her."

She stared silently at him and despair rushed through him. "Please, Olivia, tell me where she is. I promise I won't hurt her again."

She sighed loudly. "You really do love her, don't you?"

"Yes. I should have told her when she told me she loved me but I was stupid and pushed her away. This last week without her has been," he paused and gave her a plaintive look, "I need her. I can't live without her."

"She flew to Lina's Monday morning," Olivia said. "I'll give you Lina's address so you can go and grovel at Kate's feet but I swear to God, Edward, if you hurt her again I'll cut off your balls."

"I won't," he said. "I promise I won't."

He stood and checked his watch. "Is Arthur still in the office?"

Olivia nodded. "Yes. Why?"

"I need to speak with him. Can you text me Lina's address?"

She nodded again. "I won't tell Kate you're coming out, she'll just run if you do."

"Thank you," he said.

"You're welcome. Fix what you've broken, Edward."

"I will."

* * *

"Can I help you, sir?"

Edward smiled anxiously at the man standing behind the desk in the lobby. "Yes, I'm here to see Aiden, uh," - *what the hell was Aiden's last name* – "in the penthouse," he finished lamely.

"Your name?"

"Edward Turner."

"One moment please," the man said. He pushed a button on the phone and waited.

"Mr. Wright? I have an Edward Turner here to see you."

Edward, sweat starting to slide down his back, waited nervously as the man listened silently.

"Very well, sir. Thank you."

He hung up the phone and pointed to the elevators. "Go ahead. Push the penthouse button, it'll take you straight up."

"Thank you," Edward said. He nearly ran to the elevator and pushed the button. The doors closed and, his stomach churning, he waited as the elevator rose smoothly. It took less than a minute and when the doors opened, he was greeted by a massive dog. It sniffed curiously at his pants as he stepped into the foyer.

"King, go on," Aiden said.

The dog woofed as a second one, this one was smaller with a white muzzle, joined King and sniffed him.

"Daisy, you too," Aiden said.

"Hello, Aiden," Edward said as the dogs retreated.

"Hello, Edward."

"Could I speak to Kate?"

"She's not here."

Edward's stomach dropped. "Olivia said she was staying with you."

"She is. She's just not here at the moment. Lina took her out for lunch."

A small smile crossed Aiden's face. "You're lucky Lina isn't here. She wouldn't have let you come in. She is," he paused, "supremely pissed with you. Come into the living room. You look like you could use a drink."

Edward followed him into the large room. Floor to ceiling windows ran along one wall revealing a breath-taking view of the city.

"Nice place," he said.

"Thanks," Aiden replied. He moved to the bar in the far corner of the room and poured them both a glass of scotch.

Edward accepted it with a nod of thanks and took a sip of the amber liquid as Aiden studied him. "So, you fucked up pretty bad, huh?"

"Yes."

"Here to beg for Kate's forgiveness?"

"Yes."

"Well, if she's anything like Lina, she'll forgive you," Aiden said as King and Daisy crept into the room. King leaned against Edward, drooling a puddle on to his shoe and Aiden gave him a gentle push on the shoulder. "Go on, King."

Edward took another drink of the scotch. It burned like fire in his stomach but did help to quell the nerves a bit.

"I fucked up with Lina," Aiden said, "and much to my eternal surprise, she forgave me rather quickly. I never had much use for God but I find myself thanking him on a daily basis that she gave me a second chance. The Jones' women are something special."

"Yes, they are," Edward said quietly.

King and Daisy, who were lying in front of the fireplace, both sat up, their ears perking forward. King made a happy woof as Daisy ran out of the living room. He followed her clumsily, paws slipping on the wood floor, as Lina called, "Aiden? Honey, we're back."

"In the living room," Aiden said.

"Aiden, you won't believe what we saw," Lina said as she walked into the room. King and Daisy were barking and whining excitedly and she patted them absently. "We were walking down Fifth Avenue and - "

She stopped abruptly, the smile on her face turning to a scowl. "What are you doing here, you asshole?"

"Lina? Did you tell Aiden about the guy..."

Kate trailed off, her face paling as she entered the living room and saw Edward. "Edward, what are you doing here?"

"He's leaving," Lina said bluntly. She started forward. "Get the hell out of here, you dickhead. If I see you again, I'll – "

"Lina," Aiden reached out and caught her around the waist, pulling her up against him. "Give him a chance to explain."

She glared at Aiden and tried to wriggle out of his grasp. "No. He's lucky I'm not punching him in the face. You're lucky I'm not punching *you* in the face for letting him up here."

Aiden grinned and her scowl deepened. "You're walking on thin ice, Aiden Wright."

"Kate," Aiden said as he held the squirming, cursing Lina, "do you want to talk to Edward?"

She hesitated and Edward took a step toward her. "Please, Kate. Just five minutes - that's all I want."

"I'll give you five minutes of having my boot up your ass!" Lina snapped.

Aiden snickered and patted her lightly on the ass. "He flew all the way out here, princess. At least let him have his five minutes."

"You're taking his side?" Lina said.

Aiden shrugged. "I know what it's like to royally fuck up and just hope that the woman I love will let me beg for her forgiveness."

Lina sighed and stopped her squirming. "Katie? Do you want to speak to him or should I kick him out?"

"Please, Katie," Edward said.

"I'll talk to him," Kate said softly.

Edward took a deep breath as Lina said, "Start talking. I'm timing you."

"I'd like to speak to her alone," Edward said.

"No way," Lina shook her head. "Not a fucking chance. I am not leaving you alone with her so you can – "

"Come on, kitten," Aiden said, "give them their privacy." He picked her up and she smacked him in the chest with her small fists.

"Aiden, put me down or I'll – "

"It's fine, Lina," Kate said. "I want to speak to Edward alone."

"Kate – "

"It's fine," she repeated. "Please, Lina."

"We'll be right in the kitchen if you need us, okay?" Lina said.

Kate nodded and Aiden, still carrying Lina, whistled for the dogs and headed to the doorway. Lina glared at Edward as they left and despite his anxiety he couldn't help but smile when she flipped him the bird.

"How did you know I was here?" Kate asked when they were alone.

"Olivia told me."

Kate sighed loudly and he gave her a nervous smile. "Don't be angry with her. I begged her to tell me."

She didn't reply and he studied her pale face before saying, "So, your sister kind of hates me, huh?"

"She blames herself," Kate said softly. "She was the one who encouraged me to talk to you because she thought she saw something that was never there."

"I'm so sorry, Katie."

"I know you are. Is that why you came here, Edward? To tell me you're sorry again? You wasted your time. I know you're sorry and I understand where you're coming from, really I do."

"Then why did you leave?"

"Because I love you and I can't be around you right now. I don't know if I ever will."

"You still love me," he said with relief.

She frowned at him. "Of course I do. Did you think I could just turn it off like a faucet?"

"No, but I hurt you so badly that I thought you wouldn't – couldn't - love me."

She laughed bitterly. "It doesn't work that way with me, Edward. Frankly, I wish it did. It would be a lot easier to hate you."

Tears started to slide down her face and she wiped them away angrily. "Only I can't. I actually feel sorry for you. Do you know that? You're in love with someone who you can never be with and my heart hurts so badly for you that I feel like I'm going crazy."

"I love you, Kate," he said.

She froze and the look of anguish on her face nearly tore him apart. "No, you don't."

"I do. I was just too afraid to admit it to myself. I was so afraid that I was using you as a replacement for Tabitha that I wouldn't let myself admit that I loved you. I was so stupid, Katie, and I knew I was being stupid but it wasn't until Tabitha told me – "

"What?" Kate interrupted.

His cheeks flushed. "I have conversations sometimes with Tabitha in my head. She – she told me I was being an idiot and that I needed to tell you how much I loved you."

She stared silently at him and he cleared his throat. "It sounds crazy, I know, but – "

"It doesn't," she said. "It doesn't sound crazy, Edward. I know how much you miss her and love her."

"I do miss her and I do love her and always will but since I met you," he gave her a helpless look, "I close my eyes and try to picture Tabitha and I see you. I used to dream about Tabitha every night, now it's you I dream about. I want to be with *you*, Kate. I love you."

"Edward," she said sadly, "you've gone from saying you don't love me to saying you do love me in less than a week. I don't – "

"I quit my job," he said abruptly.

"You what?" Her eyes widened and, his stomach churning, he stepped forward and put his arms around her waist.

He rested his forehead against hers and took a deep breath, feeling a little light-headed from her familiar scent. "I told Arthur yesterday that I was quitting because I loved you and wanted to be with you."

"You – you didn't," she whispered.

"I did."

"But being a partner – it was your dream, Edward."

"Without you, it's nothing," he said. "I'll find another job. It doesn't matter to me if I'm a partner or not, Kate. All that matters is that I have you with me."

"Edward," Kate whispered.

"I love you, please forgive me," he said before pressing his mouth against hers. She didn't respond and fear raced through him.

"Please, Kate," he whispered against her mouth. "Please, I'm sorry."

His pulse leaped when she put her arms around him and returned his kiss. He kissed her frantically, thrusting his tongue into her mouth and licking at hers before planting kisses on her cheeks and wet lashes.

"I love you, Kate Jones."

"I love you too."

She smiled at him as he wiped at the tears on her cheeks. "Please don't cry, Katie. I'll never hurt you again, I promise."

"I know," she said. "But you really shouldn't have quit your job, Edward."

"Arthur wouldn't technically accept my resignation but when I don't show up for work on Monday, he'll have to."

She blinked at him. "He didn't accept it?"

"No, but – "

"Good, because I'm quitting."

"No, you're not," he said immediately. "You're not quitting a job that you love just because – "

"Oh, so it's okay for you to quit the job you love for me but not okay for me to do it?" She said before arching her eyebrow at him. "I'm quitting, Edward, and you can't stop me. I can work as a PA somewhere else."

"Kate, you love your job," he protested.

"I love you more," she said. "I'll give Arthur my letter of resignation on Monday and you can tell him you changed your mind about leaving."

"Does that mean you'll come home?" He asked.

"Yes," she replied.

"Good," he whispered before hugging her tightly. "I'm never letting you go, Kate Jones."

She buried her face in his neck and kissed his warm skin. "I like the sound of that, Edward Turner."

Epilogue

"Nervous?" Kate asked as she straightened his tie with a quick tug to the left.

"A little," he admitted. "The groom isn't supposed to see the bride before the wedding."

"It'll be okay." She gave him a quick kiss on the cheek and tugged on his tie again. "You look great. I'll see you in there."

"Right." He gave her another nervous smile as she left his side and crossed the foyer of the church. She opened the door of the small room and smiled at Olivia.

"How's he doing?" Olivia asked.

"Nervous. He accidentally saw Lina so I think he believes they're cursed now."

"Oh please," Lina said airily as Julia helped her into her wedding dress. "That's nothing but an old wives' tale. I'm more concerned that you're going to give birth while I'm saying my vows."

Kate rubbed her rounded belly. "That won't be a problem. I'm beginning to think this kid's never going to make an appearance."

"You were nearly two weeks late and Lina was a week overdue," Julia said. "We don't have babies early in our family."

"You say that now," Lina said as her mother started to button the long row of pearl buttons at the back of her dress, "but won't you be eating crow when I'm right in the middle of professing my undying love to Aiden and end up soaking wet from Kate's water breaking."

Kate laughed. "That is not going to happen, Lina. Besides, it's not like it's a flood."

There was a knock on the door and Edward stuck his head into the room. "How's it going in here?"

"Good," Kate said as he walked up to her, put his arm around her waist and rubbed her belly. "What's up?"

"Nothing. I just checked on Aiden - he's a little green around the gills but no vomiting yet."

Lina laughed. "My poor Aiden. He's so worried he's going to mess up the vows. I swear I heard him reciting them in his sleep the other night."

"If I was him, I'd be more worried that my kid's going to make her grand appearance and stop the wedding," Edward said with a grin.

Kate smacked him lightly on the chest. "I'm only eight months pregnant – I'm not going to give birth at the altar."

"How do I look?" Lina said as she smoothed her dress down with her hands and turned to face them.

"Oh, Lina," Kate said softly. "You're gorgeous."

"Thanks, Katie," Lina said as Julia hugged her tightly. "Mom, don't you dare cry. It'll make me cry and I'm not getting married with swollen eyelids."

Olivia kissed Lina on the cheek. "I'm going to go grab my seat. Jon will be wondering where I am."

She left the room as Alvin walked in. He took one look at Lina and burst into tears.

"Dad! Don't cry!" Lina said frantically. "Mom, make him stop crying!"

As Julia and Lina consoled the sobbing Alvin, Edward pulled Kate to the far side of the room. "You look beautiful, Mrs. Turner," he said.

"Thank you, Mr. Turner. All I can say is thank goodness Lina picked stretchy material for the maid of honour dress."

He rubbed her belly again before pressing a brief kiss against her mouth. "I was thinking about a name for her."

"Oh yeah?" She said.

"Yes. I was thinking we should name her," he paused and gave her a wicked smile, "Matilda."

"I am not naming our daughter after your car," she said.

"It would be after my grandmother, not my car," he said innocently.

"Nice try," she said. "Now, go take your seat. I've got to help Lina and mom with dad."

Edward laughed. "You know it won't make a difference. He sobbed like a baby the whole time he walked you down the aisle at our wedding. I actually felt guilty that I was taking his daughter from him."

She smiled and pressed a quick kiss against his mouth. "I love you, Edward."

"I love you too, Katie-did."

He kissed her again before leaving the room. Kate smiled at her dad as her mother handed him another tissue. "Okay?"

"Yes," he said. "This is a very emotional day for me. I can't believe both my baby girls will be married after today."

He started to tear up again and Julia patted him on the back. "Your first grandchild will probably be born today too."

"Mom!" Kate said as Lina snickered loudly.

As her father hugged her mother, Kate took Lina's hands and squeezed them gently. "Are you ready to become Mrs. Aiden Wright?"

"So ready," Lina said. "Are you ready to be a mom?"

"Yes. But not today," Kate said with a grin.

"I love you, Katie."

"I love you too, Lina."

END

Please enjoy a sample of Ramona's newest novel, "Sharing Del".

Sharing Del will be available in January of 2017.

SHARING DEL

Copyright 2016 Ramona Gray

I'm twenty-five years old and I'm not a nice girl. Even my mama says I'm not nice. When I was sixteen she sat me down and told me I was going to hell. Told me that if I didn't see the light and walk the straight and narrow, God would strike me down with every bit of righteous vengeance he possessed.

At the time I just chalked it up to her being mad. She had, after all, just caught me sucking Tommy Robertson's cock in the confessional booth at our church. I can't help it. I like boys. I like them a lot. I'm not really into what you would call the monogamy relationships. I've tried. I swear to the Mother Mary I've tried but after a few weeks or a few months, I get bored and I'm moving on to my next conquest.

I tried girls for a while. Figured maybe my problem wasn't committing to one person but committing to one man. I hooked up with a bad girl named Raquel in my first year of college. Oh my sweet blazing Jesus, could that bitch eat pussy. I mean, the girl's tongue was *magic*.

Turns out though, my issue wasn't with men. After only a few months I was starting to get bored. I would have left Raquel if she hadn't left me first. Well, maybe her leaving me isn't exactly right. I packed my stuff and left when I came home one night and found her tongue-deep in the pussy of her lab partner. She called me a few times, begging for forgiveness, and I told her it was fine. I didn't tell her I was about to leave her anyway.

Even though she cheated on me, I didn't want to hurt her feelings and I'm kind of worried you know? Worried that there's something wrong with me that I can't commit to just one person. I have three older sisters and all of them are happily married to good Catholic boys and popping out babies like they alone are responsible for keeping the earth's population going.

Last weekend I visited my oldest sister Angela. I left the city and headed for the suburbs, saying a silent prayer every few miles that my rust bucket of a car would make it. I sat at the dinner table, two toddlers clinging to my legs and a baby throwing up on my shirt, and listened as Angela lectured me.

"Del, you're going to kill mama and daddy. You know that right? They worry about you constantly. Mama spends all her time at mass, praying for your eternal soul. You need to find the right person, settle down and have babies. Children complete your life – trust me on this."

I rolled my eyes and wiped at the spit-up on my shirt. "Yeah, this feels like a really great time."

Angela frowned and took the baby, cooing softly to him before wiping his face clean with the hem of her shirt. "I mean it, Del. Daddy's been having anxiety attacks and mama hardly sleeps at night. At least come to church with us once a month."

Good old Catholic guilt. It's alive and well in my family. My parents have seven children and I'm smack dab in the middle and the only one they fret about. My baby brother Mitchell gave them some trouble for a few months in high school but they straightened him out pretty quickly. I'm the only one they've never been able to figure out or fix. The fate of my eternal soul causes them a lot of heartache.

Of course, my eternal soul is the last thing I need to be worrying about right now. Paying my rent, eating more than one meal a day – now those are the things that I really need to concentrate on.

I moved to the city on a whim. I was tired of living in the suburbs, tired of living in my parent's basement and listening to the lectures about why I failed at college, why I failed at relationships, hell, why I failed at life.

I've been living in a tiny little apartment on Fifth Street, the walls so thin you can hear my neighbour Jerry whacking off every night to reruns of the goddamn Golden Girls, and working at a dive bar on 17th Avenue. It isn't the best area in the city but I carry my mace and know how to use it.

The problem is that I was barely scraping by to begin with and now my landlord's decided to raise the rent. Nine hundred bucks a month for a shit-ass apartment so tiny I can barely turn around in it without banging into the walls. Nine hundred bucks so that I can take a two-minute shower before the water turns cold, watch the cockroaches running across the floor at night, and listen to an old balding man named Jerry cry out Bea fucking Arthur's name in orgasmic pleasure every goddamn night.

I'm not going to miss it. Well, maybe Jerry.

I have two weeks left before I need to move and I haven't found anything in my budget. I'm left with two choices – take a second job or get a new apartment with a roommate. I chose a second job because honestly? I don't play well with others. Except I haven't found anything yet and time is rapidly running out.

"Del! You thinking of working tonight or ya just gonna stand there diddling yourself?"

I scowled at the bartender. Mark could be a real asshole sometimes. The owner Bill wasn't around a lot and Mark liked to pretend that he ran the place. I adjusted my short skirt, picked up my tray of drinks and crossed the crowded bar.

It was Saturday night and it was going to be busy. Once a month Bill brought in a local band to play named "Killjoy". They always brought in a huge crowd. Their lead singer Jesse had vocals of gold and filled out a pair of leather pants better than any man I knew. The first few months I seriously considered trying to get into those leather pants but after watching the groupies throw their panties on stage and flash their tits I stopped even considering it.

Not that I don't have a kickass body. I might be short but I'm curvy in all the right spots with a set of tits on me that could make a grown man cry. Long dark hair, bright blue eyes and, thanks to my mama's side of the family, milky-white skin. Maybe if I wasn't about to be homeless, I'd have thought harder about seducing Jesse.

I set all the mugs of beer but one down on a table full of frat boys.

"Sweetheart, you get better looking every time you walk over here." The leader of the group grinned at me with perfect white teeth. He was cute in a frat boy bratty kind of way. I briefly considered taking him home and showing him the night of his life, and then rejected it. Fucking some random guy was no way to avoid my problems. Besides, he was too pretty for me. I liked them big and rough. Still, it didn't mean I couldn't flirt my way into big tips.

"Why thank you, handsome," I purred and leaned over him, letting him get a good look down my shirt at my tits before I plucked the bills from his hand.

I turned to walk away and when he smacked me on the ass, I rolled my eyes before turning and giving him a wink. "You'd better watch it, big boy. You never know what I'll do with that hand."

"You can do anything you want to it, sweetheart." The frat boy grinned again as his friends laughed loudly.

I set the last beer down on the table in the corner farthest from the stage. "Hello, Cash."

"Del." The big man nodded and took a drink of beer before handing me a few bills. I counted out the change and held it out to him but he shook his head. I nodded gratefully and shoved the bills into my apron pocket.

Cash came in once or twice a month and always sat in my section. He was quiet, kept his hands to himself, and was a big tipper. My favourite kind of customer. I waited a moment to see if he would take a look at my tits but his gaze had already shifted to the stage where the band was starting to set up.

I headed back toward the bar. Cash never looked at my tits, never made rude comments and never drank more than three beers. At first it kind of bugged me that he never made a pass but after a while I found it refreshing. Not that I wouldn't have taken him up on it if he had. I mean, the man practically screamed sex. And he was exactly the kind of man I liked. Big and broad shouldered, a permanent five o'clock shadow and tanned skin. Dark eyes and full lips, and if he didn't have a nice hairy chest that a girl could run her fingers through, I'd eat my own apron. He always wore a scuffed leather jacket with jeans and worn cowboy boots and once, when I had snuck out back for a cigarette near the end of my shift, I had seen him leaving on a motorcycle. A big old Harley that roared loudly in the cool night air.

My pussy pulsed at the thought of riding behind Cash and my panties were suddenly wet. Christ, I really did need to get laid. I didn't have a chance with Cash but the frat boy was starting to look better and better. There were sudden shrieks and I knew without looking that Jesse and the rest of Killjoy had taken the stage.

I leaned against the bar and watched for a few minutes. Jesse was wearing his usual leather pants only this time he had decided to go without the shirt. He usually ended up half-naked before the show was over anyway, guess he just decided it was pointless to even wear one. As he swayed in time to the music, I studied his upper torso. He was lean and absolutely ripped. Forget six pack, the man had a goddamn eight pack. His nipple rings glinted in the light and I thought about how nice it would be to pull on those rings with my teeth.

I shook my head. Jesus, I had to get control of myself. My panties were soaked through and I was still leaking. I caught the eye of the frat boy and he gave me a wide grin. I smiled back. Frat boy wasn't my first choice but he'd do.

* * *

I slipped out the back door of the bar and lit a cigarette, inhaling deeply. The smoke hit my lungs in a soft rush and I blew it out gently, loving the sweet hit of nicotine. It had been a long night and my feet were killing me. I had just finished cashing out and decided to have a quick smoke before I grabbed my things and took off. Frat boy and his friends had disappeared about ten minutes before the bar closed. I was disappointed but the part of me that wasn't a complete whore, knew it was for the best. A night of fucking sounded good but it wasn't going to solve my problems.

I sighed and took another drag on my cigarette. Tomorrow morning I'd –

"Hello, sweetheart."

I spun around. Frat boy was standing behind me, leaning against the wall and smiling his straight-tooth grin at me.

"Well, hey there." I socked out my hip and lifted the cigarette to my lips. He watched me take a drag, watched the way my lips sucked at the thin white cylinder, and his grin widened.

"Tell me, sweetheart, you got plans after work?"

I shrugged. "Depends."

"Depends on what?"

I stubbed out my cigarette and stepped closer. "Depends on you."

He kissed me, his tongue pushing into my mouth immediately. He had a large tongue and he was too eager, too determined to show me that he was a good kisser. I pulled back and wiped my mouth off discreetly. Perhaps tonight wasn't going to be as fun as I thought.

"I've been wanting to kiss you all night." Frat boy grabbed my breast and squeezed it roughly.

"Slow down, handsome." I tugged his hand away. "Not so fast."

He pushed me up against the wall and cupped my breast again. "Please, you've been practically begging me for it all night."

I rolled my eyes, suddenly remembering why I didn't fuck college boys. "Give me a minute to – "

He kissed my neck, his teeth nipping at the skin and I pushed him away. "I said, slow down."

"Fine," he pouted and crossed his arms over his chest.

"Let me just grab my things and we'll go," I said.

He grinned and glanced behind his shoulder. I followed his gaze, frowning when I saw his three buddies climbing out of the car.

"Do we get a group rate, sweetheart?"

Anger flooded through me and I spit on him. "I don't do groups, you little prick."

He wiped the spittle off his cheek looking at the liquid on his fingers in disbelief. "You bitch! Did you just spit on me?"

I reached into my apron for my can of mace, remembering too late that it was in my jacket in the bar. I backed up in the general direction of the door, glancing around as frat boy and his dickhead buddies drew closer.

"Listen, sweetheart, you're going to come back to our place and you're going to show us all a good time, okay? In the morning we'll, I don't know, take you out for breakfast or something to say thanks."

"Fuck you, asshole," I snarled. Without taking my eyes off them, I reached behind me for the door handle, cursing in my head when I felt nothing but the rough brick wall of the bar. Where was the goddamn door?

With surprising speed, frat boy lunged for me. I opened my mouth to scream and he clamped a hard hand over my mouth. "Don't do that, sweetheart. We just want to – "

He was ripped violently away from me and I pressed my body against the wall as he was thrown to the ground. He hit the pavement with a loud thud and cursed loudly.

"I don't believe the lady is interested, little boy." Cash towered over him, his hands folded neatly behind his back.

I stared at him in relief. I think this might have been the first time I had seen Cash standing up close, and I was shocked by just how large he was. My small frame was dwarfed by his and his hands were twice the size of mine.

The frat boy stumbled to his feet, his hands clenched into fists, and backed up until he was standing with his buddies.

"Get out of here, man. This doesn't concern you." He tried to sound tough but even I could see the way he was trembling.

"Oh, I think it does," Cash replied mildly. "You and your little friends get in your car and get the fuck out of here."

Frat boy glanced at his friends. They nodded and he grinned at Cash. "There's four of us and only one of you. It seems you're outnumbered."

Cash didn't reply. I was standing frozen against the wall, my heart beating too fast in my chest, and my mouth tasting like frat boy and cigarettes.

"You know what they say, don't you?" Frat boy sneered. "The bigger they are, the harder they fall."

"Why don't you stop your babbling and bring it then, little boy," Cash said quietly.

The frat boys ran forward and I watched flabbergasted as Cash kicked the shit out of them.

* * *

"Sharing Del" will be available in January 2017.

If you would like more information about Ramona Gray, please visit her at:

www.ramonagray.ca
or
https://www.facebook.com/RamonaGrayBooks
or
https://twitter.com/RamonaGrayBooks

Books by Ramona Gray

The Escort
Saving Jax
The Assistant
One Night
The Vampire's Kiss (Other World Series Book One)
The Vampire's Love (Other World Series Book Two)
The Shifter's Mate (Other World Series Book Three)
Rescued By The Wolf (Other World Series Book Four)

CPSIA information can be obtained at www.ICGtesting.com
Printed in the USA
BVOW01s1819280716

457212BV00022B/138/P